The Mummers' Curse

The Mummers' Curse

AN AMANDA PEPPER MYSTERY

Gillian Roberts

BALLANTINE BOOKS • New York

Library of Congress Cataloging in Publication Data
Roberts, Gillian.
    The mummers' curse / by Gillian Roberts.
      p.   cm.
    ISBN 0-345-40323-1
    1. Pepper, Amanda (Fictitious character)—Fiction. 2. Women detectives—Pennsylvania—Philadelphia—Fiction. 3. Philadelphia (Pa.)—Fiction.   I. Title.
PS3557.R356M8   1996
813'.54—dc20   96-3472

Manufactured in the United States of America

First Edition: August 1996

10 9 8 7 6 5 4 3 2 1

For Tobi and Jerry Ludwig
with abiding love
for both of you
from both of me
(even though you wouldn't strut New Year's morning)

Acknowledgments

Heartfelt thanks to the staff of the New Year's Shooters and Mummers Museum, particularly Jack Cohen, Library Coordinator, Palma Lucas, Executive Director, and museum volunteer Bill "Curley" Conners of the Ferko String Band for providing me with memories, stories, articles and studies, and for being so patient and helpful with my questions. A special debt of gratitude to Dr. Charles Welch, who not only wrote the book on Mummers on which both Mandy and I relied, but who duplicated an invaluable tape for me when I needed it most.

To Pat Fleck, for research assistance beyond the call of duty and geography, to Amy Reisch, for providing a fresh viewpoint on Philadelphia, and to Sheila Winokur for knowing "the neighborhood"—many, many thanks.

As always, it is a joy to have such generous and talented writer friends as Susan Dunlap and Marilyn Wallace sharpen my focus when and where it blurred.

And to Jean Naggar, my agent, and Joe Blades, my editor, thank you, thank you, for being who you are and thereby making telling stories a pleasure as well as a profession.

Lastly, gratitude to Nancy Ramsey and Rusty Schweikart for sharing the saga of their cat's final chapter, and greetings to Sid, wherever he now is . . .

The Mummers' Curse

One

"You'll catch your death." My mother had lived in Florida a long time, and her weather perspective was sun-damaged.

I said nothing.

"Would it be a bad idea to listen to me once in a while? Might make a good New Year's resolution."

In hindsight, that wasn't a dumb suggestion. Alas, one doesn't get hindsight until it's too late to use it, so I didn't listen to her suggestion to listen.

Nor did she stop nagging. "I can't believe you're dragging a grandchild of mine along with you," she said. "The *high* is supposed to be five degrees. It says so in the paper here."

The Southland paper was always full of happy news and it was always the same: EXTRA, EXTRA! ROTTEN WEATHER EVERYWHERE ELSE.

And, indeed, damp, bone-crunching misery had been our lot for a while and was predicted as well for the first day of January.

"I told you to come here for winter vacation," she said. "It was eighty-four today."

I had called to wish my parents a happy New Year and had, in a desperate but ill-chosen attempt to make conversation, mentioned that Mackenzie and I were taking Karen, my sister's older child, to the Mummers' Parade the next morning. In fact, we three parade-goers were spending a quiet New Year's Eve together at home, the better to have hangover-free eyes and ears the following day.

I thought my folks would be impressed with this show of domesticity. I was spending New Year's Eve with a six-year-old. I thought they'd happily misinterpret that as a sign I was headed in what they perceived as the right direction. But the only direction my mother ever clearly perceived was hers, be it philosophical or geographical.

"Five degrees there and beautiful here," my mother repeated.

Ever since she moved south, the woman has suffered from the delusion that I crave data on comparative atmospheric conditions. The greater the disparity between the mercury hither and yon, the more urgent her need to share this news. Had they only invented the Weather Channel sooner, she'd have been a natural as its anchorwoman.

"We took a walk," she said. "On the beach. At sunset. Daddy and me. Tonight." Semaphore-speak, telegraphese, teensy sentences, as if my mind were too frostbitten to absorb more than one fact at a time. "It was balmy. I was sweating by the end."

"Make sure to wear sunblock," I said briskly. "You don't want your face looking like beef jerky. Meanwhile, I'd better check on Karen and . . ."

"Poor child will freeze."

"Stop making her sound like the little match girl. It's her cultural heritage."

"Freezing or matches?"

"The Mummers' Parade. If we needed to strut our stuff on a warm day, we would have been born in New Orleans. We're tough, we're *Philadelphians*. Having our parade on the least likely day of the year seasons us, makes us all that we are."

"Karen doesn't live in Philadelphia," my mother said. "She lives outside the city. They have their own traditions."

I pictured the Main Line denizens in their duck-patterned golf pants playing banjos and doing the Mummers' strut around the eighteenth hole. It did not compute. "I think clipping coupons is their folk tradition, Mom, and it's not entertaining to watch."

"Oh, Amanda," she sighed. We were ending the year as we'd begun it, with my mother vaguely disappointed in my choices and actions. At least there was symmetry.

"HEY, KAREN," I said the next day as we shivered on the sidewalk. "What's two and a half miles long, sixty-nine feet wide, twelve feet high, and covered with feathers?"

"A riddle," she said. "Good! But is there a knock-knock part?"

When I shook my head, she gave up. "The Mummers' Parade!" I said, although it was difficult making merry through clattering incisors. As we watched the last of the parading comics, I recalled why I'd skipped the last several dozen parades. The air and wind acted like a sushi-master's knife on my skin. The environment was sufficiently evil to make in-person parade-watching a spectator sport for masochists, but not evil enough to postpone the event. Parades were rescheduled when rain or snow endangered the expensive and fragile costumes and instruments. Nobody worried about endangering spectators.

"What this city needs is the sense to stage an outdoor extravaganza when the weather's decent." Mackenzie said this with a wink and a good-ol'-boy drawl that was meant to, but didn't, take the edge off his words.

It would, indeed, be lovely if so oversized and lavish a spectacle were held when there was a hope of benign weather. Instead, it's an annual challenge, our gritty Yankee street game—Mummers vs. Mother Nature. Both show up in full regalia and do battle from dawn to dark. The contest generally ends in a tie.

But this isn't something else to blame on Philadelphia, something the city could arbitrarily change. "It has to be now," I said.

"Why?" Karen asked.

Mackenzie cringed. Or maybe it was only the cold that put the crease between his eyebrows and made him say, "Not again."

I ignored him and turned toward Karen. "Because mumming has roots back a thousand years or more," I said. "The Druids made noise to scare off demons in the dark part of the year. People in different parts of Europe wore masks and costumes—in fact *mumme* means mask or disguise in German. They gave plays for their neighbors, all at the time when the old year was dying."

Mackenzie slumped as if his backbone had abruptly dissolved.

Why had I suggested this outing? As I recalled, it followed a heated debate over whose parade was better. This was based on pure hometown boosterism, given that neither one of us had ever actually seen the other's event. But Mardi Gras gets such excessive PR, I had virtually spectated.

"Obviously," Mackenzie had said, "Mardi Gras is better known because it's better."

I had to educate him. "Wrong. Mardi Gras is a capital-S social event—as in Society. It's status to belong to a certain Krewe, and I'm sure not just anybody can join. The Mummers put on as spectacular a production—but they're working class and always have been. This is a folk celebration, not chronicled in the Society pages. These are people who don't keep detailed records of their every move or declare that there's a pecking order of social correctness within their clubs. There are rivalries—good-natured and based on skill or success or style, and the members have to like a new guy before he's accepted, he needs to be sponsored, to come to a few meetings—"

"So it's a closed world, too."

I shrugged. He was correct, but it was a different sort of closed universe, and there was still a vast difference. And so I had dared Mackenzie to a parade-exchange. As a bonus, I tossed the detective a professional incentive, the question of what had become of one Theodore Serfi.

The Tuesday before Christmas Serfi had attended a weekly meeting of his Fancy Club, then disappeared without a trace. Since then, there'd been persistent rumors that he was now being served as a pasta topping, an ingredient in a rival family's blood sausage. Bus and billboard ads for King's Sausage had been unofficially augmented, so that they now read *Whose Blood is in King's Sausage?* The understood, if unverified, answer was *Ted Serfi.*

I had a different theory. "Years ago," I told Mackenzie, "Mummers kidnapped men and held them hostage until New Year's morning, when they'd make their captives march with them. Maybe Serfi will reappear with a new brigade. Maybe this is a gimmick, a historical reminder."

Mackenzie thought Ted Serfi, who was reputed to have been "connected," had been "Hoffa'd," as he put it, and at any rate, was a missing person and not a homicide detective's concern. But in a show of good will, he'd said that if Ted Serfi came strutting along, prisoner of a rival brigade, he'd be happy to apologize for his cynicism.

Another reason for my attending was an article I was writing about the Mummers. Correction: an article I intended to write. As faculty advisor to the school newspaper, I was dared by the editor-in-chief to verify or disprove the expression, "Those who can, do; those who can't, teach." He was writing a feature about our faculty, based on that dreadful maxim, so what could I do but accept the challenge? I, too, would commit journalism. I would write and sell an article of my own.

Although I'd already prepared my Pulitzer acceptance speech, I actually hadn't yet had time to write more than notes. What I had done instead was share each interesting factoid I discovered. In the course of doing so, I also discovered that Mackenzie and I did not always agree on what was interesting and what was not.

Even as I watched a ribbon-bedecked passel of comics strut by, I had three-by-five cards at the ready. Unfortunately, it was too chilly and complicated to take off my mittens and retrieve the cards from my bag.

"Are those men Druids?" Karen asked.

"Aunt Mandy will answer all your questions in her article," Mackenzie said. "That is, when she finishes it. Which will, of course, be some time after she begins it."

"Your mean streak is wider than Broad Street, Comus." I gestured at the parade route.

"Mean?" Mackenzie said. "Comus?"

A year and a half of guessing what the damned C. K. stood for, and I was no closer. "Comus was the god of revelry. Of mirth. Song, dance, and wine. But you're too mean to have that name."

"He isn't mean," Karen said.

He wasn't either mean or Comus, simply the unbearable sort who did what he said he was going to and who thought everybody else should do the same. He expected me to write the article, wanted me to because I said I was going to and because I wanted to. And he knew I was afraid to actually do it, to risk proving that nasty adage true. And so he tweaked and poked, and I acted outraged and found excuses galore, and the article continued to pend.

"Are they Druids, Aunt Mandy?" Karen asked again, giving me a reprieve.

"No, but they might be the great-great-how-many-great-grandsons of Druids. And of a whole lot of other people who brought their New Year traditions to the new country. The Finns masqueraded, and the Swedes started the year by shooting off guns—in fact, the people we call Mummers really call themselves Shooters."

"But they will *not* be shooting today," Mackenzie said. "They don't do that anymore. Haven't for a long time."

Karen looked relieved.

"The English put on a Mummers' Play, Scotch-Irish men dressed in women's clothing—"

"Like that," Karen said, pointing at a male comic dressed in the traditional Wench style, with a flouncy dress, golden shoes, and long pigtails. She and her male counterpart, The Dude in a sequin-trimmed tuxedo, were out of the minstrel show tradition, but

Mackenzie shot me a look and I didn't say that out loud. Instead, I stayed with the European influences. "As I was saying, the Germans wore masks and disguises, including one as an early kind of Santa, called a Belsnickle."

"He was one mean Santa," Mackenzie said.

I beamed at him. He wasn't sneering, or yawning, he was participating.

"I think maybe I could write your article myself," he said. "In fact, maybe I should."

I turned off the beam.

Karen looked wide-eyed at the idea of a mean Santa.

"Like Santa, the Belsnickle wanted to know who'd been naughty or good," I said, "but unlike Santa, when he found the naughty ones, he whipped them."

"And the good ones?" Karen asked. "Did they get presents?"

"Their present was not getting whipped. Santa quality control has improved a whole lot over the years. And looks. He had ugly, strawy hair and beard, and a mean face and plain clothes, except for his fur-trimmed pants . . ."

Fur. I shivered. Even the nasty Belsnickle got to wear it. It was not P.C. to think of it, but I did. However, the only fur I own was home, meowing and clawing the furniture.

In all honesty, it would have been nice if those Scottish, Irish, English, and German people had decided to celebrate the spring solstice. Then, I might not feel as if a Phillips screwdriver had been inserted in my forehead. How had New Orleans known to pick up on Lenten traditions instead? I flashed with irrational resentment—those rich Southern folk had snatched the good season and left the freezing cold for poor, hard-working Philadelphians.

"Anyway," I said, "people have been celebrating this time of year, and in ways like this almost forever, but in Philadelphia, all the separate traditions combined and became this very special parade."

Mackenzie looked near-comatose. He spoke in a flat voice, as if telegraphing news to me. "You needn't feel obliged to tell the child everything you know."

"She asked."

"When kids ask why things are the way they are, grown-ups say, 'Because I said so,' or, 'It's how we do it, that's why.' "

"That'd save a lot of time in the classroom as well." Suddenly, I'd become The Woman Who Tells Too Much. My desire to share ideas hadn't annoyed him until we were living together. "And you say you love history," I muttered.

"I do. As well as the saying: 'Everything in moderation.' And that includes Mummers and exposure to foul weather." He pulled up his parka hood and faced a group of comics who were ridiculing none too subtly some national political leaders.

We stamped our feet and rubbed our hands while our breath made smoky patterns. Savvy Philadelphians cultivate friends with apartments or offices overlooking the parade route. I resolved hereafter to base friendships on real-estate access, not compatibility.

I had been concerned about how a six-year-old, conditioned to special effects via TV, movies, computer screen and control pad, would react to an ancient, handmade spectacle. We'd come after the Police and Fireman's bands had passed, and a goodly portion of the enormous comic division as well. Since then, we'd inched forward as early-arriving spectators left. We watched, as best we could, a troop of comics in season-denying hues—intense apple green, hot pink, butter yellow, and electric blue—both on their satin and sequined costumes, their triple-tiered umbrellas, and often on their faces.

Before the civil rights movement of the Sixties, many of the clowns would have been in minstrel's blackface, but nowadays their makeup was less offensive and more interesting.

And years ago, whatever the color of their faces, the comics and everyone else in the parade would have been male. Dressing in drag was and is a favorite way of clowning around, and female impersonators were still preferred to the real thing, but female-females, after their own struggle, could also now participate.

The family in front of us—friends and relatives of the spring-time group—called it a day and we moved up to the barrier. Karen giggled as a straggler comic—his face something other than human behind its frosty lilac glitter—reached out his forefinger and painted a lilac stripe down her nose.

And all of a sudden, the chilly nonsense on the street seemed the only right way to bring in a new year and I understood its evolution and rationale. Outside beyond us, the forest was deep and frightening and frozen. Anything could happen in its dark recesses. But not here, with its insistence on bright color and sound, its smiling music and clowns. Not here.

"How soon will your buddy be on?" Mackenzie was not a parade person. To me, there is something magical about people putting their hearts and imaginations on display, turning their raucous happiness into music. And there's something mystical about living behind a mask, creating an entirely new identity, not necessarily human, if only for a few hours. So much of our lives seems devoted to insisting on who we are, on asking to be noticed—and then, this, an encasing, removing, reversal, one day of the year.

All that leaves Mackenzie cold, no matter the temperature. He fidgeted much more than Karen.

The buddy he referred to, Vincent Devaney, was a Philly Prep teacher who'd helped me with my research. He had, in fact, suggested the topic, and he was the main reason we were shivering our way through the first day of the year. Four months ago, he'd joined the faculty, after majoring in biology at Temple University and, as far as I could tell by his interests, minoring in Mummering. Or maybe it was the other way around. A third-generation New Year's Shooter, he was bent on educating people about things both scientific and mummerific.

"Vincent's in a Fancy Club," I said.

"And that means?"

"There are four divisions. We're still watching the first, the clubs in the Comic Division." I waved toward the street, where more comics, the Mummers closest to the original carousers, the least organized, the most spontaneous, and the most numerous on New Year's Day, strutted by.

"And the Fancy Division is second—next?"

"Yes. The Fancy Clubs, the ones with the frame suits."

"Which means Vincent will be on soon, then?"

It was like talking to a child, except that the real child was less of a pest.

Mackenzie pulled a paperback out of his pocket, looking up only when a new group approached and sometimes, a second time because of the quality—as in excellent or horrifying—of the band hired to accompany them. The Comics and Fancies are allowed to have music played—but only on instruments not used by the String Bands. The combination of bongos, bells, and whatever else was left, was often less than pure delight.

Nonetheless, Karen, mouth half-open, eyes wide, watched a very young boy done up as a stylized Harlequin. His small suit was a mosaic of spangled diamond shapes that made him look like a fluid stained glass window topped by a glittery cap. "I would like to do that." Her voice was hollow; she sounded like a possessed baby in a horror movie.

"It probably looks like more fun than it is," I said. "It's even colder out on the street, the suit's heavy with all that stuff sewn on it, and they still have a long way to go before they reach the judges' stands."

"I would like to do that," she repeated in her lovesick, mesmerized voice.

No wonder. The splendiferous boy glittered and sparkled. He wasn't bundled and huddled on the sidelines. He was the center of attention, a star, making merry, dancing to the music. High on his life and not yet, presumably, on the spirits that reputedly kept his elders warm this winter's day.

"Yessss," Karen said.

My sister would probably never let me see her daughter again. I was supposed to support the idea of a Main Line life, beige and tailored, not one featuring feather boas and golden slippers.

Mackenzie was less entranced. "Wish they'd speed things up," he said.

"Why? Does the Mardi Gras rush by at Mach speed?"

By way of answer, he took a tissue out of his pocket and blew his nose. "This is on TV," he said softly. "The whole thing. We could go home, light a fire, make a pot of coffee, snuggle on the sofa and see it. Or better still, tape and fast-forward it. Make them strut double-time. One turn and twirl per man allowed. It's not like you're takin' notes or doin' anythin' you couldn't do at home."

Guilt, guilt. Didn't he understand that my hands were too cold to hold a pen? "You Southerners are hothouse flowers," I said. It wasn't a rational answer, but it was my only counter-argument to his irresistible idea of being comfortable.

But just as I felt on the verge of retreating, the first Fancy Club's banner car arrived. Not Vincent's club, however. People applauded as they sighted the sea of approaching figures, hundreds of undulating feather-trimmed jewels.

I, too, felt a rising excitement. I hoped I never became too sophisticated to be dazzled by the pure extravagance of the spectacle.

"I have to go to the bathroom," Karen announced. "Bad."

"We'll have to hurry," I said.

"Don' I wish," Mackenzie said. The speed of the parade had not picked up, which was lucky, because it felt a very long time making our way out through the crowd. "Excuse me, excuse us," I said countless times, weaving through the now-deep throngs. Mackenzie remained at the barricades, holding our space. After we'd tripped over dozens of feet and annoyed countless spectators forging our way out and around the corner, we waited in line near urban outhouses rocking in the wind. And despite the distance and bluster, we could hear the pleasant cacophony of the music. I kept one ear tuned to it, trying to tell if a new group was nearing.

The music was temporarily stilled when Karen had completed her task, so on our way back, we stopped for hot pretzels with mustard for all, but mostly for Mackenzie as a peace offering.

We munched, stomped feet, and waited for the next group, timing the wait with puffs of frosty breath. Mackenzie, with no subtlety, looked at his watch. "How about lying and saying you sat through the whole thing?" he asked behind Karen's back.

"I can't leave before Vincent marches. What if the camera doesn't come in close enough to see him? How will I tell who's who?"

"Why would it matter?"

It seemed a debt I owed. Vincent Devaney had let me peek into his world. I could at least witness its day of triumph.

Teaching was important to Vincent. It supported him, his wife, and young son. He seemed good at it and enthusiastic. But mumming was his passion, the world of the Mummers his community and true village, the Mummer's year his meaningful calendar. He was nearly distraught when rivalries, both personal and financial, surfaced within his club and threatened to end its existence. They'd patched themselves together enough to make it to this day, and it was important that I be here, because nobody was sure they'd survive till the next parade.

Mackenzie's mournful exhale resembled a dragon's snort. Then, despite the fat pretzels and the thermos of hot chocolate I'd brought, he went off to find more food. To kill time, I thought.

The light became subdued, as if the sky were on a dimmer, and the wind continued to pick up, blowing a debris-laden swath down the wide wind-tunnel expanse of Broad Street. I thought about the String Bands, the Clubs still back at the starting point with miles to maneuver before they reached the judges' stands at City Hall. What did they wear under the satin and feathers to avoid freezing?

And then the next banner car slowly approached, and it announced Vincent's club. His group—several hundred strong—approached with difficulty. A fancy suit is as ornate as its name implies—a piece of handiwork, with towering plumed and constructed "hats," or backpieces, face masks, ruffed collars, and trains often so enormous they require page boys. And every inch of man and suit is lavishly decorated.

But a Fancy Club member could also wear a frame suit—a hundred pounds of wood and metal covered in silk and lace, like a hoop skirt that begins at the neck. It takes strong shoulders to carry a structure two dozen feet in circumference all the miles and hours of the parade, even with wheels on the vertical struts. And that's on a still day.

In a stiff wind like the one now blowing, capes can act as sails and frame suits seem hell-bent on either skidding out of control, taking their man along with them, or collapsing into heaps of wood, steel, and fabric.

A frame draped and covered in iridescent panels approached, surrounded by men in silver suits with feather-trimmed capes made of filmy layers of shimmering colors—a rainbow billowing over gold and silver cloth. The frame suit replaced the recognizably human with pure texture and ethereal color. It was a moving octagonal tent with a gryphon head, a glorious monster whose chiffon and feathers blew wildly in the wind.

This, then, was the real descendant of the medieval demons the ancient noisemakers held at bay. Here was the monster, possessed and owned. Under control.

Almost. The suit lurched and bucked, as did another suit, a variation on this one's mother-of-pearl coloration. It was a mark of pride to be strong enough to endure hours of carrying the weight of a frame, plus a headpiece that could add another hundred pounds, but today, being trapped in the center of one must have felt less of an honor and more of a punishment as the forms waged war with their wearers.

One tent seemed in more trouble than the others. The men around him, capes flapping, helped steer the frame, which careened like a ship in a storm. Civilian helpers crossed the barricade and added their strength to steady the form.

The one visible part of the man was a portion of his face, weighted below with the enormous frame and dwarfed above by an outlandish headpiece that threatened to buckle or take off in flight. He was painted as Pierrot, with dead-white makeup and features drawn in black. Below the right eye was a fifty-carat "ruby" of a red tear.

The head, overshadowed by its costume, looked toylike.

Another frame suit approached. I scanned for Vincent Devaney, but it was impossible to distinguish features with collars and panels blowing every which way. And, in fact, I didn't know if Vincent was wearing a frame. He had worked on one with a friend, but they had also worked on a regular suit, deciding to toss at the last moment for who would wear which.

Karen's teeth chattered. I sniffed the hollow smell of approaching snow. Enough was enough. I couldn't spot Vincent, even though I knew this was his club, but I could nonetheless compliment him on his splendor. Time to go enjoy another all-American tradition, like central heating. "After C. K. gets back," I said, "it might be a good time to—"

"Not l-l-*leave*," the wanna-be Mummer wailed. "I'm n-n-not cold!"

"I don't want us to get sick, and—" I became aware of a rising murmur across Broad Street, a something-is-happening sound. I expected to see an overturned or wrecked frame suit, but I didn't.

People pressed forward. The noise level increased.

Mackenzie returned, both hands holding hot dogs.

"I c-c-can't see!" Karen wailed. We'd lost our vantage point as people jostled for a better view of . . . something.

Mackenzie passed me the franks and lifted her onto his shoulders, making her a human periscope. "Now, can you?" he asked.

"Yes, but there's only the same stuff." She'd stopped stuttering, but now she sounded peevish. The noise across the way became less diffused, sharper, marked by shouts. "And people pointing."

"At what?" Mackenzie asked with more interest than he'd heretofore demonstrated.

"At the barrel-man," Karen said. I assumed she meant a frame suit. "He's disappearing."

"Falling down?"

Mackenzie sounded frustrated. He did not like viewing things secondhand, but at the moment, his sight-line was blocked not only by an enormous man who'd moved in front of him but also by Karen's mittened hands, which she held across his eyes.

"Yes," she said. "No. *He's* not falling down. His head is."

And then I, too, saw it—just as spectators on the other side screamed and surged onto the street. The gryphon-headdress sank, lower and lower, until the man's face was swallowed by his frame. His headpiece banged on the suit, ostrich feathers and golden sequins skewed and wobbling. The pearly lace tent swayed but stopped moving, and as if a contagious and debilitating disease had spread out from it, the other marchers, in ragged sequence, slowed, then stopped, and the music of the hired band dribbled to a halt.

I looked at the other Mummers, tried to make them out, but their disguises worked and I had no clue as to whether I was seeing Vincent Devaney.

"Is there a doctor here?" a voice shouted from the ranks of the Mummers. "Heart attack! Help!"

His words carried on the wind. The unnatural silence had slowly spread backwards up Broad Street as clubs and spectators realized something was wrong.

A woman pulled free of the crowd, a young boy holding onto her hand. She lifted a silver-embroidered panel and put the boy's hand on it, as if mooring him, while she ducked under, inside. How strange, I thought, to have to examine a man with a cloth-covered jungle gym on his shoulders. I wondered for how long the noise, the wind, the wheels, and the strong support of his suit would carry along a man having a heart attack, a man who was unable to gesticulate or to be heard above the music and the crowd.

The woman climbed back out, shaking her head. Now, the area grew preternaturally quiet as everyone leaned forward to hear. Mackenzie quietly transferred Karen back to the ground. I could sense his muscles tighten inside the parka.

The doctor's words rippled across the street, carried on dozens of voices. "Sorry. Sorry. Sorry."

"He's . . ."

Dead, dead, dead. The word was passed with dull finality. "Dead" in near-whispers that reverberated as each person took hold and transferred the word to the next.

I wondered how the doctor had reached her conclusion so quickly. Had she tried to revive him? Used CPR? How could she be so sure?

Someone may have asked her that, because she put up a hand. Once again, her words were relayed back and across, making what she said all the stranger and more upsetting.

"This man was shot."

Shot! Shot! Shot!

It seemed impossible. He'd been in the midst of hundreds of thousands of people for hours, and not uninterested passersby, but spectators watching him, his chest surrounded by steel rods, wooden framing, and cloth.

But it had happened. The Shooter had been shot.

My mother had been right. He'd caught his death.

Two

KAREN and I made our way through a silent city to the loft. I yearned for a public hue and cry, a real reaction. Something dreadful had happened, and only the air currents—both atmospheric and electronic—seemed agitated.

I turned on the TV for a quick look. "Murder at the Mummers' Parade," a voice said on the hour. "Details on tonight's Headline News." And on another channel, "The Mummers' Curse? That's what some wags are calling today's tragedy, the second in two weeks involving a Philadelphia Mummer."

The second tragedy. But Ted Serfi had disappeared, and he hadn't been mumming at the time. Besides, there were those rumors, suspicions that he was "connected." That was nothing like being shot dead in full view of watching crowds.

I turned off the TV. I didn't think Karen needed her day's horrible images reinforced. We could talk or play games, while I waited to find out if my co-worker was still alive. I was sure they knew by now—his fellow Mummers would have ID'd him in an instant. But there was the notification of next of kin. That sort of thing.

"The parade!" Karen said as I turned the TV off. "You said we could watch it."

"But that was before . . . don't you think . . . how about a change of scene? We could read, or play a board game, or—"

"The parade! You said." She pushed out her bottom lip in a clear, if unendearing, she-who-is-peeved pose.

It didn't strike me as wise to remind her that the parade had turned sour, terrifying, or that she was *upset*. I turned on the television again.

From then on, we snuggled on the sofa and watched while sipping from steaming mugs of chicken noodle soup. Outside the loft's high windows, loose pages of newspapers and decimated bits of city trees whipped by, reminding me of the cyclone in *The Wizard of Oz*, except that Mummers didn't get shot in Kansas.

It was a good time to be behind doors, inside walls. It would have been a better time if all three of us were there, but Mackenzie considered finding himself at the scene of a fatal shooting a divine—or a least a legal and professional—sign that he was required to remain. He was correct, but that didn't make me love the fact.

At the time Karen and I left it, the parade had well and truly stalled. Nobody knew what to do beyond clearing the crowd sufficiently to allow the body to be taken from its awkward cage and moved to a cross street where an ambulance waited.

The Mummers, vulnerable and stricken on their merriest of days, had milled uncertainly, except for the men in the frame suits who did their damnedest to stay upright and didn't dare any fancy milling.

I wasn't ready to leave when Mackenzie suggested it. I was still scanning for Vincent, fearing, when I didn't find him, that he was the caged-in corpse.

But Mackenzie had been right to say we should leave, if not for my peace of mind, then surely for Karen's. From there on in for a goodly time, the Mummers, from what I could glean, went into limbo, unsure of what was the right, legal, or smart thing to do. They decided to stop out of respect. But before word could travel through all the ranks, somebody realized that the Comic Clubs and one Fancy had already passed City Hall and performed their four-minute routines for the judges. Prizes had probably been decided for the Comics. Stopping penalized this and the two remaining Fancy Clubs, all the String Bands, and the Fancy Brigades. A year's labor, a year's passion, gone. Whoever had murdered the Mummer had thereby simultaneously murdered the entire parade.

Or maybe the equation went something like: twenty thousand living marchers, one dead. Besides, even to the corpse of a Mummer, being responsible for canceling the parade would be ignominious, a fate truly worse than death.

So by the time Karen and I arrived back at the loft, the parade was in motion again, and now, the lords of Broad Street, the String Bands, were in full swing. Karen watched TV, her mind obviously only partly with Macavity and me. She kept one hand on the cat's back, as if securing herself to something yielding, safe, and soft.

I checked my answer machine, hoping Mackenzie had called while we were en route.

He hadn't. My mother had. I listened to New Year's wishes and muted distress, commenting that since I wasn't home to take the call, I had decided once again not to listen to her, and she hoped I was at least enjoying the parade. "Something sad around here," she said. "Remember I told you about Dr. Landau's cat?"

I shook my head at the machine. I didn't remember any of this, nor did I feel guilty about this failure on my part. And in any case, I knew my mother would review the data she felt important. Again and again. Precisely the way Mackenzie said I did about the Mummers. I didn't want to think about that. "She went away," my mother's voice said. "Dr. Landau, not the cat—to visit her married children for Christmas, and hired her regular cat-sitter, Violet."

If I sped it up or simply walked away, would I be teaching my niece to ignore her elders? I stayed and listened.

"Violet called me all upset. Sid—Sid's the cat—is sick. Terminally. I'm down as the emergency number. There's no way to reach Allen—"

Who was Allen? Another kitty? Another kitty-sitter?

"—because they went to somebody's ski place, can you imagine? Snow!—and the vet thinks Sid needs to be put to sleep, the dear thing. Sid, I mean. Not the vet. Isn't that awful? In a way, I'm glad she doesn't know, she loves him so much, and my goodness, she's a doctor, dedicated to preserving life, she'd be—"

I gave up on who the *she* was, along with the idea of being a role model for my niece, and I fast-forwarded to the remaining message, hoping again that it might be Mackenzie. Again, it wasn't. It was my least favorite student, Renata Field.

I upset myself when I actively dislike a student. It feels unethical, as deserving as the antipathy might be. Luckily, it doesn't happen often. But it had surely happened with Renata, and the feeling was set in reinforced concrete.

"Happy New Year, Miss Pepper." Her chilly voice made it abundantly clear that she in no way meant her words. "I hope you've been thinking about me. I was thinking about you because it is a new year, and a new start, and my last year in high school, and I'm hoping it will be a happy year for me, too. See you soon." And that was that.

If Renata would put the energy into classwork that she put into trying to avoid the consequences of doing nothing except cheat, she might have an academic chance. But instead of doing her homework, Renata had repeatedly claimed I'd lost it, then handed in one take-home essay after she'd copied it, verbatim, from an A student.

I split the A between the two of them, which gave each a 50, which in turn translated into F's. That was before winter break, and Renata had called me every other day since. The calls did not make me fonder of her.

I left the answer machine and sat down next to Karen, who still stared straight ahead. We both oohed and ahhed, although her oohs and ahs seemed a bit forced, at the sea of glittering instruments backed by equally ornate musicians.

Mackenzie had been right. This was the way to watch the parade—and if we'd done it his way all along, he'd be with us now. I tried not to think about that.

Four or more generations danced before us, from a child barely out of toddlerhood all the way up to a man who moved with the careful deliberation of old age. Their theme was "The Peaceable Kingdom," and fantastic lions with feathery "manes" drilled beside silver and white lambs. The band members wore capes the colors of the U.N. flag, and their headpieces had platinum doves stitched on the satin.

I love String Bands. Their one-of-a-kind music is the sound of the parade and to me, its heart.

I'm not sure, however, why they're called String Bands, because in addition to guitars, mandolins, banjos, bass viols, and violins, there were stringless clarinets, saxophones, flutes, and keyboards, both the metal ones of glockenspiels and the faux-ivory of accordions, plus drums—bass and snare. Stringed or not, those haphazardly collected and oddly combined instruments gave the bands their unique, upbeat sound.

The String Bands' anthem, the one song every band includes in its repertoire, is "Oh, Dem Golden Slippers," which contains the essence of their sound—exuberant, irrepressible, overflowing happiness. Not a music designed for tragedy or anything less than high-stepping.

"Time for your initiation," I told my niece. "Now that you're at least partly a girl of this city, it's time for you to do a strut." I leaned close to her. "The people in New Orleans do not have this at all," I added, and then I stood up and demonstrated, doing my own variation, which boiled down to whatever felt good and moved in time to the music, and wishing I, too, wore blue and white mirrored sequins and didn't feel so plain and unadorned.

And after a brief interval, Karen stood up and grinned as she took one step forward and half a step back, lifting an imaginary cape, bending forward and simply moving to the music.

We both giggled, and I didn't explain—not a syllable—that the strut was probably an imitation of the African-American cake-walk of long ago. This bizarre and wonderful celebration is one of the few places the stuff tossed in the pot had actually melted. But I kept it to myself.

And when we had made our way around the entire loft and collapsed back onto the sofa, Karen exhaled in a massive, shoulder-lifting, ultimate sigh and looked at me. "That was very bad, what happened," she said with great solemnity.

I agreed.

"I was scared. The people screaming scared me."

I nodded.

"Even though I got to be on C.K.'s shoulders."

"That part was good." We held hands.

"He said there wouldn't be any shooting this year. That all the shooting was a long time ago." Karen's tone was solemn. A great deal was at stake.

"He thought that's how it would be. That's what everybody thought, because this was *not* how it is, or was. This never happened before. This will never happen again." Please, oh, please, don't make me a liar on that last count, I silently begged. I needed to know that almost as much as Karen did.

"I wish I didn't know that Mummer was dead."

"Me, too."

"I wish he wasn't dead."

The phone rang. I bolted. This had to be Mackenzie.

But the voice had no southern softness, no bass undertones. "Mandy!" my sister said. "You're home. Karen's there, too, isn't she?"

"Yes, we're—"

"Thank goodness you didn't go to the parade. I'm so relieved!"

"Actually, we—"

"Did you hear what happened? Somebody shot a Mummer!"

"Yes, I—"

"Killed him! He's *dead!*"

"I know. I—"

"That *city!* How can you *live* there?" She sounded more like our mother every day, a fact that would curdle her blood if she were aware of it.

Certainly, the city isn't often mistaken for Utopia, but my sister's method of disengaging, standing back and pointing didn't help. Besides, I was tired of blaming everything on geography. Cities don't kill people, guns do. I hoped the murderer turned out to be one of Beth's suburban soulmates.

"Karen's fine," I said. "But we were there."

"There? Where? Not at the—"

"Yes. At the."

"Nowhere near what happened, I hope."

"Right there. When he fell into his suit. She seems okay and we're talking about it, but you should know, in case she has bad dreams or anything."

"Mandy!" Her inflection suggested that I'd purposefully exposed my niece to urban slaughter.

"It wasn't like we could see anything gross." A weak defense, but the best I could manage. "And we're comfy up here now, and talking it through, so don't worry."

"I don't feel good about her in an old warehouse in that city. No offense intended."

"I'm taking some, anyway. This is historic Old City. Where I live once was a warehouse, but now it's a loft. This is *chic*, Beth. This is Philadelphia's SoHo."

"I don't go to New York's SoHo," she snapped. "And I certainly don't take my babies there."

This was a bad way to start the year, and the basis of it, the problem of the increasingly fearful suburbanite, of walls real and imagined, deserved a bigger chunk of time and thought than I was willing to donate at the moment.

"I'm sorry you were so worried," I said as sweetly as I could, given that she hadn't even *asked* whether I was all right. Let alone Mackenzie. "Would you feel better if I brought Karen home right away? We're settled in with hot soup and the TV, but . . ."

25

She was too well-bred, or at least too cowed by what my mother had said was the code of female politeness—never inconvenience anyone but yourself, a code my mother did not necessarily follow, by the way—to say what she meant, which was "bring my baby home *now* and I don't care what you want."

Beth sighed. I waited, counting on her excellent, if antiquated, standards. I wanted to stay put until I found out more about the Mummer. "No, no," she murmured. "I didn't mean . . . Thanks for offering, but I guess I'm being . . . I know you didn't put her there on purpose. I tend to be over-protective at times . . ."

And thus do the city sister and the country sister once again stave off a value clash; plus, the trip to the hinterlands was suitably delayed.

However, two hours later, I'd had my fill of sequins, struts, and strings, but I hadn't gotten a call from Mackenzie. His unpredictability and unaccountability were speed bumps on our path through life together. I was working at adjusting, not only understanding the demands of his profession, but honoring them. I took deep breaths and made a heartfelt New Year's resolution to stop resenting Mackenzie's job.

I instantly resented the need to make such a vow.

"Had enough parade for a while?" I asked Karen, who looked groggy. "Ready for the glories of Gladwyne?"

She regarded me blankly. We'd finished our soup and bread and topped it with ice cream and Oreos. Perhaps too many, her glazed expression suggested.

"Home. Yours. How 'bout it?"

She nodded. She was a big girl, not a baby like her brother, she was fond of reminding us. But she'd been on the town for twenty-four hours, slept in a strange bed in a former warehouse, seen a parade and a murder, and she was tired and homesick, although, like her mother, too polite to say so outright.

EVEN NOW, at the frozen nadir of winter, Beth's suburb maintained a green lushness, although I don't know how. Trees lose their leaves even on the Main Line, and climbing vines freeze.

The residual greenness must be further proof of how money colors everything.

I sighed and rang her bell.

Beth had a visitor, a slender woman with hair the color of pink grapefruit juice and features sharp enough to slice paper. As we unwrapped Karen, who had been packed off to my place wearing enough to survive a month of snow camping, we were introduced.

"This is my friend, Quentin Reed," Beth said.

I'd already met women friends of Beth's named Sidney, Michael, and Claude. Perhaps she collected the ambiguously named, but what to make of a day spent watching men dressed in sequins, feathers, lace, and satin, and an evening with a woman named Quentin? Perhaps we were headed for androgyny at long last, but was it a good thing?

"My parents really, really wanted a boy," Quentin-the-girl said with an engaging grin.

True equality will be had when I meet a man named Rosabelle or Tiffany who says, "My parents really, really wanted a girl."

"Quentin's a therapist," Beth said in an overly calm voice, after Karen had run upstairs followed by the household's galumph of a dog, Horse. "You've probably heard her."

"Yes," I said. "Of course. That's why you sounded familiar."

"Good day," she'd say on the radio, "This is Dr. Reed On the Air." I had come to think of *Dr.* as her first name and *Air* her last. But as I'd drive wherever, listening to her ripe, fruity voice giving urgent advice and telling her "true stories"—nasty-funny case studies of neurotics she'd known—I'd imagined her fuller, older, much more subdued-looking.

"The radio doctor."

She smiled. "Among other things, yes."

"Pleased to meet you." I was, even though I'm leery of the sound-bite solution, of keeping therapy zippy enough to maintain ratings.

"I felt it would be good to have someone at the ready if Karen needs to ventilate," Beth said.

Ventilation seemed the concern of steamfitters. Besides, was it wise to hire a shrink before there was any sign of emotional problems, like purifying drinking water just in case? Or did it instead insure that there would be problems?

"I agreed," Quentin Reed off-the-air said, not surprisingly. "Given the dimensions of the child's trauma. To be an eyewitness to such a dreadful event. The death, in essence, of a beloved icon, a clown." She looked devastated herself.

"Not a clown," I began. But that was irrelevant and arguable. "More to the point, we weren't precisely eyewitnesses to the crime, only its results. I suspect that nobody actually saw it happen. After all, there were thousands of people watching, and not a peep until he collapsed, so it couldn't have been too obvious when he was shot. Mostly, this is going to be a gigantic headache for the police." And create more nights alone for me.

"Forgive me, but I find that a purposefully dispassionate—no, let us say dissociated—appraisal of a human tragedy," she said in her mother-knows-best voice.

I felt properly rebuked, improperly perverse. "I didn't mean it the way it sounded. I meant, the good news for Karen is going to be what makes it a problem for the police because there was precious little to see. No blood, no fearsome dying. All you could see was a painted face, and then it slipped down inside his costume. His headpiece stayed on top and the costume still stood up. It almost all looked unchanged. Much less violent than TV cartoons, to tell the truth."

Quentin Reed's mouth curled into a beneficent I-have-compassion-and-pity-for-your-unbelievable-ignorance smile. "I'm sure you'll agree that a six-year-old is a much more vulnerable spectator than you would be. And death is so final, so absolute."

Not a whole lot of room for debate there. What could I retort? That now and then there were temporary deaths? She'd have me shrink-wrapped in a white jacket within seconds. So I smiled, nervously, agreeing with who knew quite what. However, even if she'd said something grossly incorrect, how can you convince a serenely self-assured, certified mentally healthy professional that you are fine if she doesn't think so? The more intense the protests, the more smugly superior the pro becomes. Nonetheless, probably because I am demented, I pushed on. "We didn't see the shooting. We didn't see his wound. The actual crime probably didn't take place anywhere near where we were. The wind and momentum and maybe tradition kept him moving, possibly for blocks. We only saw him slide—"

"Yes, yes," she said. "You've made that clear. I must say that I'm not only worried about Karen, but about you. Perhaps more so. You are in serious denial. You've been on what was intended to be a happy, bonding outing and instead, you've witnessed a hideous murder."

"I've been trying to say that we didn't witness the—"

"And you have the maturity to comprehend its full significance," she barreled on. "Not only was the man murdered, but so were your dreams and hopes for the day."

Were the two things equal? One dead man versus my soured plans?

"It isn't healthy to stuff feelings," Quentin Reed said. "Makes you sick."

Was she actually Beth's friend? Did they talk this way to each other all the time? And weren't shrinks supposed to *listen*? "Doctor," I began, then I had a thought. She was going to be peering into Karen's psyche. "Your specialty—your branch of medicine . . . that's an M.D.?"

Quentin cleared her throat.

"In . . . ?" I was being rude, but so was she, reaming my brain with a pickax and without invitation. "Child psychiatry?"

"A D.P.M, actually. I was originally a podiatrist."

A foot doctor, indeed.

"Of course, I then got a master's in therapy."

From a diploma mill, I'd be willing to bet. I flashed my sister a look. Was she listening?

Horse-the-dog clomped back down the stairs, his rump wiggling with each step. My mental health didn't trouble him in the least, and he came over and sat on my feet.

"Sweetie," Beth said over-brightly, in a tone she generally reserved for her children. I understood how mentally mature she considered me. "Why so resistant? Why not take advantage of Quentin's presence?"

The rock-bottom truth is that I believe that stuffing and stifling selected feelings can work toward the general good, also known as civilization. *Not* stifling leads to freeway snipers, mail bombs, and talk shows. Be honest, who'd you rather have across the table for the long haul? Queen Victoria or Geraldo?

What's so great about mental health, anyway? For starters, what would it do to literature? What kind of novel would a self-actualized Anna Karenina produce? What play would be left if Quentin Reed had worked through Macbeth and his lady's power drives? How interesting would a serene Holden Caulfield be? A Joan of Arc medically relieved of those voices?

Stories require neurosis, psychosis, obsession, and delusion, so why abet anyone attempting to squelch those things?

The dog was the only perfectly adjusted creature around, and while he was delightful in a canine way, you really couldn't base an opera—even a soap opera—on his life and times. We *need* mental disturbances and stifled emotions.

But my sister looked so desperately concerned that I apologized for my perversity. "I knew—know—one of the Mummers in that club, so I have a personal reason and concern in addition to normal worry."

I had made things worse. "You *knew* him?" Beth looked ready to cry.

"I hope not, but I don't know. I don't know who was shot. The costume, you know, the makeup. The distance. That's why I don't think Karen was overly—"

"You knew a Mummer?"

"I hope I still do."

On the Air looked as astounded as if I'd claimed familiarity with a Martian, not somebody from the other side of City Line.

Beth shut her eyes. As if by knowing one of *them* I'd been contaminated, and much more significantly, had endangered her daughter. That because I knew one, had a link, the dead man had chosen to die at Karen's feet.

Beth was a basically good person. Even more than basically—she was a good on-the-top person, too. But her domesticated life in the green suburbs was corrupting her, leaving her too surprised by and incredulous about reality.

"Time to head back," I said. "Mackenzie will be home any minute." I wiggled my toes, signaling Horse to dislodge. He turned his head and licked my fingers.

"Where is he, then?" Beth asked worriedly. "I thought he had the day off. I thought the two of you were taking Karen to the parade. Is he *working*?" Beth turned to Dr. Quentin. "Her, um, boyfriend. They live in a warehouse."

She made us sound like squatters huddling in the deserted shell of a building. She had never been snotty about my tiny Trinity house. Its three and a half rooms wouldn't have filled a quarter of the loft, but living in the cramped former abode of a poor Colonial person obviously had more panache than living in the spacious former residence of Oriental rugs.

And *boyfriend*? C. K. was thirty-five. I was thirty-one. A little long in the teeth for boy- and girlhood.

I gritted my long teeth and reminded myself she meant well. "We were there," I explained. "At the parade. As observers. But Mackenzie's a homicide detective. There were thousands of people freaking out, a blocked street, a dead man. He went to help. He has to." Here I was, justifying behavior I otherwise complained about.

"Ah, a homicide detective. And by attempting to identify with him, no wonder you can be so . . . matter of fact about death," Quentin Reed, healer, said. "But the strain—you're a teacher, a nurturer, not someone accustomed to death. In any case, your friend's at work and it's cold and dark outside. Why don't you stay? Have a cup of tea, put your feet up. Ventilate. Pals talking. This isn't a session, merely a chance to unburden yourself."

It would be rude to suggest that she wasn't my pal. "I appreciate the offer, but I'm fine." I was about to remind them that the Doc, needed or not, was on call for my niece, except that I had a moment's horrified speculation that maybe Beth had summoned her for me all along. "Karen will be fine, too," I said, sidling as close as I dared to suggesting that no shrinks—or podiatrists—were required.

Ah, but I had forgotten that my niece, once again mesmerized by the never-ending parade in the next room, wanted to be a Mummer. Wait till she told her Mama. Dr. Reed would go off the air and become a permanent resident, a household appliance.

"Never hurts to be cautious, does it?" the doctor asked with a knowing smile.

I'm not certain caution ever helped, either, but instead of saying so and appearing even more contrary and city-ruined, I made my farewells.

The dog seemed truly sorry to see me go.

Three

B Y the time Mackenzie actually came home, the sky had fallen. The howling wind whipped snow around buildings, and my man looked as if it had mugged him.

His red nose contrasted dramatically with his frost-bleached skin. "Took forever," he groaned. "Nobody wanted to move, to lose their spot, in case the parade was still on or in case TV cameras were coming. Nobody had seen anything more than what we saw."

"Please—I hope this isn't rude, but can we cut to the chase? Who was it? What happened?"

When Mackenzie is stressed, his Southern speech patterns intensify, which is to say, slow down, slur out, and take too long for this short-tempered Yankee to bear. And Mackenzie was most definitely stressed. I offered him mulled wine in partial atonement for my inherent impatience.

"Fellow named Patricciano," he said.

"Thank heavens!" I realized how cold-hearted that sounded. "I mean—"

"I know. It wasn't your friend or anybody you know."

But as I poured a mug of the hot spiced wine, I saw a face. Dark hair, dark eyes. Puckish features filled with ready charm. Patricciano. "What's his first name?" I asked.

"James."

I inhaled long and heavily and remembered the evening Vincent had taken me to his Fancy Club. His friends and fellow members didn't want me inside at first, and then, when they relented, it was only for a controlled and censored peep. They were afraid a journalist—for so Vincent presented me—an outsider, and worst of all, a female, might describe the suits they were finishing. Their themes and designs were secret, known only to them and a priest whose job it was to tell clubs if they'd inadvertently chosen the same idea. That's as far as the information was supposed to go until the New Year's Day parade. The competition between clubs might be good-natured, but it was also real. The prize money was minimal compared to the cost of the suits, but winning was important. Designs and details were as carefully guarded as state secrets.

But later that evening, several of them had coffee with me at the Melrose Diner. I met Vincent's wife Barbs, who was overly cordial and nervous. Also a silent, dull fellow named Fabian with a silent, dull chip on his shoulder, and a brother and sister, Stephen and Dolores Grassi, both dark, fine-featured, and quiet, although Dolores's hair was spectacular, rising above and around her small face like a Mummer's headpiece. Dolores's fiancé was also there, and he was the man whose puckish face attracted me, not because of its features, but because of the personality behind them. He was also the most helpful and charming of the assembled Fancy Club members.

"They called him Jimmy," I said. "Jimmy Pat. He was a nice guy—cute and funny. Very animated. Engaged to a girl named Dolores Grassi. They're getting—they were supposed to get married soon. Poor Dolores! He drives—drove a produce truck for a group of Jersey farmers. What a shame."

Mackenzie looked gratifyingly amazed. "While acquiring his entire family history, did you also find out why somebody'd want to kill him?"

"Vincent must be distraught. They've been friends since childhood. So were their fathers. Tommy Pat, Jimmy's father, was like a dad to Vincent after Vincent's own father died. That's how come Vincent joined a Fancy Club, even though lots of his relatives are in String Bands. Because Tommy Pat belonged to it and brought him in when he was fourteen."

I could sense C. K. listening only halfway, waiting with unpleasant information to hand me in an unwelcome trade. "What is it?" I asked.

"Devaney was the only name I knew in that club, so when we were surrounded by upset, not particularly sober Mummers and spectators, I thought maybe I should talk to him."

I didn't like his sidewinder approach, slowly told or not, didn't like the hedging, conditional ideas, explanations, and phrases like *I thought maybe.*

"His bein' a teacher and all," he continued, "I hoped he'd be less incoherent. Calmer by trainin'. An' I thought, his knowin' you, there'd be a connection, maybe he'd talk more freely." He rolled his head to the left and right, as if his neck hurt.

"Yes, and?" I said it even though I suspected I might be happier not knowing what came next.

"Couldn' find him." Mackenzie paused, one eyebrow raised as he watched me.

"Meaning what?" I tried to keep my expression impassive. Mackenzie couldn't see my blood pressure rising, and what Mackenzie couldn't see or intuit didn't count.

"His buddies," he said, "were confused about his whereabouts. When he finally appeared, one asked where he'd been, and another said the first was too drunk to see somebody next to him. He may have had a point. I'm not sure how much they can notice besides the weather and the music after a few good hours. But apparently, there are diverse opinions as to Vincent's whereabouts when his fellow Mummer bit the dust."

"Why do you sound that way? Why apparently? Why are they divided on his whereabouts and what does it matter?"

"Muddies things further, is all. Was he or wasn't he there?"

"If he wasn't, then he couldn't have shot anybody."

"So you'd think he'd make it real clear where he was, but he wasn't partic'ly communicative, even before he realized what'd happened and went into shock, supposedly."

Supposedly? "And even if he was there, he wouldn't shoot anybody—certainly not Jimmy Pat—so why do you care? Vincent can't be a suspect."

"Everybody's a suspect at this point, everybody who had opportunity." He wearily ran his fingers through his hair. The salt-and-pepper curls had much more resilience than he seemed to. "Of course," he said, "if he left the street, we will surely find somebody who saw him elsewhere. It's not easy bein' inconspicuous in feathers and shimmery stuff. Of course, even in the parade, there were ten or so of them around the frame suit, all dressed like Devaney, so who's to know who saw what when?"

"Does anybody know where Jimmy was shot?" I asked.

"Stomach."

"I meant at what point on the parade route."

He shook his head. "He was joking and fine when they set out, pretty drunk within a few hours, but a party boy, according to all, able to handle liquor. And then he was dead. Friends thought at first he was passing out. They thought he'd get it together in time for the judging, and they'd rib him about it all next year."

"What about the noise of the gunshot?"

Mackenzie shrugged. "There are silencers. Besides, given the racket with the brass band and people whistlin' and callin' out, who'd hear anything? Who'd think it was unusual if he did hear something?"

"Is anybody considering—don't laugh—suicide?" I found the idea ridiculous myself, but still and all . . .

Mackenzie sighed. "Where's the gun, then? And what would be the sense of that, anyway?"

"Well, how could a killer be invisible?"

"What if he wasn't? What if he was right there, twirlin' and marchin' and doing his thing, like another Mummer would be?" The suggestion was made in a soft voice which did not make it less ominous. "How about somebody with a weapon under his costume? There are enough flaps and gussets and plackets and whatever-you-call-'ems to hide a cannon."

"How about the people who rushed to steady the suit?"

"The official helpers?"

"Some looked unofficial, too."

"How about somebody ducking inside the suit?" he asked. "It's the size of a room."

"Why would anybody? And wouldn't everybody notice and remember?"

"I have been told that despite the rest stop on Washington Avenue, there are those who use the commodious frame suits as mobile outhouses."

The idea was disgusting, but then, so was the gigantic urinal-tent on Washington Avenue, and Lord knew where females went when nature called.

Mackenzie had an eloquent, continental shrug that expressed infinite weariness with the world's evil potential. This time it probably also encompassed the idea of men disappearing into the pleats and panels of frame suits.

"Wouldn't Jimmy Pat have shouted? I mean, being shot . . ."

"Shot several times, in fact, but who'd hear? Who'd know it wasn't a normal feelin'-good expression? Also, Jimmy Pat might have been so tanked he didn't feel the bullet, or he could have gone into shock, or at least not understood what was happenin', until it was too late."

"Then what are you going to do?"

He finished off his mulled wine. "We need a whole lot of forensics, like calculations of how fast or slow that kind of bleed would go given the temperature, the fact that the victim was in motion, and some kind of reconstruction of how fast or slow the brigade was moving. Blood alcohol level. Wind-chill factor. We need to check the street for blood, but how many people strutted over wherever he bled, and now, this snow is not helping. And then, what I'm goin' to do is pray for a miracle. If anybody saw it happen, why didn't they make a fuss? And if nobody saw it happen, then what?"

"Surely somebody saw it happen, but they didn't know they were seeing it happen."

"If a person sees a crime in a forest, but doesn't know he's seeing a crime, did he see it?"

"What is the sound of one homicide detective being snotty?"

He yawned, and I felt a twinge of compassion. He was tired, disappointed, and frustrated at the prospect of a difficult, if not impossible, investigation.

He sank into the downy softness of our most recent extravagance, a sofa made of leather so butter-soft and palely glowing, I was sure it had been the hide of something gentle and mythical, most likely a unicorn. I hoped it had died of old age.

"Ahhh," he said. "Quiet at last. It hurts to listen to that many people. I must have gotten five hundred names. Not that anybody had much to say, except how horrible this all was and that they didn't know what the hell happened and they were royally freaked out."

"I met somebody named Quentin who'd love listening to their traumas."

He rolled his eyes. "You going to tell me his history, too?"

"Hers. And the only part I know is that her parents really, really wanted a boy."

"Wouldn't anyone's?"

I sat down next to him, the better to throttle him.

"You're so easy," he murmured. "Any time I want to see a cute knee jerk . . ."

"I was thinking . . ."

He sat up straighter. His hair seemed to uncurl and go on alert. Despite his avowed preference for "smart women," they sometimes frightened him. Or at least I did.

"It's a brand new year," he said. "Surely Philadelphians have more than Mummers by way of tradition. Don't you folk make resolutions? How about you make a serious one to—"

"Stop thinking?"

"Stop thinkin' about what you're thinkin' about, which is what I'm supposed to think about an' concentrate instead on thinkin' about what you're supposed to be thinkin' about."

"If I could follow you, I'd try. But all I meant was that I know some of the people involved, so could I help you?"

"Sure. I'd like you to tell me whatever you know, just the way you did about Jimmy Pat. But if you mean could we job-share, then the answer is no. Adamantly. Definitely. Absolutely."

"Get off the fence, Mackenzie. You want me as a partner or not?"

He had the grace to grin.

"So, then," I said. "Don't you think I could—"

"I think you, or somebody, could make dinner."

"Dinner?"

"You remember. Food. The stuff that gets rid of that yawningly empty sensation. This somebody doesn't have the energy to cook tonight, and don' know who's open for takeout on New Year's Day."

Given that the cat was unlikely to whip up a repast, that left me as the somebody. I am a moody cook. I have my moments, but only when I feel like it. Mostly, I don't. The grinding dailiness of food preparation makes me feel trapped in an alimentary canal. I can hear the hollow boom of empty stomachs, the gurglesong of digestive juices. Buy ingredients, they warble; prepare them, serve them to me in a new form, clean up from the serving and the cooking, and then—well, I don't want to think about the finale of the roundelay. And if you listen to it, obey it, do it— then you have to start all over again. Couldn't we take care of all that and save a whole lot of time if we were fitted with long-term batteries instead? I think Mother Nature was on the phone when the idea of sustenance came by for review, and she waved it on.

Besides, even though we now shared the loft, the kitchen was still, unmistakably, Mackenzie's. He tried to be nonchalant about it, but I could feel him watching that I didn't scratch the tin lining of his beloved copper pots, and that I left the counters sterilized in case we'd have to perform brain surgery later in the evening. I like to slop things around, feel industrious through an abundance of clutter, then do a decent cleanup. Life is too short to polish a copper pot, which, just like the rest of the food cycle, needs constant re-doing.

Luckily, we still had the chicken-vegetable-noodle soup, most of a good crusty loaf of bread, and a bottle of Pinot Noir. On my less inspired days, whatever I cooked seemed like leftovers—even when we'd never had the food a first time.

"You have to remember," Mackenzie said from the sofa, "that somewhere is a person who shot a man in front of hundreds of thousands of spectators. A person, therefore, who isn't easily intimidated. Cold-blooded. Not a person to frighten by pushing on him or meddlin'."

"Meddling! You make me sound like a—"

"Meddler."

"I wanted to help. That was all."

"Does it have anythin' to do with your friend's being involved?"

"Why are you picking on him? You said everybody was a suspect. You don't know anything except that Vincent was hard to find today. Which argues in his favor, anyway."

Mackenzie nodded. "He's a suspect, then, is that okay?"

"Why? You sought him out because he teaches at my school and you knew his name. Teaching with me isn't a crime, but you're making it one. That's why I feel involved."

"Far as I can see, you always feel involved. Have you ever considered puttin' this quirk to use?"

"You called it meddling."

"Not that way. You could turn a profit by labeling it a problem, a societal ill. You know the drill. Females who love crime too much. Homicide-addiction. Women Who Snoop Too

Much. Write a book, go on talk shows. Confessions of a crime-junkie."

He pronounced it as *crahm*, but a slur, slurred, doesn't sound less offensive.

"A twelve-step program," he went on with low-grade Southern glee, "startin' with step one: one crime at a time. You'll make a fortune."

"Never mind. It was an offer, nothing more. End of topic." I said it mildly, actually meant it, although I was still worried about Vincent Devaney's whereabouts and/or why Mackenzie was suspicious of him. But in the meantime, peace was restored in our little household. After awhile, we even remembered that there were things to do together that were more fun than discussing crime and punishment.

Later, Mackenzie napped. He had to go back to work at midnight. I lay on the bed, watching the digital adjustments of our Doomsday clock. We'd gone to a Boxing Day party after Christmas. Each invitee brought his worst gift for a blind swap.

I wound up stuck with the Doomsday clock, and nobody else tried to trade for it. No wonder. And no wonder somebody had gladly given it up.

It sat on the dresser, either a grisly piece of humor or just plain grisly. On a black marble slab, a lighted panel said:

YOU HAVE
359,160 HOURS
15 MINUTES
27 SECONDS
LEFT IN YOUR LIFE. ENJOY THEM.
THE TIME IS NOW: 10:47 P.M.

Enjoy them, indeed. Who had thought the device up? What kind of person bought it as a Christmas gift—and for whom, with what motive? As I watched, my remaining time dwindled, second by second. Three hundred and fifty-nine thousand hours didn't seem enough, particularly when I could watch them diminish. I worried whether the clock maker had accounted for the leap years in my future, for daylight saving time, for medical break-throughs and random violence. Did this mean it didn't matter if I exercised or started smoking again or rode a motorcycle without a helmet or jaywalked?

When the telephone rang, I realized that I had dozed off. The Doomsday clock said 1:05 A.M. Also that I had two hours and eighteen minutes less to live.

The caller brusquely asked if Mackenzie was there and told me that if so, I should immediately wake him.

We'd overslept. The alarm on the real clock, hastily and wrongly set for an A.M. instead of a P.M., had remained silent. Actually, only one of us had overslept since I'd never intended either to go to sleep at eleven or to be up at midnight.

Mackenzie looked so exhausted, I felt cruel for waking him. It didn't seem fair that baddies got to do their thing whenever they so pleased, and goodies had to play the game according to the criminal's timetable.

I saw him off, then shuffled back to bed, intending to sleep straight through the last day of my vacation, even if it meant missing hours, minutes, and seconds of remaining life.

It had taken me awhile to get used to the wide-open expanses of the loft after years in my historic but constricted house. When I first moved in here, I felt stranded in a wilderness. Nothing above the high ceilings but roofing, nothing below but other spaces, too often silent, and an art gallery that was closed at night. For a month, I half hoped the walls would close in, like something out of Poe, but now, I was accustomed to a skylit ceiling and plaster and brick horizons I could barely see at night. The dangerous expanse had become breathing space.

Macavity, who was supposed to be the skittish one, had taken ten minutes max to call the place home.

All of which was to say that both the cat and I were soundly asleep when the door to the loft opened.

I wouldn't have noticed, it was done so quietly, except that Macavity did notice and pounded over my hip and chest en route to his under-bed hiding spot. It's amazing how much a cat makes itself weigh when it's stomping you. "Detour, you inconsiderate beast," I groaned. The cat spoke back.

"Since you're already up . . ."

I screamed. And lost a huge number of seconds and minutes of the potential joy I had left.

"Din' mean to startle you, thought I heard you—"

"For God's sake! How could you not think you'd scare me? What are you doing here? You just left! Why didn't you knock, or make noise—what are you *doing* here?"

"Workin'. And now that you really are up . . ."

I was. Definitely. All systems jump-started even though, squint as I might, I couldn't see a hint of daylight through the windows, or even through the skylight. "It isn't tomorrow yet."

"It's four forty-six A.M.," he said in a bright voice that assumed I was lucky he hadn't let me sleep past this fabulous hour. "I'll make coffee," he added, and he relocated to do so.

There followed an inordinate amount of grinding, tamping, clattering, and cabinet-slamming for so minor a task.

I dragged my bod out of bed, into the arctic of a brick-walled expanse whose heat had been turned down for the night. I insulated my feet with a pair of Mackenzie's ski socks and pulled a hooded sweatshirt on top of the oversized T-shirt I wore as a nightie. I did not look like an ad for eternal womanhood, but I was warmer. "What is it?" I muttered. I caught the first fragrant fumes of brewing coffee. "What's going on?"

"I missed you, so I made a detour. Nice that we live so close to headquarters."

"I'm always glad to see youuuuu . . ." The *you* turned into a gigantic yawn. When it was finished, I continued. "Only, sometimes more than other times. I thought you were working."

"I am." Enough had dripped into the pot to pour us each a cup. I felt more nervous with each nuance of coffee-serving minutiae, as if Mackenzie were inventing a ceremony for an onerous event. Something was amiss if the man visited this way at this hour while on a new homicide case.

He rummaged around until he found leftover bagels, then he sliced two and put them in the toaster oven.

"You're gonna get a call," he said, "later, from the department. Billy Obenhauser, okay? Wants to talk about your buddy. Devaney."

"Why?" I knew that business that Mackenzie had said earlier, but I didn't know *why*. "As a character witness?"

"As an alibi." He sat down across from me and sipped his coffee, never taking his eyes off my face. I hoped the attentiveness was love, not surveillance.

"Whose?" I asked. "For what?" Those weren't over-bright questions, but I was sleep-deprived and even if I hadn't been, the idea still wouldn't have made ready sense.

"Vincent Devaney's. He insists—not to me, to Billy, who was questioning him, that he was not around for the probable time Jimmy Pat was shot. Says he was with a teacher from his school. Namely, you."

"But I was with you!"

"I know that and you know that. Devaney seems the only one who doesn't know that. Of course, there are gaps like when you and Karen left. I can't vouch for then." He waited.

So that hadn't been love light in his eyes but the gleam of professional observation. "What are you intimating? We stood in line for the Porta-Potty, and then we stopped at a pretzel vendor's."

"And the other time was when I went to get us hot dogs."

"What are you saying, C. K.?"

"Just the facts, ma'am. The thing is, Vincent doesn't appear to have known that we were parade-viewing together. Or that I'm a cop. You never told him about me?" He seemed to feel slighted.

"About you? Told him what? I notified him of your existence. Of our relationship. And probably about what you do for a living." We'd talked lots in the months during which I was supposedly writing my article.

The article. I felt an avaricious and shameful flash. Would it be more salable because of the murder?

I had to think about precisely what I had told Vincent. Before school ended for winter break, I'd mentioned that I was taking my niece to the parade. I had no idea whether I'd said Mackenzie would be there, too. Probably not, because I couldn't have known for sure two weeks ago. The man's schedule is not exactly predictable. So it could have appeared I'd be at the parade with Karen and no one else. The implications of this made me sad. "He's not a killer," I said.

"Nobody is. Everybody is, pushed enough."

"They were like brothers."

"So were Cain and Abel."

"Come on. Best friends, then."

"Fighting over everything," he said, surprising me. "Pretty heatedly about who would be the next club Captain."

I waved that away. "Good-natured rivalry, that's all."

"Even about who would wear the frame suit. And Jimmy Pat had a habit of always winning their contests. This could have been one contest too many."

"You're pushing too hard. Not Vincent."

Mackenzie raised an eyebrow.

"That's all I know and now I've said it. So why does somebody else have to question me?"

"Ethical gray area if I question you about your whereabouts. I was part of them, remember?"

"Then why this visit? Surely, warning me about being questioned is even grayer."

"I'd never warn you about police procedure. That'd be wrong. I'm here because I can't bear bein' away from you too long."

"Am I supposed to know that this Billy person is going to happen?" I asked. "Or that Vincent named me as his alibi?"

"Kind of slipped out, didn't it. Post-pillow talk. Maybe it would be best not to mention it when Billy calls, which won't be for a while."

"He's actually waiting until daybreak?"

"He has other things to take care of first. A lot of what he'd want to know from you about timin' depends on forensic results."

So I was privy to something that wouldn't be called upon for a while. Why let me know this? Wasn't this the man who a few hours earlier had advocated recovery from meddling addiction?

He must have seen the questions bopping through my brain, or at least had enough brains of his own to recognize that they needed to be addressed. He leaned over the little table to put his hand on mine. "You may think I'm about to eat a bagel, but it's more like crow."

"No metaphors or similes until daybreak," I said.

"He trusts you, this Devaney. He didn't call and alert you to his considerable lie, did he?"

I shook my head. It felt heavy with woeful suspicion.

"An' it is a lie, isn't it?"

I exhaled with annoyance.

"Had to ask, is all. See why I can't interrogate you or take a statement?"

Point well made.

"Thing is, he trusts you to protect him. Which is to say, with a relationship like that, maybe you'd find things out that we aren't going to, like why he's lying and what's really going down. At least, you might find out more quickly and easily than we could. Save time. He owes you that, doesn't he? You could be helping him out of big trouble."

"Officer, are you saying what I think?"

"Who ever knows what you're thinkin'?"

"Are you not he who forbade me even to speculate?"

"Live and learn."

I shook my head. "Nope."

"You won't? But . . . but you always . . ."

"Not unless you say it. Out loud."

"Aw, please . . ."

"Clearly, comprehensibly." I folded my arms across my chest.

He swallowed, scowled, took a deep breath, and looked as if the required words might gag him. But Mackenzie is a brave and practical man.

"Okay," he said. "To speed things up, and since he has already involved you in this, and if you feel you could or should, would you talk to your friend Vincent?"

I considered this a moment. "I'd like a declarative sentence, not a question."

He tapped his fingers on the table. "I could use—"

"Say my name, would you?"

"Mandy, I would appreciate your help on this."

"No problem." The light through the window facing east was pearly. Almost dawn. I went over to his side of the table, sat down on his lap, kissed him, and whispered in his ear. Not sweet nothings. Reality. "You are a most excellent man, and right about many things, but you are wrong about one thing. You're not about to eat either bagels or crow. Your only option is charcoal."

I stood back up and extracted two cremated bagels from the toaster oven.

Sometimes it takes entirely too long to get a man to admit he needs you.

Four

VINCENT wasn't answering his phone. I'd waited a decent interval until households with early-rising tod-
dlers would be up. Then I'd waited longer, until even
households with hungover adults would be up. But all I got in return for my patience was a machine that promised to get back to
me. It lied.

"It's me, Vincent. Me, Mandy." I sounded like I was audition-
ing for a Tarzan movie. "It is I, Vincent," I said next go-round.
Maybe he only responded to the grammatically correct.

Why did I have to tell him that we had to talk? I wasn't even supposed to know that he was using—abusing—me as his alibi, but he certainly knew it. We were friends. Why hadn't he called me?

From outside and below, I heard the whir of snowplows and the occasional scrape of a shovel hitting sidewalk. The part of the sky I could see was soft gray. The sun had risen and presumably was up there somewhere, but in a reclusive mode. Probably waiting until later, when its overdue appearance would slush up the snow in time for it to freeze into a layer of ice by nightfall.

Things are bad when you're miffed with the sun.

Two hours and four more messages later, with Billy Obenhauser's interrogation looming, I'd had it with Alexander Graham Bell. I'd communicate the old-fashioned way, in person, braving the not-so-great outdoors.

I couldn't imagine Vincent committing a cold-blooded murder, or fleeing. I could, however, picture him biding his time at home, in shock at the implied accusation of having committed a crime.

I didn't want to drive on unplowed streets, so I waited for a holiday-schedule bus an inordinately long time. This sleuthing stuff, even this talking-with-my-friend stuff, was less than convenient. Vincent had better be worth it.

He lived near Ninth Street, in the same neighborhood as his parents did and his grandparents had. His in-laws lived five blocks away and his wife's brother and family, a few blocks over. In South Philly, a remarkably constant and intact world of its own, there was nothing exceptional about this ongoing proximity. While the rest of the country subscribed to the different-is-better theory, following jobs and whims to all corners of the earth, South Philly remained amazingly cohesive, generations choosing to live close to one another—young men ignoring Horace Greeley and never going west, not even as far as West Philly.

Many of the houses around here were never on the market. They were inherited, passed on to family, sold directly to a known quantity, preferably a relative.

In contrast, my parents had left home, hearth, and offspring for the sunshine of Boca Raton, and Mackenzie had loped out of the Louisiana Bayou for college in Texas and crime-busting up north. He had a brother in San Diego, a sister in Minnesota, and other siblings and siblings-in-law scattered hither and yon. The thing was, neither of our families found it odd that we were fragmented, but the Devaneys would have considered it heretical, close to tragic.

I contemplated these various cultural norms so intently that I missed my stop, and in walking several blocks, I had more chance to wonder why they called our climate temperate, when it was anything but. Maybe it meant the climate had a temper. A bad one.

My favorite part of Ninth Street was the market, where buying food was personalized and close to enjoyable. As opposed to the sterile all-business atmosphere of a supermarket, this marketplace is a blur of noise and movement as people push their way between small shops and stalls set out at the curb. Vendors hawk specials; chickens squawk; cottontail rabbits and piglets and lambs hang limply from butchers' hooks; fish gleam in woven baskets; and the aromas of oregano and ripe cheeses flavor the air. The Italian Market, we used to call it, but it has become more international, with Puerto Rican specialty shops and a definite Asian edge. Today, the market seemed tired, dazed, recuperating from New Year's parades official and traditional, both the one up Broad Street and the nonstop hometown revelries afterwards on Second—known as Two—Street.

I passed a building with a large and colorful mural on its side. It depicted the market and, looming in front of it, Frank Rizzo, former police chief and mayor. The scale was odd—the stores, small, and Rizzo, enormous, hundreds of times their size. A new Wonder of the World, the Colossus of South Philly.

Vincent lived on a side street of flat-faced shallow homes that rose abruptly from the pavement. No trees, no front lawns, no grass or low bushes softened the meeting of hard surfaces. Each home had three marble steps leading from pavement to front door, a window to the left of the door, and two windows facing the street on the second floor. Some were natural brick, others had been painted or stuccoed over. All were lovingly maintained, except for one whose paint was peeling and crackling, but it was for sale and would undoubtedly be brought up to speed once it found an owner.

Philadelphia's row houses were the local equivalent of New York's high-rising railroad flats. Manhattan Island had nowhere to go but up, but here, with all the space in the world, when quarters for workers were required, we expanded horizontally. Two or three bedrooms, one bath upstairs, living room, dining room, kitchen, one behind the other, downstairs. Houses sharing common walls to conserve heat and expense.

Over the years, the people of Vincent's neighborhood had personalized their addresses in ways apartment dwellers never could, with window boxes, shutters, wrought iron stair rails, metal awnings, and aluminum or fake stone siding. Each street of homes wore many faces, and for better or for worse, South Philly was an idiosyncratic patchwork. At this time of year, it was particularly exuberant with colored lights outlining doors, windows, and rooflines above which, often as not, sat Santa and all his reindeer and below which were front-window Nativity scenes. That and last night's snow moved the neighborhood to within shouting distance of a Currier and Ives.

I banged a brass knocker attached to an evergreen front door. The brick facade of the house was the color of aged burgundy, and its shutters matched the door. I could tilt sideways and peek through lace curtains into a living room dominated by a heavily decorated Christmas tree and the spastic sounds of TV cartoons.

I banged more heavily and pressed the doorbell, twice. The noise of cartoons raged on, but I also heard human voices.

Vincent's face appeared at the same window I had peered into. Not a subtle lookout system. I waved and pointed at the door.

He looked resigned, not thrilled, to see me.

"I've been calling you," I said as soon as he admitted me. "We have to talk."

His son, a bowl of pink and yellow dry cereal on his lap, sat on green carpeting in the middle of the precise room with its yellow brocade sofa and end chairs. Even TV snacks were color-coordinated here.

The boy turned toward me. "Hi," I said, remembering my manners. "Chipper, isn't it?" His name was Vincent, Junior, and they were avoiding the Little Vincent syndrome, although I think they could have found a more appealing substitute than Chipper. "I'm Amanda Pepper, and we met when your Dad brought you to see where he worked, remember?"

Chipper squinted and said, "Hi." Then, since I was not nearly as interesting as a cartoon, he turned away.

"Kids!" Vincent raked his hair with his fingers. "No manners." I didn't think his son's deportment was what troubled him. "We've told him a thousand—"

"I have a question, Vincent," I said. "I need to know why you're using me as an al—"

"Barbs, this is Mandy Pepper, remember her?" Vincent spoke too loudly and emphatically. His nervousness bounced off the pale green walls. I turned and saw her, plump and apprehensive, in the arched entry to the dining room. "Teacher at Philly Prep? You met at the diner that night?"

"Sure," Barbs said quickly. "Good to see you again. Excuse the mess. We weren't expecting anybody. Take off your coat, why don't you?"

I unbundled myself and looked around. It was not a house where I'd drop outer garments on a nearby chair, even if I were staying for two minutes. Barbs put out her arms and I handed most of my wardrobe over.

"Your house looks beautiful, and that's a gorgeous tree." Enough niceties. We had a murder suspect here, the posse was on his trail, and I'd been given oblique and short-lived permission to save both the day and the friend. "I'm sorry to barge in," I said. "I left messages on your machine, but perhaps it isn't working?"

Without commenting on the condition of her answering machine, Barbs left, arms full of my coat, hat, and bag. She was back in two or three seconds.

"I called all morning. I was worried."

Barbs's eyes flitted from her husband to me, and she rubbed the knuckles of one hand with the other. Perhaps she had a tic.

Perhaps arthritic pain. More likely she was suspicious of both her husband and, now, of me. Of having had the vacuumed rug pulled out from under her secure world.

"Why?" Barbs asked after a too-long pause. "Why would you worry?"

Hadn't Vincent told her he was in trouble? Had he told her he'd been with me? What reason would he have given for seeking me out during the parade, and wouldn't she know it wasn't true? No wonder she watched me warily. I tried to ease her palpable fear. "I guess, considering what happened to . . . to Jimmy Pat," I said. "Practically in front of me. It leaves a person twitchy." That should be sufficiently obvious and non-threatening.

"You *were* there, then?" she blurted out.

So I'd been right. She didn't believe her husband. She knew his story was suspect.

"I *told* you she was!" Vincent said sharply.

"I meant . . ." she began lamely, then she gave up looking for a face-saving edit. She blinked a few times and switched to a hostess mode. "Did you enjoy the parade?"

"Did you enjoy the parade?" Vincent echoed. "Aside from that, Mrs. Lincoln, how'd you like the play? Jimmy Pat got killed, Barbs, so how could she enjoy the parade?"

Whereupon he took my elbow, steering me away. Barbs stood with her mouth agape. "Sorry," he said to her. "Didn't mean to be short. Kid's making me nuts. Those shows! Come down—but bring coffee or something?"

"Sure, Vinny," Barbs said over-eagerly.

I wanted to tell her she didn't have to atone for spousal disbelief. Her spouse was lying. But instead, I said, "Please don't bother yourself. I don't want a thing." Actually, I felt the vague nausea of too little sleep, and the idea of food was not pleasant.

"Any fruitcake left?" Vincent asked.

"No, please, I really don't feel like eating."

"Or how about whatever's left of your Christmas cookies, or the Bûche de Noël? Hey!" he said with special emphasis. "It's lunchtime, so how about Pepper Pot?" He put a finger up and declaimed:

Here we stand at your front door
Just as we did the year before.
Open the door and let us in,
Give us all a drink of gin.
Or better give us something hot,
A steaming bowl of Pepper Pot.

"What could be more appropriate for our Miss Pepper, huh, Barbs?" He sounded feverish, manic. "It's probably named for Mandy's family."

Nothing was named for my family, except me.

Barbs continued to look apprehensive. I didn't blame her. Vincent was rushing out words in a nervous torrent, as if he were on amphetamines or his first date.

Or as if he were nervously trying to stave off a deserved accusation.

"Truly, I'm not hungry," I said. "Thanks, but—"

"It's traditional," Vincent said. "New Year's Eve open house with Philadelphia Pepper Pot soup. New Year's Day, too. Lots of people, they don't make it anymore, even on Two Street. Nowadays, it's more cold cuts, but Barbs and me, we like traditions."

I wish something more glamorous than a soup made of the muscular lining of beef stomach bore my family name. Prince Orloff got veal, Melba got a peach dessert, Caesar got a salad, and I got tripe soup. Oh, it's historically interesting, being said to have turned the tide of the American Revolution. When Washington's troops were starving, often deserting, all the cook had on hand was tripe, peppercorns, and scraps. His improvised soup saved the day and maybe the whole campaign at Valley Forge. Maybe, therefore, the country.

I'm glad we're no longer a colony of Great Britain's, but all the same, tripe is tripe. I had never tasted the stuff, and had no desire to begin today. Nonetheless, Barbs was headed into the kitchen, so I followed Vincent to a door in the dining room, and down a staircase. Under fluorescent lights, boxy banquette seats lined two of the narrow room's paneled walls and faced an oversized

TV and a collection of CDs and tapes on another. The floor was covered with black and white vinyl squares.

"Did this myself," Vincent said. "Look here." He lifted the seat of one of the benches to reveal toy storage. "Kid's supposed to use this room to play, make his messes, watch his TV—put in an entire entertainment center, but does he? No, he has to be where the action is. Barbs and I—we escape down here from him, he's such a terror." His pride in both his handiwork and his son was evident.

"Maybe when he's older." I inspected the paneling. "You're really good with wood, aren't you?"

His look was wary, on alert. I couldn't imagine why until I remembered that he built his club's frames because of his carpentry skills. Everything in any way related to the fatal parade must feel fraught with dangerous meaning now.

"We have to talk fast," he said. "I told Barbs all that food on purpose, to delay her."

"Why?"

He turned away, walked over to the entertainment center, and ran an index finger over the TV screen, as if removing dust. "Damn," he said. "I can't explain. That's the problem, you see?"

"Not at all. Not any of it, starting with why you said you were with me."

He turned to face me. "If I swear I didn't do a thing to hurt Jimmy Pat—never would in this lifetime—could you believe me?"

"I already do." Kind of. Mostly. Pretty much.

"Good. But I can't say where I was."

"So you weren't in the parade, beside him?"

"Why don't you believe me!" It wasn't a question and it wasn't plaintive—it was an accusation. "What am I, a liar?" He slammed his fist into a wooden support beam. "How come I'm on trial, even with you? Why do I have to justify my every—"

"Hey!" I held my hand up like a traffic cop. I also maneuvered so that he was no longer between me and the staircase. "I'm not the enemy. Simmer down."

He took several deep breaths. "Sorry," he said.

So was I. I'd caught a glimpse of an explosive temper I would not have suspected.

"I'm really . . . strung out. But I couldn't have done it, even if I'd gone crazy and wanted to. It's easy enough for people not to know if somebody ducks out for a minute. Guys do it, you know, to take care of calls of nature or get a little cheer."

What he was saying was that nobody had a clue where you were at any given time when thinking back. What he didn't say was that it was therefore easy to concoct any alibi you liked.

"I was away, and I wasn't toting a gun or hurting anybody. They tested me last night. There wasn't any residue on my hands."

Would there have been on a man wearing gloves? I'd have to ask.

"Anybody could have done it, anybody who was there, or watching."

Very helpful.

"All I know, it wasn't me. I thought I could cut out for a few minutes, nobody'd notice or care . . . and look at this mess. If I *lie* and say I was there, then they say I did it because of stupid stuff. Jimmy and me, we were always having contests, friendly rivalries, you know, but they don't understand. If I tell the truth, I can't prove it."

"All the same, I can't cover for you."

"Why not?" He seemed astounded.

"Why are you asking me to?" I had to know, and quickly. We were racing ahead of the speed at which soup reheats, but also, whether or not Vincent knew it, ahead of Obenhauser.

"Barbs . . . she's an insanely jealous woman."

This wasn't exactly news. Barbs hadn't tried to be subtle about her suspicions upstairs. But all the same. "Jealous of me?"

"God, no!" He smiled.

For a nanosecond, I was relieved that his wife didn't consider me a threat. But that was instantly replaced by burning resentment that the idea seemed ridiculous, laughable, to Vincent. What was I, chopped liver? At thirty-one, I was older than he by half a decade—maybe more, but so what? Didn't that give me seasoning?

"The thing is, I used to go with Dolores. Jimmy Pat's fiancée. In high school. Six years ago."

Dear Lord, he *was* young. I had assumed that with a house, a wife, a toddler . . .

"You know how wives are about old girlfriends."

Wifely attitudes are not my special area of expertise, but I did think that high school romances were like training wheels on your first bike. Valuable helps for getting up to speed. Beyond that, they provided fodder for scrapbooks, reason to mist up at old songs, and cause to act-out during a midlife crisis. Vincent was too young for the last option, and I couldn't believe he was honestly suggesting that his wife, his real-time love, the mother of his son, thought he might have killed Jimmy Pat in order to get Dolores back or avenge her being claimed by another. That was ludicrous, or at least I sincerely hoped so.

"So what?" I finally asked. "What relevance does that have?"

"Everybody knows. It's not like the cops aren't going to find it out right away."

"Find what out? That was then and this is now. What does high school or Dolores have to do with this murder?"

"Nothing. But, see, when I ducked out—before anything happened, Jimmy Pat was fine—I checked, because, well, I left to see . . ." His voice dropped to a whisper. "Her."

"Dolores?"

I had spoken in a normal tone, and he winced and glanced up the staircase before he nodded.

"Why?"

He shook his head. "She was in distress. I can't explain. Made a solemn promise."

"To her?"

"To myself and my God, that's who."

"Okay, so tell the police the truth. She's your alibi. Let her tell the secret, whatever it is. It can't be as bad as murder."

He shook his head again. "I can't." He looked toward the staircase.

"Barbs will have to understand."

"Dolores dropped me. Dolores is that kind of girl, being so

pretty, being a Grassi, having everybody look up to her, her family, having things easy, whenever she wants them. Fickle, you could say. But in the end, even if you know all that about her, and I did, all along, being dropped still hurts, and hurting makes it different, not really over, you understand? Barbs still worries about it, but when Jimmy Pat started dating Dolores, what, was I not supposed to see him, my best friend, because of who he's with? *I* adjusted, but Barbs, we could go out with Jimmy Pat and Dolores a million times and she's still never relaxed."

I couldn't help but note that he hadn't said his feelings for Dolores were no longer romantic, only that he'd adjusted to being with her as Jimmy Pat's girl. I wondered if Barbs's suspicions were justified, even if it was only dumb yearning on Vincent's part.

"As long as Dolores makes it clear why you were looking for her," I said, "then Barbs won't have anything to be upset about. Am I right?"

"She can't. Dolores can't. Wouldn't. It'd shame her, asking to secretly see me while she's engaged and all. And now, with Jimmy Pat . . ."

"But she asked to meet you?"

"What did I say? Didn't I say that?" The temper was back on a high simmer, ready to break into a boil.

"Whoa," I said again and waited till he stopped overreacting. "She asked to see you at a specific time, right?"

"But, the thing is," he said, "she wasn't there, so I didn't see her and she can't say where I was, so why stir up a hornet's nest, create shame? Because you know, people will talk—if it's me, and then Jimmy Pat dead and all."

"You never found her?"

He shook his head.

"So after a while you gave up, went back, and found Jimmy dead?"

He nodded mutely, sorrowfully.

"Bottom line is, you have no alibi."

"I'm innocent, I swear on my son's head. But when the cops kept asking me where I was, I panicked. All I could think of was you were there, I was there, why couldn't I have been looking for you? Why won't you cover for me?"

"Because it isn't true."

"It could have been true."

"Besides, my—" I faltered, as always searching for the missing term for the Mackenzie roommate. Society's word makers don't create nice labels for things they aren't sure they want to have, like romantic partners living together while legally single. "The man I live with was with me," I said. "And he's a cop. On this case."

Vincent looked as if I'd slapped him, as if I'd taken away his only chance at avoiding the guillotine. And I suddenly wondered if perhaps he had shot his old buddy.

Who had ever said or known *when* it had happened? Why was Vincent so eager to establish that he was away when nobody yet knew when that should have been? Maybe he was in the parade the whole time, next to Jimmy Pat, close enough to brush by on a twirl and plant a bullet. Maybe it did matter enough who became Captain of the club, whose father didn't die young, who wound up with Dolores Grassi. Maybe the wearing of the frame suit was the final straw.

"I'm sorry," I said. "Truly. Even if I don't understand why you're in this mess, I'm sorry you are. But my hands are tied. Aside from ethics, there's no practical point to my lying. It won't work, not for a minute."

"Oh, God," he said, "what am I going to do?"

"How about trying the truth?" I asked softly. "It's so much easier."

"I told you. I'm not going to shame her, particularly now that he's dead, it would be . . ." He might have explained more, but just then, after an overly loud warning knock—what did she think/fear was going on down here? And why warn us so loudly that she was about to witness whatever it was?—Barbs began her descent carrying a tray laden with steaming bowls and baked goods.

That was the end of Mission: Devaney. It hadn't been a particularly rewarding time. I still didn't know whether I believed my fellow teacher and friend. I only established that he had a temper sudden and fierce enough to make me wonder, and what seemed a long-lasting yen for Dolores Grassi.

Ah, yes. I also established that I wasn't at all fond of Pepper Pot soup.

Five

IT was now late morning. Barbs's soup and fruitcake lay heavy, greasy, and overly present on the floor of my stomach, and even so, provided scant insulation against the cold. I had no idea what I should do next, so I called home for further instructions from My Leader, who wasn't back yet.

Which is when I remembered that I didn't have or want a leader. But neither did I have a sense of direction, and I would have liked that.

I reconnoitered and figured out that I was pretty much nowhere. And so was Vincent, far as I could see.

I didn't understand. Shouldn't a decently working marriage be able to withstand the innocuous truth? So maybe he carried a torch for an old girlfriend. Not optimal, but was it such a world-shaking big deal? Did it really matter all that much as long as he held the torch and not the girl?

Or was Barbs onto something, and was Vincent lying? What was it really with the old girlfriend, his good, now dead, guy-friend's fiancée? Did he mean he wouldn't shame Dolores with the truth, particularly now that her fiancé was dead, because he wanted to stay in her favor? Or because the truth would reveal him as a man having an assignation with his best friend's fiancée, and make him seem even more suspicious?

Dolores seemed the key to everything. If Vincent were telling the truth, then where had she been? Why was she "in distress," as he'd put it? Why had she summoned him if admitting it publicly would "shame" her?

Still, I was certainly not going to barge into her home and demand answers while she was in mourning.

The night we'd all gone with Vincent to Melrose Diner for coffee, I had remarked on her luxurious black-brown hair, more out of awe than admiration, although I didn't say so. I was rendered momentarily silent by how high and wide it flung itself, like a self-contained organism, an other that accompanied her, not something that grew out of her head. She was a small, delicately made, and fragile-looking woman—until you factored in the hair, which added a good half a foot to her height.

She had a natural flair, a gift, she said with innocent pride. And she could make my tresses just as bouffant as hers. Dolores, it turned out, was a hair stylist at a place called Salon d'André. The name had stuck because it seemed to combine a lot of pretension with no imagination. I envisioned André in a pencil-thin moustache and a beret.

I assumed it wouldn't be difficult to find his salon.

It wasn't, particularly after I finally looked it up in a phone book and got on a bus. That came after a half hour of cold and aimless wandering.

It wasn't until I reached the store that I remembered it was Sunday.

But the shop was, miraculously, open, with a small hand-lettered sign taped to the window. "For the convenience of our loyal customers, we will be open Sunday, January 2nd until lunchtime." Although I felt as if the day was already 50 hours old, it was not yet lunchtime at André's.

"Hi, there. Help you?" A woman in a bubblegum pink smock and Jean Harlow hair flashed a smile as she worked the chair nearest the door. Then she turned back to her client, scissors in one hand. "Your ends are a mess," she told the owner of the hair. "You're not conditioning like I said, are you?" Her client mumbled apologies and lowered her eyes.

There were four other work stations, three other operators clipping, blow-drying, and hair-setting, respectively. There did not appear to be a receptionist, so I walked over to the pink lady who'd hailed me. "It's last minute and all," I said, "but being as it's after New Year's, all the parties over—" as if I'd just completed an exhausting round of silver-spangled galas. Aside from the Mummers, I'd had a spangle-free vacation.

"I thought, maybe, I could be worked in." Winding up with a hair high-rise seemed a fair admission price. I was counting on clichés being true, on the neighborhood salon being the epicenter of gossip.

"Dunno," the woman said. "I doubt it, today. This is only, like, emergencies. Being as we were closed and we'll be closed tomorrow, Monday, too. Still, let me take a look." She flashed another smile. She had a deep and appealing dimple, and I suspected it caused her to smile whatever her mood. "Be one sec," she told her client, who looked unhappy.

"You have gorgeous hair," the pink lady said to me. "Great color. That auburn looks almost natural."

"It is natural."

"Could use styling, though, a little oomph." She strode to a small desk and checked the appointment book. "I'm Andrée," she said as she flipped pages. "Two e's, accent on the first one. Andrée Jansheski. Left the second e off the sign. It was easier."

It appeared that I, not Andrée, was the one with too little imagination. How silly to have assumed that the cross-naming phenomenon was limited to my sister's friends on the Main Line. Was it a fad I'd missed? An underreported aspect of the women's movement that I could pretend to write another article about?

"You're in luck. I have a noon with Marty. Right now." She twinked another Andrée smile. It was a most impressive dimple. "Depending on what you want, how long it would take."

"Darn, I wanted Dolores," I said. "I met her awhile back and told her I'd be in for an . . . um . . . a styling."

Andrée turned dark-circled eyes toward me. "I'm real sorry, hon, but Dolores isn't available."

"Should I make the appointment for later in the week?"

She shook her head. Her crimped bob didn't move at all, as if it were a molded part of her head. "She won't be in for an indefinite spell. Today, we're only open a few hours anyway. But Marty's good, too. You'll like her."

The woman at the farthest end of the shop stopped clicking her scissors and instead waved them at me. I waved back and smiled.

"All our operators are expert beauticians," Andrée said. "Ask anybody in the neighborhood."

"I'm sure, but all the same, I had my heart set on . . . when will Dolores be back?"

Andrée's bottom lip raised until her face was pure rueful resignation. "Who can tell, hon? Wish I had a crystal ball, but till I find one, I don't know any more than you do. When things like this happen . . ." She shook her head again. The white-gold waves remained in place like an ad for fixatives. "Out of the blue . . ."

"Is she ill?"

"You didn't hear?" Her brown eyes grew wider with a gleeful willingness to share bad news. I had hit pay dirt.

"Hear what?" I tried to look confused and a bit alarmed.

"Ohmigod, and you her friend and all."

"Actually, I've only met her once. We went out for coffee."

"What, that isn't friendly? You saying you don't like her?"

"I didn't mean . . ."

"Of course not! Who wouldn't like Dolores?"

"Andrée?" The woman on the chair swiveled around. "Phyllis will throw a fit if I'm not done in time."

Andrée nodded. "In a sec, Stel. It's real bad," she said to me, her voice lowered to a stage whisper. "Hate to be the bearer of bad news, especially about somebody you know."

Her client was a buxom woman whose flat features looked naked and overblown under her wet hair. "Excuse me?" she said, loudly. "Andrée?" She tapped her watch with a polished fingernail and looked meaningfully at the hairdresser.

"Yes, right. Sorry, Stel." Andrée turned to me. "Stand next to me, hon, while I finish her up. Toss your things over there. That's Dolores's chair. Too hot for coats in here."

I put my things on the bright blue chair. A photograph was tucked into the mirror above the work station. I recognized Jimmy Pat's puckish features and Dolores's enormous hair.

I went and stood near Andrée. The three other operators looked me up and down during this process. I got the feeling my hair, which more or less does what it wants to on its way to my shoulders, wasn't passing muster.

One of the other operators, a hennaed redhead in her early twenties, was setting an elderly woman's hair in pin curls. I had no idea those tiny implements still existed, let alone were still used for styling. And Marty, the middle-aged, no-nonsense sort, was finger-fluffing and arranging the still-wet frosted hair of her client. The third beautician looked like she'd been airlifted from a war zone to the salon for safekeeping. She was agonizingly thin, with enormous eyes and pokey elbow bones and a hairstyle that possibly aimed for punk, but emerged as waif. Her client had a manicurist working on her at the same time.

"Hear about the guy in the parade got killed?" Andrée asked as she separated out a lock of Stel's hair. "Guy in a Fancy Club?"

"I saw it," I said.

"Who didn't? The TV showed it enough, didn't they? Hope the bad publicity doesn't ruin future parades." Andrée watched me in the mirror, much more attentive to my potential reactions than to her snipping. Stel was about to have a bad hair day.

"Couldn't do away with the Mummers if they wanted to," Stel said, caught up in the conversation, "and who does? It's like . . ." She couldn't think of anything. "It's like a tradition."

65

"Exactly." Then Andrée looked at me in the mirror, meaningfully. "That guy who died was Dolores's fiancé." She paused for effect.

I opened my eyes as much as they could go. That seemed to be what Andrée'd wanted, and she nodded, vigorously.

"Supposed to marry him on the fifteenth of this very month," she said, "and now he's dead. Like that. If you could have been here for her planning and preparation. The lace for the train, her mother's veil, the bridesmaids' dresses—oh, and then one of them, Stacy, found out she was going to have a baby, she'd be in her sixth month by the wedding, and all the fuss about how to have her wear the same dress and not show because Dolores wanted every single second to be picture-perfect. 'The day of my life,' she called it."

"I heard rumors," Stel said.

Andrée ignored her. "Dolores is like that. Whole family is. Attention to details. Everything has to be just so. If the Grassis do it, you know it's done the way it should be. Always been that way. Proud people. And you have to believe that in a family of four sons, the youngest one, the only girl, their baby daughter is going to be sent off in style. The flowers—if you could have heard the talk about what kind of bouquet for her, for the bridesmaids—"

"I heard there was trouble. Big trouble." Stel was feeling shut out and petulant.

"Trouble? I'll say there's trouble. He's *dead*!" Andrée said.

"I mean before," Stel insisted.

I was a front line correspondent in the war of the gossips. Who'd be the victor who'd get to charge the hill first with news of The Big Trouble?

"A makeup specialist was going to come in that morning," Andrée continued. Stel, I suspected, sagely remembered the scissors in Andrée's hand and kept quiet. "I was flattered, she wanted me to do her hair. But even that, we talked about the styling for weeks. It was going to be gorgeous, piled up, with curls on the side, just so, and now, look, everything gone because of some lunatic."

"Andrée—" Stel whined. "You know. About Jimmy?"

Andrée was not about to turn over the flag, give the field to Stel. She upped the volume and continued her advance. "Who'da thought of such a thing—killing a Mummer goin' up the street? I tell you, people have gone crazy. And Dolores such a sweet one, too. So sad. A widow before she's a bride."

"But I heard—you must have heard, too . . ."

That was clever. Stel outflanked her opposition with her prior knowledge. We both know this, she was saying in essence, I admit it's not fresh news, so why don't you let me say it?

"You never heard anything that said Dolores wasn't a sweetie, did you?" Andrée's smile, despite the deep crease of dimple, was slightly frosted.

Brilliant defensive ruse. She had refused to answer the obvious, and had instead deflected the question by protesting a completely imaginary argument. Andrée didn't subscribe to the idea that the customer was always right.

Stel shriveled, became less inflated and buxom. "Of course not," she said. "Don't I know the Grassi family? We go way back, and I would never say a word against them. Nobody would, but with me, it's even more. My mother's second cousin is married to Dolores's father's sister's brother-in-law. We're *related*." She took a deep breath. I could almost see her weigh her options. How bad a haircut would she get as punishment for stealing Andrée's thunder? How much would it bug her to keep her gossip to herself? To allow someone else to usurp it?

She chose being the first to say over placating her haircutter. "But I *did* hear," she said emphatically and loudly, "there was trouble. Who knows if there would have been a wedding?"

"What kind of troub—" I began, but Andrée talked over me.

"Everybody heard, except I wouldn't have said." The stylist tightened her lips into a tightly pressed *o* as she snipped an edge of hair. "Andrée Jansheski doesn't speak ill of the dead. And Dolores never breathed a word of it herself, so who's to say if it was so?"

Trouble. Wedding-preventing trouble. Did that translate into Vincent Devaney?

"She doesn't deserve this, the sweet thing. That's the shame of it," Stel agreed.

One law of gossip is to pause and say sympathetic things about those you are about to dismember, thereby demonstrating that you are not biased.

"Don't you think she's a sweetie?" Stel abruptly asked me.

I nodded. "Sure." A *sweetie* isn't the way I'd instinctively label anyone, but Dolores had seemed a pleasant, self-satisfied, gruff but well-meaning girl. Not that I could remember much that she'd said or done. She'd been mostly a table ornament, frankly. In fact, both the Grassis had been silent observers. It had annoyed me, because theoretically, Stephen was there to help me with information about his club, but instead, he seemed reluctant to give me the time of day. Neither of them was a sweetie.

"In fact," Andrée said, "we're going to see her in a few minutes. That's why we're closing the shop. You come, too. Cheer her up. Make a little visit."

"Oh, but I—"

"It's not far. Girard Estates, you know? Nice house, too."

"It's not that, I—"

The redheaded operator, who'd been murmuring quietly with her client, joined our conversation. "Look, they can't even have a wake yet, let alone bury him. The cops, the tests they have to make, you know. Makes it extra hard on her. There's like no way to end it, no real place or time for people to say how they feel."

"A sweet girl," Andrée said. "A hard worker. So come. Spend an hour, make her feel better." A big smile this time.

"I don't really think I should—"

"What, you maybe have something more important to do than comfort a friend in mourning?"

"I would go myself," Stel said. "If it weren't for Phyllis." She sighed loudly, rolled her eyes toward me. "My sister has a condition, depends on me for everything."

I murmured in what I hoped was a sympathetic manner. I felt sucked into the vortex of a lot of lives.

"I went over last night." This from the pin curl woman as an old-fashioned hairdryer was lowered over her head. The redheaded operator turned on the machine and the pin curl woman continued to talk. Shout, actually. "The family is so upset! What a shame! Her father—I thought he'd have a heart attack!"

And at that point, they all seemed to abandon the subject of Dolores. The only sound in our little corner was the snipping of Stel's bad ends.

I was afraid that having danced around the heart of the matter, everybody was now content. I didn't want to push, to interrupt, but I surely wanted to know why it had been suggested that Jimmy Pat might not have become Dolores's husband even had he lived. I wanted to hear that Vincent Devaney was not the answer. I could still see Barbs's fearfully suspicious eyes.

Andrée broke the tense silence. "Now that Jimmy Pat's gone, nobody but Dolores will ever know for certain what was going on in their hearts."

"If she even knows. Knew," Stella said. "I mean, really knew."

If Dolores knew? Wasn't she the problem?

"I heard it from Molly, you know her?" Stel asked.

Andrée shrugged irritably. "Who doesn't know Molly? She has a big mouth, and I'd tell her that to her face."

"She's good friends with Dolores's mother. She was upset."

"She didn't tell you what was going on?" Andrée asked me.

"Dolores? We'd just met, you see. I'm writing this article about—"

"It's the Semow girl's fault," Stel said.

"What Semow girl?" Marty, the black-haired operator, asked. "How come I didn't know?"

"Because this is not a place of gossip," Andrée said with not a trace of shame or self-awareness. "Besides which, we're all grown-ups and we know it takes two to tango. Can't go blaming only one of them."

"Okay, but who Semow shouldn't I blame?" Marty asked.

"With the card shop on Christian, between Two and Third," Stel said. "Kind of a dump, that store. I don't know how they stay alive, maybe just by being open all the time. Anyway, she's always been wild for Mummers, living near so many clubs, but particularly for one of them, Jimmy Pat. I guess this was like her last chance for him."

"He shouldn't have had a thing to do with her," Andrée said. "He shouldn't have played that game."

"Bachelors sow wild oats. It's the girl's responsibility."

Goodness me. Not only pin curls but the double standard was alive and well. And what did this mean? Another woman was involved. How embarrassing would it be for Vincent to realize that his other woman's man had another woman? Infuriating enough to off the other man?

Cherchez la femme was the old rule of detection. How would that work here? Would Jimmy Pat's other woman cause Dolores distress and make Vincent's rescue and love fantasies all the more vivid and urgent? Make Barbs the more furiously jealous? Make Dolores shoot her fiancé? Or make Dolores's rival shoot her seducer? Or make Barbs shoot the fiancé? Or make Vincent . . .

And in any case, how, with everyone in Philadelphia as eyewitnesses and none seeing?

"And what's she going to do now?" Stel asked Andrée.

"Emily Semow? Who cares? She made her bed, now let her sleep in it."

"But I hear . . . what if it's not just her," Stel said. "What if there was going to be a . . . what if she's having a . . ." She finished the sentence with a roll of her eyes and a knowing grimace.

Emily Semow was pregnant. This was not good for anybody.

"That'd be Emily's business and her problem," Andrée said. "And," she added, facing me, "not a word to anybody. We don't even think Dolores knew."

Fat chance that every single person for miles around didn't know, but I played along. "Of course not."

"It's a mess, with Dolores in mourning and all. I say let Jimmy Pat rest in peace and let bygones be bygones. Let her get on with her life. Otherwise, what's the point?" Andrée poked and prodded Stel's hair. All the women in the shop nodded and sighed in agreement. All except the one under the dryer, who had no way of knowing what was going on.

But there *was* a point. Jimmy Pat hadn't expired of shame or overactive glands. Somebody shot him, and there seemed to be a growing number of people who might have wanted to do it, from Vincent to Dolores to Emily Semow.

"What's she going to do with the gown?" the blonde client asked. Dolores's secrets might as well have been broadcast on CNN. "Can you return wedding gowns? Who'd buy such a bad-luck thing?"

Andrée shook her head sadly. "Who ever heard of such a thing." Then she shook her entire self, the way a wet dog might shudder moisture off, and looked at me. "So you can tell why we think she needs a little cheering. You'll come with us."

I'd learned everything I needed to know, and I wasn't even sure Dolores would remember me, so I again demurred. "You know, I only met her because I was working on an article about the Mummers, and she was—"

Andrée's thin eyebrows raised. "You're a writer?"

"Well . . ."

"This is some story, isn't it?"

"I'm not writing about Dolores or any particular—"

"A major motion picture, if you ask me," Stel said.

I shook my head. "I'm not a—"

"Going to let somebody else grab it? Think about it. Movie of the Week. It's got everything. All the more reason you should come along, get more background, think about settings."

"No, really, I don't think it's appropriate." Mostly, I didn't think Dolores would feel it was appropriate.

"We made food. This way, they could go to church, not worry about what to eat after. Potluck, way too much. Marty made her four-cheese casserole, and Rae"—the waif-woman nodded and smiled shyly—"makes a devil's food cake you wouldn't believe." Given Rae's sharp angles and prominent skeleton, I wondered whether she'd ever tasted her own baking, even sampled the icing with her fingertips. Ever eaten anything, in fact. "And Jo—"

Joe. Ray. Marty. Andrée. It sounded as if they would be more likely to run a car repair shop than a salon, sexist as I knew that thought to be. How had Dolores with her non-ambiguous name gotten a job here?

"Jo did her killer guacamole dip," Andrée continued. "Hot but delicious. I'm doing garlic focaccia bread."

A meal for the cholesterol-challenged. My stomach, already burdened with Barbs's Pepper Pot soup, asked if I wanted to begin the year by dying. Much wiser to go home, think about the meaning of these convoluted connections, and resume that sleep I'd intended as the main activity of the day. "Thanks a lot, but I've already eaten," I said. "New Year, new diet. You know how that goes."

"So don't eat, although I don't know why you should diet. Come anyway. You'll be a nice surprise, a special treat. Feels good to be thought about, and heaven knows, she could use a little feeling good these days. Make her remember there's life beyond Jimmy Pat. That's why we're going. To remind her that men come and go, but there's always hair."

Then Andrée looked at me, and I saw a glimmer of why she so wanted me, a stranger, along on an awkward, stilted mission. I'd be a buffer, a distraction, a point of focus. They were all understandably uncomfortable about going to pay a confused condolence call—should they be happy or sad the no-good fiancé is dead? or worried about who did him in?—to a woman they liked, but didn't really know except as an expert hairdresser and co-worker.

I waffled about what to do. Billy Obenhauser was due to question me, but since I wasn't supposed to know that, why should I stay home and await him?

I mentally explained myself to Mackenzie, as if he were inside my ear, reminding me that enough was enough. I had already exceeded my unofficial mandate—to see Vincent—with pitiable little to show for it, and I should thank these women and leave.

Oh, but, Dolores was the pivot, the center, and this chance to see her had fallen into my lap. How could I refuse?

Besides, going along with these women had to do with human kindness—to Andrée, if not Dolores. This had nothing to do with snooping.

Somewhere in my imagination, Mackenzie raised one eyebrow and crossed his arms in a pose of disbelief, so I clicked off my mental TV screen, picked up my coat and bag, and followed Andrée.

Six

I SURFED along with the wave of determined hair stylists, even though, no matter what I had mentally told Mackenzie, I felt hypocritical joining them.

Actually, what really swept us along was a gigantic wind-shove at our backs. I was relieved that Dolores lived leeward of the salon. As it was, nobody talked because you had to think hard before opening your mouth and freezing your fillings.

Buoyed along, I worried double-time. Would Dolores want to see me? I had actually met her twice. Once at the diner, and once when I'd gone with Vincent and Barbs to a fund-raiser for his

Fancy Club. Even to winners, the city's cash prizes on New Year's Day didn't begin to cover their expenses, so there were events all year long devoted to closing the deficit. In spite of all this, members have mortgaged their homes or borrowed from banks against their businesses in order for their club to march on New Year's Day.

The event I'd attended was a dance, cake sale, and raffle for prizes donated by local merchants, and Dolores, whose father, brothers, and fiancé were in the club, had been there.

But both times, she'd been part of a group, not my new best friend. We had exchanged a few perfunctory words, and those only because I knew Vincent, the man she now might suspect had killed her fiancé. Those credentials didn't warrant a welcome mat.

On the other hand, from what I'd heard in the salon, her fiancé didn't seem much of a loss, although I didn't know why I was even factoring that in. What did the worth of a man ever have to do with how much he was valued by his true love?

"Another two blocks," the redhead said.

Dolores lived close by, at least in geographical terms. Economically, we'd moved into a different galaxy, an enclave of large, semidetached homes set back behind front yards on tree-lined streets.

Girard Estates, somebody at the salon had said. Named for Stephen Girard, the first American multimillionaire, a French rags-to-riches immigrant who almost single-handedly bailed out the U.S. after the War of 1812. There's a Girard bank, bridge, street, school, but here, indeed, according to a sign, was Stephen's Estate. Or one of them.

Set in the midst of a large park was an impressive sprawl of a Revolutionary-style house that belonged in *Architectural Digest,* not blue-collar, closely packed South Philly.

This, plus lots more of the surrounding land, had been his farm, the sign said. I tried to imagine South Philly as open corn or pumpkin fields leading to the ports on the Delaware. My imagination couldn't handle that much of a stretch.

We walked another short while and entered the left half of a solid-looking Dutch Colonial two-family home. The front lawn looked as if it bloomed with roses and forsythia in warmer times.

The Grassis had twined greenery and lights around the porch's heavy wooden railings, and a wreath lush with marzipan-like fruit was on their front door.

Inside, the house had a well-preserved sense of the early days of the century. We walked into a small entryway that ended in a frosted-glass door designed to catch the wind and protect the house from the cold.

The inner door was opened by a dried apple doll dressed in black, with eyes half-hidden by weathered crinkles of skin, and a dumpling body below. "Oh, yes, oh, yes," she said. "Dolores told me you were coming. It's so nice of you." Her voice was pleasantly crackly, the way I'd imagine an apple doll's would be.

Behind her, I could see the living room and behind that, a huge dining room with walnut wainscoting that matched the living room's high baseboards. A fire flickered in a green tile fireplace in the corner opposite the front door, but it appeared the shallow variety originally designed for coal, and the flames looked heatless, the log really an ignited gas line. The ceiling trim was festooned with still more boughs of greenery, and a string of blinking green and red lights encircled the arch into the dining room. A Christmas tree, surrounded by a Nativity scene, dominated the non-fireplace corner.

"Mrs. G.," Andrée said by way of greeting. "So sorry to come for such a sad occasion. You remember Marty, Rae, and Jo from the shop, don't you? And this here is Amanda, a writer friend of Dolores's who came looking for her. We made you a little something, too, hope Dolores told you we were going to and hope you aren't insulted, you're such a famous cook."

"Come in! Come in!" Mrs. Grassi waved her arms toward herself and her home, but as we surged into the living room, she reversed the motions of her hands. "Leave your things there, in the vestibule." We did, dropping and hanging hats, mufflers, coats, boots, and bags in the closet and on a bench there for that purpose, while Mrs. Grassi talked nonstop. Her words felt like a hot shower on this freezing day. "Dolores is on the phone upstairs," she said, "you can imagine the calls, but in a minute she'll be down. So nice of you! You'll make my Dolores a little happier, too." She wiped at her eyes with the sort of lacy handkerchief I thought extinct. "Those dishes must be heavy!" she exclaimed.

"No, no—plastic containers," Andrée said.

"You carried them all the way over! Angels, that's what you are. Let me—or here, into the kitchen. We'll heat them up. They need heating up? I have a microwave. Here, you'll get a hernia!"

"I could set the—" Nobody heard me. The group, led by the indomitable Mrs. Grassi, headed for the kitchen, which was commodious and breathed the very essence of hearth. This, I was sure, was where the family lived.

"Such an awful thing!" the lady of the house said. "I can't believe it. Just last week, Jimmy Pat was right here. In my house where you're standing . . . This smells delicious, what is it? Your mother's recipe? How is she? The arthritis still bad? And in this weather, too—can you believe how cold it still is? I went outside this morning and thought I'd . . ."

The shower of words had become a tsunami. I tried to tune her out. She was the spirit of generosity with words and affection, but probably not a good source of hard information. Besides, I had need of a rest stop.

Mrs. Grassi noticed my questioning expression. "Upstairs," she said. "First door on the left. But you know what? Dolores is up there, and the boys, so use the one in the rec room. Down these stairs."

This time, I entered what felt like a night club. A plush and mirrored, carpeted retreat, with a curved chrome bar, fully stocked. The room was lush, overdone maybe, but not stuffy, with magazines left tossed open onto tables and sofa pillows, a black and white check sweater dangling off the corner of a chair, a pair of running shoes with a shimmery throw of fabric tossed on top. Not like Barbs's precise and anxiety-ridden household.

On the mirrored coffee table stood a small porcelain sculpture of a comic Dude, with his trademark golden slippers, glitter-trimmed tuxedo, and pink and green three-tiered umbrella.

And on the walls, a baroquely framed Mummer rendered in oil

paint and what looked like gold leaf, and more plainly framed photographs of men in full regalia, arms around each other's shoulders, toasting the camera. And a plaque honoring Edward Grassi, Sr. for his donations and service to the Philadelphia New Year's Shooters & Mummers' Association.

Dolores's father, I'd been told, was involved with launderettes, but obviously, he seemed equally involved with Mummering.

Even the powder room mirror had been made to look like a backpiece, butterfly shaped and trimmed with carved feathers.

Once I was upstairs, the women of the kitchen shooed me out. "You're a guest," Mrs. Grassi insisted. So were the other visitors, but they were different—from the neighborhood, familiars. "Sit in the living room. Be comfortable. Dolores will be down in a minute."

The overcrowded room was a contrast to the rec room one story down. The chairs looked too stiff and delicate for a house in which four sons had been raised. The end tables were completely covered by a lamp with a fringed shade and sculpted silver-framed photographs of babies and brides, the coffee table had a collection of glass kittens, and the fabric on the sofa was a scratchy cream brocade that practically begged you to stain it. You weren't going to curl up with a magazine or leave your shoes behind here. This room was a show of possessions, a formal statement.

I heard the comfortable laughter of women working together and the clunk of dishes and pots and pans from the kitchen, and I considered braving Mrs. Grassi and reentering that warm and much friendlier space. Instead, I surveyed the snapshots on the end tables. Spotting Dolores at four or five stages of her evolution was like watching a stop-action nature special, but I was more taken with a photo of Jimmy Pat in jeans and a T-shirt, leaping into the air, both arms extended. I picked it up and examined it. The camera had caught that hyper-alive, appealing electricity I remembered. The man had had a rakish charm, maybe too much for his own good.

"Yeah," a growly female voice said from mid-staircase. "Lookin' at Jimmy Pat, aren't you? That was at the races—he won that day, that's what the jump was about. There you have him. He always said that's who he was and who he'd be till he died. And he was right." By the end of that practiced-sounding speech, Dolores had reached the bottom of the staircase. She blew her nose, blinked tearily, and looked ready to greet me.

Then she did a double take. *"You?"* she asked. "You? In my own house?"

This was worse than any of my imagined scenarios. "Hello," I said, "I went to the beauty parlor to extend my condolences, and Andrée insisted that I come over here with them, and—"

Just then, what sounded like a herd thundered down the staircase. When they'd reached bottom, and the dust cleared, they turned out to be only two men, both probably in their twenties.

"Yo," one of them said to me. "Yo," the other agreed with a laconic hand wave.

They were fine-boned and good-looking. I recognized one and could assume who the other was even before Dolores grudgingly introduced us. "My brothers," she said. "Two of my brothers. This is Stephen—" the younger-looking of the two, the one I'd had coffee with, although he didn't seem to remember me with any enthusiasm "—and George. This here is Amanda Pepper. She works at Vincent's school, only she teaches English."

"Oh, Jeez. An English teacher," George said. Having heard that one line, I felt as if I could write his biography. Class clown all through school. "I'd better watch my p's and q's, whatever the hell that means," he said.

There were several theories of the meaning of the expression. One simply had to do with the confusion young printers' apprentices had setting the similarly shaped letters. A more interesting theory held that bar accounts were tallied with a *p* for a pint and a *q* for a quart, and that in figuring how much you owed, you had to mind which was which. However, I squelched my impulse to pass on the wisdom. "I'm on winter break," I said instead. "Have no fear." I'll bet he talked straight through every English class he'd ever had. But having beaten the system and graduated, he now became tongue-tied in the presence of the breed that had failed to quiet him down years back. You get wary in the presence of those you've successfully bamboozled.

"Yeah, but all the same," George said. "Grammar. Parts of speech. Ooh-ee! Man, I'm still in trouble about them. Like with propositions?"

I almost corrected him, but realized in time that this was the start of an oft-told part of George's repertoire.

" 'A proposition relates its object to something else in the sentence,' " he said. "That was one of the only things Sister Prudence said that made sense to me. So when she asked for examples, I said, 'Madam, should I be behind you? Above you? Under you? Between you and your sister, Sister?' And Sister Prudence suspended me."

I'd heard equally pathetic variations on that theme, and I was coming to feel a lot like Sister Prudence about it.

Stephen, the younger brother, ignored the banter and seemed less than delighted by my presence. In fact, he looked as if storm warnings should have been posted beneath his face. That was pretty much as I remembered him from the evening at the diner.

"Amanda is also a *journalist*," Dolores said. She sounded as if that were akin to having a social disease. "She's writing about *us*."

"Not really," I said.

"Not really what?" Stephen demanded.

"I'm not a writer yet, only trying to see if I could do it, could sell an article."

"You're trying out the idea by writing about us?" Stephen asked.

"Don't you remember anything?" his sister demanded. "You were there at the diner when she asked all those questions and things?"

Stephen gave a so-what shrug. Another young male I'd failed to impress. "I'm not writing about specific people," I said. "I'm writing about Mummers."

"Shooters," Stephen said. "You should know at least that much."

I nodded. "Sorry," I said.

"That sure as hell is us," George said. "Every one of us. Ask my mom—she's a Mummer widow, all right. Never sees Dad, he's so busy with his committees at the club."

"*I'm* the Mummer widow," Dolores growled.

There was an awkward moment, which I tried to end by dragging us back to the topic. "I'm interested in Mummers as a group, as a cultural phenomenon, a tradition. Outside of Philadelphia, not all that many people know about—"

"About who?" Stephen again. "Don't you people get permission before you barge in on somebody? We aren't guinea pigs, you know."

"About what *Mummers*—Shooters—are," I insisted. "How the parade evolved, who's involved in it, what it means to your lives, how hard you work all year. You know."

Dolores's mouth tightened. "About Jimmy Pat," she said.

"No. Not at all."

"And not about my sister, right?" Stephen asked. "Not about Jimmy Pat that way, either, am I right?"

"Of course." These people were incredible egotists, unable to see beyond their own little fiefdom. "I was never interested in—"

"George . . ." Stephen changed concerns abruptly. "George, we're late. Supposed to be there already."

"Sorry." George zipped his leather jacket. It was impressive, burgundy with a fur lining and GRASSI'S LAUNDERETTES embroidered in lemon yellow on the back.

Stephen pulled an identical jacket out of the vestibule closet.

"That you, boys?" Mrs. Grassi, wiping her hands on a dish towel, called out from the dining room.

"Yeah, Ma," they said, almost in unison. "Bye, Ma. Back soon. Nice meeting you, Amanda." That last was from George. I had a sense that once again, Stephen didn't think it was nice to have met me. In either case, first the inner, then the outer doors slammed behind them.

"Boys," Mrs. Grassi said. "All noise. I was downstairs, lookin' for a picture to show the girls. Dolores, you all right? You're pale. I'll get you something hot."

"Ma—" Dolores began, but Mrs. Grassi was gone again, and the widowed bride turned on me with viper-speed. "You should be ashamed of yourself, coming here," she spat out in a rush. "If you were decent, you'd leave now, right away."

"Why?" But I knew I was an interloper. She was honest about it and I wasn't.

"We treated you right, told you what you wanted to know, had a few laughs together, so what kind of person are you? Why'd you do a thing like this? You don't like us? Don't like me? Want to make everything worse for me?"

Dolores was petite, a feminine version of the fine features and delicate bones that made her brothers so attractive. She wore an understated black tunic and leggings and no visible makeup. You saw her and thought of vulnerability, fragility. Today, even her hair seemed subdued, its parameters narrower, as if it, too, were in mourning. But as soon as she opened her mouth, now and the earlier evenings I'd spent in her company, an oversized, gruff, and intimidating bad-girl spoke out. If you didn't look at her, only listened, you'd envision someone huge, merciless, and murderous, or at least, a seasoned moll.

"I know you think I understand what you're talking about," I said softly, "but honestly, I don't."

"It's not like I don't know. I just got off the phone."

"With whom?"

"Whom, schmoom. I'm not of the fancy talkers. I'm not an English teacher. This is my house, I can talk like I want. You have no right to snoop."

What had I done? I hadn't inspected a thing except those out and on show, so where was the harm or the offense?

"Hot chocolate." Mrs. Grassi's voice preceded her around the corner from the kitchen. "Drink." She stood in the dining room, at the table, which was covered with a crocheted cloth. "I brought one for you, too," she told me. "Do you good on a freezing day."

I thought it impolite to point out that we were all in an overheated house. Iced tea might be more like it.

"Sit, sit," Mrs. Grassi said. "We're almost finished in there."

"Couldn't I help you?"

"Visit with my baby girl," Mrs. Grassi said. "My little princess. That's the help you can give." Dolores snorted cynically at the idea of consolation from me. Apparently, Mrs. Grassi didn't hear. "Besides," she continued, "you're a guest in my house. Sit, sit!"

We sat.

Dolores waited till her mother was back in the noisy kitchen. "You're a nosy bitch," she snapped.

Everybody in the shop had described her as sweet. Vincent was her once and possibly future admirer. I wondered why. I tried again. "You said you were on the phone with someone. Who was it?"

"I thought it was *whom* was it," she snarled.

I waited.

"Vincent," she finally said.

"He called you?"

"Like you don't know. You were there today."

"What does that have to do with anything?" My mind made loopy figure eights. Was there, then, something real between Dolores and Vincent? Were Barbs's suspicions on target? Why would Vincent, the prime suspect, call Dolores unless his story was altogether true? But what about Barbs? And why would Dolores seem sympathetic to the man? Loop, loop, getting nowhere but back to "go."

"Stop seeing him," she said flatly.

"Wait a minute! Me? Stop *seeing* him? Meaning what? Why?"

She leaned closer, across the crocheted cloth. I smelled her cologne, an aroma that would be blue violet if it had a color. It didn't suit her personality. "You want me to spell it out? Okay, teach, here goes. Because he's married, because you're messin' with his head. Because you'll ruin his life if you keep this up."

I became wistful for my figure eights, because now my brains were shapeless, a sort of lava lamp of the mind.

"Barbs might not be a mental giant, but she isn't stupid."

Barbs was jealous of Dolores, not of me. Or what kind of game was Vincent playing? "Vincent and I—we teach together. We aren't—it isn't that kind of a—" I stopped myself. I needed to think more about what this meant, and how much I should say.

"The least you could do is cover for him. Or do you want him to spend the rest of his life in jail?"

"If he killed Jimmy Pat, then I don't know what I want," I said slowly. "I would think you'd feel that way, too."

She glared.

"You don't think he did it?" I asked.

"What does it matter what I think? The police think he did, and he wasn't where he should have been because he was with you."

"But he said . . . he told me . . ."

"You're a user, know what I mean? You used Vincent and Jimmy Pat and me and everybody else to get your precious story. And you're still using us. Great. You'll make money and get famous, and he'll go to jail."

This was about my story? That was the snooping she resented? "I'm not writing the article," I said. That appeared to be true, even if unintentional.

"Like I believe that. Anyway, the damage is done, you asking all those questions and playing up to Vinny for information, and then there he is, trying to help you out during the parade and you won't even admit it and maybe save his life."

"Wait," I protested. "Now I'm even more confused." He'd told me that she'd made an appointment with him. She was his missing alibi, not me. Except she seemed oblivious of that. Was this pretense? A cover-up? An attempt to avoid whatever shame Vincent said such a date would engender? To whom had Vincent lied?

Since Vincent hadn't seen Dolores when he said he was supposed to, that meant she had no alibi for the time of the murder, either, and I believed that in the hell-hath-no-fury department, Dolores would be Chairwoman. I looked at her with new interest.

"Like I care about your being confused," she said.

"Are you under the impression that Vincent Devaney was with me when Jimmy Pat was shot?" Surely she was bluffing, creating a smoke screen for herself. She had probably suggested this scenario to Vincent. Unless, of course, he was playing a game I truly couldn't follow.

Dolores was an Olympic-level glarer.

"In the first place," I said, "nobody yet knows when Jimmy was shot. In the second place, I wasn't with Vincent at any time during the parade. And in the most important third place, I *was* with somebody, with my . . . my boyfriend. Who is a cop. A cop who knows Vincent was not with us. How could I lie about that?" I hated how my voice rose toward the stratosphere, as if it were trying to find a place to hide.

She just plain didn't care about logic or reason and, in fact, brushed it away with a sideways motion. "We aren't real to you, just bugs to study, freaks of nature."

"Not at all, that isn't . . ." But I had wanted to look at this culture within a culture, at a closed society centered around something unusual and exotic, like mumming, and looking at it meant backing off, being apart from. Maybe she had a point.

"Stop, already," she said. "Haven't we suffered enough? I was supposed to have a wedding in two weeks and instead, there'll be a funeral."

"I didn't kill Jimmy," I said, even as I wondered if she had. "Don't you want to find out who did?"

Her eyes flashed. "How'm I supposed to manage that?"

She actually waited for an answer, but I shook my head.

"Everybody liked him," she said. "You had to like him."

I nodded. I, too, had been aware he was something special, that he wore a likableness that was almost tangible.

"I'm not saying he was a saint," Dolores said. "He was a good-time boy, never worried about tomorrow. That can make problems, but not so bad that somebody'd . . ." She seemed unsure of her own words, then shook her head again. "Nah."

"What kind of problems?" Was this an oblique reference to the scarlet Emily Semow?

"Vincent must have said. Everybody knew. Jimmy lived fast. Loved risks and chances. On anything. The horses, Atlantic City. Hell, if he'd lived through the parade, he'd have had a wager on how much snow would be outside this time of day today. Sometimes, a man like that, he loses the bet. He wouldn't take money from me to pay his debts. Said it wasn't right, we weren't married."

"He used loan sharks?" I envisioned hatchet-faced men, knee-breakers, one loan too many.

She shook her head. "But what with getting married and every-thing, what I'm afraid of was that sometimes, if Jimmy wanted something real bad, like having people forget he owed them money, he could believe that they wished it just as much as he did. Like I said, he wasn't a saint, but you had to like him all the same."

"Do you know who loaned him money?"

Her answering shrug suggested everyone, anyone.

Charming Jimmy's postmortem portrait grew darker by the moment. A compulsive gambler, he cheated his friends over money and cheated his fiancée with another woman, but might be marrying her because she could pay his gambling debts. What a prize. I wondered if Dolores, knowing all that, wasn't a little re-lieved to be freed from this marriage. "Are you saying a friend killed him? Do you know who?"

Dolores sniffled. "Talk about jumping to conclusions! Who said anything except that nobody would have wanted to hurt him that way? I loved him," she said mournfully. "He was supposed to be the father of my children."

That seemed an ill-advised description, given that he was re-ported to be the father of Emily Semow's expected child. "Doesn't that make you even more eager to know who did such a—"

"Yeah, well I'll read it in the papers. I'm not saying another word. You're pretending to care. You're interested in your story. In the money you can make out of us."

"I'm interested in the truth. If Vincent left the parade the way he says, it was because he was trying to find *you*, not me."

"Says who?"

"Vincent."

"Get outta here!" She'd told me to leave as soon as she'd seen me, but this time the words expressed incredulity. I thought.

"I gather you used to date and maybe something was starting up again?"

"Get outta here!" she said again. "Jimmy Pat and me, we were getting married in two weeks."

An oven timer dinged. The food troops would march in any second now. I stood up.

"You're saying Vincent's still carrying a torch for me?" Dolores's voice was foggy, bemused. She waved her hand dismissively. "Ahhh ... that's crazy." But she sounded lighter, and definitely interested. Fickle, Vincent had called her. He seemed right on the mark. "Nah," she said, continuing her internal debate. "That's too crazy. Get outta here."

This "get out of here" was the charm. With a few apologies, and fewer regrets, I got out of there.

Seven

TWO P.M. in South Philly. I'd taken a bus to Third and was waiting to transfer to the connecting bus home, but even though I could state my locale, where, really, was I?

"Hey, lady, you nowhere."

I wheeled around to see who had read my mind and answered it. An unshaven man in a raveling knit cap and layers of jackets and shirts, none of which looked warm enough to protect him, grimaced. "Nowhere?" he repeated, this time as a question.

"Excuse me?"

"The recycling center, like I said. Know where it is, lady? Do.

You. Know. Where?" He punched the side of one of his plastic bags and I heard a metallic clinking.

I smiled my relief. Know where. Unfortunately, I had no idea where the recycling center might be. In fact, I still wasn't one hundred percent sure either metaphorically or literally where I was. I looked toward the corner. Christian Street. Now I knew my geography, but that didn't help the man. He must have known how useless I'd be because he shuffled off.

I watched the retreating figure. Welcome to the Nineties, to a modern refinement of Santa-as-homeless with trash bags full of recyclables. Then I turned back toward the bus stand. But the corner signs for Third and Christian Streets hung in the gray-blue air as if outlined. Something about that location, something I'd stored away besides the fact that a north-running bus was available. But what? I looked around, trying to see if memory or recognition would be on the tape this time.

The know-where man had not given up his quest. As I watched, he stopped two men. They listened as he asked his question and shook his bag of soda cans, shook their heads, waved him aside dismissively—although one of them handed him money first. The backs of their leather jackets had writing embroidered on them.

The Grassi brothers. Why were they here, twenty-thirty blocks from home? Were they following me? Or did it have something to do with why I was supposed to remember this area?

I was losing it. They could be here for a million reasons. This was their greater neighborhood and they'd had some kind of appointment. The real question was—why was I here?

Because . . . Christian Street. Between Second and Third. This time, I heard Stel's voice at the beauty parlor saying that Emily Semow's card store was nearby and always open. I glanced at my watch and confirmed that the odds of Mackenzie's being back in the loft were slim. A case of serendipity, so a small detour wouldn't make any difference, except, perhaps, to yield something tangible. Like whether or not Jimmy Pat really had another woman plus a Jimmy Pat, Junior on the way, although I wasn't sure how I could broach a subject of such delicacy.

I walked across the street to where Semow Stationery settled grayly and unimpressively between a dog groomer and a beauty supply shop. The Grassi brothers had stopped a few paces down and were watching me.

Nothing odd about any of this, I reminded myself. Maybe they'd needed THANK YOU FOR YOUR KIND SENTIMENTS AT OUR TIME OF LOSS cards.

"Déjà vu all over again," George Grassi said. "You were just at my house, and now you're . . ."

"Shopping."

"For what?" Stephen asked. "Us? More facts for your article? That really burns me. Leave us alone, would you?"

"I had no idea you'd be here," I said. "I'm looking for school supplies."

"Why here? You're not from the neighborhood, why here?"

"I heard this store was open a lot, like today."

He nodded and scowled, then leaned closer. "It's not going to do you any good."

"What isn't?"

George tugged at his sleeve and, with one last frown, Stephen turned and walked away with his brother, but he kept swiveling to watch me.

When I opened the door, an old-fashioned bell rang in the back of the shop. However, no summons had been necessary. A tall, blue-eyed, black-haired young woman stood arranging a display of half-priced Christmas cards. She turned and appraised me. She had striking features that were probably odd and teaseable in school, but stunning now. "Help you?" she asked as I stood aimlessly near the register. She wore a black skinny-ribbed T-shirt, a black leather skirt, black tights, and clunky high-heeled black sneakers. Her hair was cut in shaggy points, so that her head looked not unlike a dark-rimmed ornament.

The ensemble could have been a form of mourning attire, or simply standard-issue black clothing worn to show you were a unique and sophisticated individual.

I remembered that I should look like a customer. "Um," I said, biding time while I waited to hear what I was going to say. "I'm looking for . . . three-by-five cards."

She sighed.

I had failed to say the secret word. Three-by-fives weren't it, weren't enough to brighten her day. She listlessly nodded toward a counter. This was one sad cookie. "White, yellow, green, pink, blue, lined, unlined, three-by-five, five-by-eight, whatever you want," she recited with no animation, for which I couldn't blame her. "Also, over with the recipe boxes we have some that say 'From the kitchen of.' "

I smiled and shook my head. "No thanks."

"Or *bon appétit*. Those, too."

I hated disappointing her.

"Not using them for recipes?" she asked.

"Sorry."

"What then? Writing a term paper?" She laughed, then stifled it. "Didn't mean to sound like I thought it was funny if you were still in school, or anything. People should do what they want to."

I shoved my mittens into my purse and selected a packet of assorted colors. It was one of the brightest objects in the store, which seemed shrouded by a veil. Maybe it was only the dark day, inadequate lighting. "I'm researching an article." I loved saying that much more than I loved doing the work.

"You're a writer?"

"Freelancer." It wasn't a lie. I was an inept, inadequate, and completely unsuccessful freelancer, but she hadn't asked for my résumé or profile. "It's all an excuse to let me go crazy in stationery stores," I added. That part was probably true.

"So go crazy," she said. "I could use the business."

I paused in front of the discounted Christmas cards. It would be smart and economical to stock up now, as the hand-printed sign advised. I would love to be a person who buys at the post-Christmas sales and has a closet filled with wrapped and carefully selected gifts and cards months in advance. But I am always broke in January. Besides, I'd worry that the catchy item I bought would be further discounted or recalled by December. Or that since it was so perfect and such a good buy, the giftee would have already gotten it for himself. Still, I paused at the half-priced card rack.

Upholding a great local retail tradition, the store's heat register was set on *equatorial*. No concessions to what customers would be wearing when they entered. In summer, the systems are equally irrational, air-conditioning set on *arctic*. Temperate, indeed.

I unbuttoned my coat, loosened my muffler, pulled off my knit hat. Winter in a nutshell: taking off and putting on insulation.

"Here," the girl said. "Toss it on that chair. I tell my dad all the time it's too hot in here, but he never listens."

So she was Emily or at least, a Semow. Who else's father would be in control of the thermostat? I put my things down—everything—nearly was tempted to pull off my lined boots and pad around in my socks.

I skimmed through sparkle-sprinkled Christmas kitties, cunning vignettes on the daily lives of grinning elves in curly-toed shoes, a handful of talking reindeer, and glimpses into the private life of Mr. and Mrs. Claus. I had never suspected how frisky Santa became once his annual workday was over.

"You're not from the neighborhood," she said.

I shook my head. Neighborhood seemed a quaint, old-fashioned, but important construct in these parts. Other parts of the city—like mine—were areas. This was a neighborhood.

"Didn't think you looked familiar."

I controlled another urge to apologize.

She hummed tunelessly while she did whatever it was with the price stickers, then she spoke again. "So who do you write for? Like magazines?"

"Like magazines," I agreed, relocating to the always-alluring pen display and trying out one, then another, on the little pad of paper provided. With the fifth try, I thought that I had found the perfect writing implement. It wrote so smoothly, felt so right in my hand, that surely ideas would transfer themselves directly from my brain to the page, and I would finish my article and write countless more and be rich and happy forever. Scribble, scribble. Amanda Pepper. A.P. Associated Press and Me. Ms. Mandy. Smooth and easy.

"Emily!" a voice from the back grumbled loudly. "I'm hungry, damn it!"

"In a minute!" she shouted.

So she was, indeed, Emily Semow.

"Do they pay a lot?" she asked me.

"Magazines? It varies." I spoke from the depths of ignorance while I doodled loops and experimented with signatures. "Some magazines and tabloids, very well. Others . . . you know how it is." I hoped she didn't, because if she did, she could ask me specific questions and find out that I knew nothing. "Nice pen," I said. Of that much I was positive.

"Damn it, Em, I don't like to wait!"

"Then get it yourself! It's in the refrigerator." She looked toward the back of the store, her mouth set and her eyes bleak. "He could reach it with one hand," she said to me. "Customer!" she shouted. "Leave me alone!"

I tried to seem unaware of the rising tension level and focused instead on whether I wanted to stay with traditional black or make a breakthrough with blue-black or even, heretically, turquoise ink. Was the new year time for a new image? Would green composition corrections seem more benign and acceptable than those made with the traditional red?

"People like you, they ever buy people's stories?" she asked while she sorted through keychains.

"I'm not a publisher."

"I mean, buy what happened to somebody."

"You mean to write it up?" Of course that's what she meant, but I didn't know. Tabloid TV and newspapers bought stories, but did freelancers? "It depends who they're writing for," I answered, hedging the issue.

"Supposing somebody had a story to sell *you*, for who you write for, would you be interested?"

"Me?" She didn't have very high standards if she would talk to someone as tongue-tied and verbally limited as I was being.

"A good story. Stuff nobody in the world but me knows. What would something like that be worth?"

What to do? How to possibly keep up the pretense? Bus tickets, three-by-fives, and the pen would wipe out my post-holiday discretionary funds. I couldn't buy her story. Ever. "I'd have to . . . do research, get a better sense of what you mean," I finally said. "Of whether a wide readership would be interested. Can you give me a hint?"

"Murder. That enough of a hint?"

"You didn't commit one, did you?"

"Like I'd tell you, right?"

"Then you know about a murder." I was practically whispering. "An unsolved murder? A wrongly solved one? An old one? A recent one?"

"All I said was I had a story. And this—even that—is off the record, right?"

If only I had a record to keep it off. I nodded. What did a real journalist do in this situation? "Is this like a . . . Jack the Ripper sort of thing? I'm . . . thinking of possible markets."

She shook her head.

"An open case? I mean, should the police be told this information?"

She raised her eyebrows. "The police don't pay a cent."

"But legally, if you have information . . ."

"So what you're saying is you don't do what they call investigative reporting. Too bad. What do you write about?"

I could have said gardening or fly-fishing or anything, except the only thing which came to my limited, somewhat frozen mind was the truth. "I'm doing a piece on the Mummers."

"The Mum—" She squinted so hard a crease appeared between her eyebrows. "Wait a minute—you're *that* writer!"

I had achieved literary fame without writing, let alone publishing, a word. Amazing.

"You work with Vinny Devaney, don't you?"

I didn't say a word or move a muscle.

"You're her, aren't you? I can't believe it."

"Why? How did you hear about me?"

"I was told you're snooping around about Jimmy Pat's murder for an article that's going to be bad for us—"

"Us?"

She shrugged. "Shooters. Us."

"You're a Mummer?"

"Not officially. But I practically live on Two Street, and I love it, the fun, the guys, the people. It's sure better than this." She opened her arms to indicate the store.

A Mummer groupie, as I live and breathe. And completely understandable, given her gray daily surroundings.

"These are good people, my people," she said, "and they like their privacy, keep it within friends, and nobody wants you airing our dirty laundry."

"I'm not. I'm probably not even going to write the article, and it never had anything to do with dirty laundry, whatever you're referring to. It wasn't going to be bad for the Mummers, it was going to be good publicity. That kind of thing."

"Like Mummers need publicity," she said. "The whole world knows about them." She smiled for the first time, and seemed to reappraise me. Then she lifted a shoulder and tilted her head. "But why should I listen to what a Grassi tells me?"

"They—" I waved at the now-empty storefront. "That's what they came here for? To tell you about me?"

She shook her head. "We had things to say. They added a warning about you for free. A bonus. But hell, why should I listen? That family hates me because . . . they do. They're jealous of me, is all. Even now. I'll say what I want to who I want."

Her grammar wasn't perfect, but the blue of her eyes was, and she had a spark that ignited her features and made her more interesting than Dolores, and I could understand Jimmy Pat's defection. If indeed such had happened. I also could understand why the Grassis would fear her.

What I couldn't understand was why they'd go out of their way to warn her against me. Or if, as she'd said, it had been chitchat, something dropped in passing . . . then, what was it they'd had to talk to this girl about?

"I could tell you something for your article," Emily said.

"The story you mentioned?"

She shook her head. "That one's for sale. This is for the Mummers article. About Jimmy Pat. Free of charge."

"My article isn't about him, it's—"

"He wasn't going to marry her. That's what Stephen Grassi didn't want me to tell you. They wouldn't want you to know that, being as they're big on their reputation. Appearances. They get what they want, you know? The Grassis act like they own us all, living up there in the Estates, having money and respect, but nobody owns me."

"Hold on," I said quietly. "Jimmy Pat was supposed to marry Dolores in two weeks."

She shrugged. "Supposed to doesn't mean going to. And she knew it. He told me he told her. So she didn't say? She's still pretending like she's getting ready for a wedding?"

"Well, given that Jimmy Pat's dead, she's not—"

"She's not telling the truth, is she? That it was off."

"Not that I know of. What's it . . . what happened?"

Emily looked at me with her dark-lashed pale eyes. "He was in love with me." She shrugged. "What can I say? He finally realized what a mistake he was making. A man can be dazzled by an important family like the Grassis. And those brothers probably strong-armed him."

"It was really off?"

She nodded vigorously. "She knew, too, but she didn't tell anybody. Not even her mother, who kept on with the preparations. All Dolores cares about is saving face. She knew a week ago. He was going to marry me once a decent amount of time passed and the gifts were returned and all. Didn't want to be rude and marry me the weekend he was supposed to marry her. Maybe in spring, we thought. I always wanted to be a June bride. I wanted the serenade, too."

The serenade was a warm-weather Mummer tradition, a private concert outside the house of the bride-to-be. I had notes about it at home. I thought about the warm weather, a season away.

Emily's face crumpled. "Now, of course . . ." She shook her head and wiped at her nose.

"So sad," I said. And so unlike what the gossips had suggested. A man doesn't delay his wedding six months to someone he *has* to marry. And Emily, despite her dreams of romantic serenades wouldn't wait that long, either. "What a shame for you," I said. "Would you mind telling me what made Jimmy Pat suddenly realize it was you he wanted to marry?"

Her peachy skin iced over and her eyes became glacial.

"It's so romantic," I said. "And sad. Tragic, even, like those old myths. Tristan and Isolde . . ."

"Who the hell are they?"

"Like Romeo and Juliet, you know?"

Her expression softened. "Except we weren't kids, and we always loved each other and our families didn't have problems with each other. See, I remember what I was taught. Jimmy and me, we dated after we were out of school, then I don't know what happened. We were immature. Dolores got Jimmy Pat on the rebound, that's all it was. Her family knew him from the Fancy Club, so they were happy about it, and they planned that wedding from day one. I don't blame them. Dolores has a bad attitude, a bad rep. Always dumping men, changing her mind. She's a spoiled brat and always was. Her family calls her Princess and they mean it. Baby Princess gets whatever she wants from Mommy and Daddy and her four big brothers. But people who aren't Grassis get tired of it, you know? It gets old real fast. A man'd be crazy to plan a life with her, and rich as she is, Jimmy Pat was her one chance—if they moved fast, while he was still blinded by the fancy Grassis."

I wondered how she knew so much about the Grassis, who seemed to live in a different world and at a different social level than Emily did. Perhaps the link was the Mummers. "This is irrelevant, but is your family also involved with a club?"

"Your article, huh? Always doing the research, aren't you?" She shook her head. "I'm it for family, except my dad. He was in a String Band. Played the glockenspiel, but he's been crippled a long time. His old club'd let him ride in the banner car, or the repair car, but he says if he can't march on his own two feet, he isn't going anywhere. Cuts off his nose to spite his face, I say."

"I'm sorry."

"So, about Jimmy Pat, I ran into him maybe two weeks ago,

and that pretty much was it. It can be like that, you know. You suddenly realize, and then, your fate is set."

Two weeks ago. And he supposedly told Dolores their wedding was off a week later. It necessitated rewriting the laws of biology to begin a pregnancy, get it verified, and rupture a prior engagement within seven days. Either Emily was fabricating a story, or the gossip was dead wrong about a shotgun wedding.

"Quite a story," I said. "You were right."

"Wait a minute—are you talking about this, or the other story?"

"I thought, since you said your story had to do with a murder, and Jimmy Pat was murdered, I thought maybe this turned out to be the story."

"This was a story. But what happened to Jimmy . . . if I knew that . . ." She squeezed her lips together so tightly that no color showed in them. "I'd get the son of a bitch who did it, and I'd cut out his heart."

I believed her. "I . . . have to think about the other story, then," I said.

"You're not interested? Do you know, maybe, if a person can call up one of those TV shows, like *Unsolved Mysteries*? Do they pay? Do you need to know somebody?"

"I could try to find out."

"Never mind." I could almost see her vivid coloring fade into the overall gray of the store.

"If you give me a clue as to what murder this is about, maybe I could—"

"Rip me off. No thanks. It's what I have, and I'm not giving it away. So . . . look around. That's why you're here, right?"

There wasn't much to see. The supplies looked old and tired. "This is it," I said. I bought the unnecessary three-by-fives and the pen with green ink.

She looked at me intently as I opened the door. I paused, thinking she was on the verge of changing her mind, of unburdening herself of the too-big story that weighed heavily on her.

Then her father's voice boomed out of the dark back room, and looking as if all possibilities had just been erased, she turned around and answered his summons.

Eight

I<small>T</small> was good to be home where the complications of my relationship with Mackenzie, endless though they often seemed, felt simple and clean-edged in comparison to the love-murk I'd waded through. Nobody out there was fully or adequately attached; nobody appeared to be cleaving completely unto, or forsaking all others. If I probed more, I'd probably find out that Barbs Devaney had a guy on the side and that Dolores also had a spare somewhere.

The phone rang at dusk. "Hi," Mackenzie greeted me. "Gonna take a food break soon, me and Billy."

"As in Obenhauser?"

"Uh-huh. Yes. He says 'hi,' too."

Very cordial for a man I didn't know, but I got the message.

"He's been back awhile, too, and he's ready for a break."

Translation: Billy had been to see Vincent.

"Been a long day."

That was the unsimple truth, not code for anything. Given that Mackenzie's dawn had been one A.M., he'd been doing whatever he does for seventeen hours now.

"How does pizza sound?" he asked. "Sausage and mushrooms. And how did your day go?"

"Middling. You want a rundown before Billy's with you?"

"Shoot."

"Okay, understanding that some of what I was told might be delusional, here goes: Vincent used to be—might still be—in love with Dolores Grassi, who was engaged to the dead man. Vincent's wife Barbs is a jealous woman. Dolores Grassi's engagement to Jimmy Pat might actually have been cancelled a week ago, even though she's not admitting it. Don't try Pepper Pot soup. Some person named Molly, a gossip, thinks Emily Semow, the other woman in the Dolores-Jimmy Pat triangle, is pregnant, and that's why he was about to switch brides, but Emily says they only just met up again two weeks ago and weren't going to get married until June. She also has a murder she wants to sell me. I mean, she doesn't want to sell me a murder, she wants me to pay her for what she knows about one so I could write about it. On the other hand, she and Dolores and Dolores's brothers are paranoid about what I might write about them."

"What's all this about writing?"

"Give me a break. They heard I was a journalist."

Mackenzie, my conscience, did not say "so did I," for which I was grateful. "So," he said instead, "that's how you define a middlin' day?"

I wasn't sure if that was praise for all I'd found out or a polite expression of tedium, or a kind of macho joshing to let Billy O.

99

know that Mackenzie and I never had talks of any substance. Whatever.

THE TELEPHONE rang again after the constables and pizzas had arrived. We'd been doing silent munching, since Mackenzie wasn't about to talk about the case, either his findings or lack thereof or mine, with the corpulent, good-natured, shrewd-looking Billy there.

The official line, or an overview of it, hadn't taken long—my whereabouts during the parade, my not having seen Vincent during that time, etcetera. I'd promised to go to headquarters and make a formal statement along those lines, and then we'd run out of chitchat and concentrated on pizza. It was an exceedingly dull dinner party, or I wouldn't have answered the phone.

I shouldn't have, and I shouldn't have been surprised that my caller was once again Renata Field. "We had an agreement, Renata." I kept my voice calm, although I felt anything but. The girl was invading my home and my life, and I felt her as a physical presence. Nonetheless, I didn't want Billy noticing my murderous streak. "*Badgering* doesn't help anything."

No, she insisted. This wasn't badgering. This was one last attempt to break through my thick-headed lack of comprehension about how a desperate person, such as she, had to bend the rules.

Because of her, I was now the desperate person and she was still a lazy, immature wretch. I had so few rules—she had no right to bend a single one of them.

But there was a new twist to her desperation. Unless I gave her a decent grade, she said in a quavering voice, her parents were pulling her out of Philly Prep. She thought maybe she'd kill herself or at least just die if that happened.

I wondered what my principal would do if I cost him a tuition. In a conflict between ethics and money, I didn't have to guess which side Havermeyer would favor.

"I made a mistake," Renata said in a vibrato. "I admit that, even though you never let me explain why. You never gave me a fair chance to defend myself."

"That exam *was* a chance, and you know it. Besides, you admitted cheating." On a take-home exam. She could have read the book instead. Or, at least, if she felt driven to cheat, she shouldn't have produced a word-for-word duplication of another student's essay. For stupidity alone she deserved to fail.

The other girl's record was exemplary. She'd be able to drop her lowest grade. Everybody could. She'd be fine. Renata, whose only earned grade was an F, wouldn't.

"There were *reasons*," Renata said. "I had problems." Renata considered life an emotional difficulty, a personal affront visited upon poor, unlucky her and her alone.

"I was *desperate*." She must have realized she had already used that line of defense in this conversation. "I was . . ." She paused, trying to find a synonym for desperation, but because she'd never paid attention during lessons in vocabulary building, she lapsed into silence.

It felt fair, then, to take advantage of the opening. "Don't do anything drastic or desperate tonight," I said, "and we'll deal with this tomorrow. As agreed."

"My life is on the line. My college career!"

I took a deep breath and continued. "After school. Tomorrow. Right now and until then, I'm on vacation, and I'm requesting that you finally respect that." I hung up while she continued to sputter, even though I knew she'd call back to protest my hanging up on her.

"I wish I could arrest lawbreaking students," I said between bites of pizza. "Lock them up the way you do. You're so lucky."

"Oh, yeah," Billy said. "It's keen fun. A million laughs."

Mackenzie nodded. "We'll give ours grades, instead. Okay, mister, this murder really pulls your average down. Clean up your act or you're going to flunk the year."

The phone rang again. "I've had it!" I said. "If there were something lower than an F, I'd make sure she got it." I grabbed the phone so fiercely, I nearly knocked over a small gargoyle sculpture that sat nearby. "Renata, I told you—"

"Mandy?" My sister's suburban voice. "Sounds like I've caught you at a bad time."

"No—sorry—that's—there's a student who's been—" I took a deep breath. "What's up?"

"I hope this isn't too much of an intrusion," she said breathlessly, "but we're going to an event downtown—a benefit for Quentin's favorite charity and she's speaking and then doing her show live, in front of us, and there are special presentations for the children, so we're all going, even the baby. If you have a few minutes, we'd love to stop by and see you first."

"See me?" See the warehouse in which her poor sister huddled. That was okay. The place was relatively tidy. I hadn't wanted Billy Obenhauser to think I was a slattern. Beth, The Perfect Homemaker, could come over. "Great."

"Only for a few minutes," she said. "We have the guest speaker with us, so we have to be on time."

"Whenever you like. I'd love to see you, and I'll be here all evening." C. K. and Billy would be long gone by the time the Wymans made it in from the suburbs, a trek that would take thirty to forty-five minutes if they left this instant.

"Super. How does five minutes from now sound?" Beth giggled. "We're in the car, a block away. Finding parking is the only problem."

Few, if any, people were rushing to park outside closed art galleries at this hour. I wouldn't even get car-circling time.

The Wyman family trooped in within seconds. Alexander, of course, wasn't yet able to troop. He might have crawled, or even toddled, but he was swaddled to the point where he was only theoretically there, so he was carried in by Sam, who was extremely proud of having found a parking spot.

I'd been living in the loft for four months, but Beth's forays into the evil city are few and far between, so this was her virgin exposure to The Warehouse. Although she tried to behave nonchalantly, she couldn't hide her amazement that bats didn't dangle from rafters and rats weren't snacking on our toes.

We made introductions all around, offered pizza remains to any takers, and I sketchily briefed my older sister on our future decorating ideas. Her preference was for exquisitely crafted and maintained antiques. Neither my wallet nor my taste pointed in that direction, nor did Mackenzie's, and I could feel Beth's discomfort with the wide open spaces, the shades that were the only window coverings, the skylight's openness, the broad expanses of uncovered planked floor between rugs. She was too polite to say anything except how airy and spacious it all was. Civilization in action again.

Quentin Reed silently examined the bookshelves and CD collection, making deductions about our mental health.

"Get comfortable. Want coffee or somesuch?" I asked.

"No, thanks, we're in a rush, actually," my sister said. "In fact—Karen?"

Karen had been stroking Macavity, who sat in a contented lump on top of my pocketbook on the table, purring.

"She made such a fuss," Beth said, "and now that we're here, look at her."

"I left my Magic Markers," Karen said to me.

"You remember where?"

She nodded, and relocated a miffed Macavity to the floor. "I took them to the parade," she explained, "but it was cold and too fun to draw, so I put them in here." She pointed at my bag. I sighed.

The soft leather pouch looked like a feed bag, and was big enough to carry a horse's or my rations, or both. Which was lucky, because it was always full. I wasn't excited about having the contents of my messy bag excavated. Karen's hands and face disappeared into it.

"Kar?" Her mother turned her nickname into a question. When no answer was forthcoming, she stated the obvious. "We're running late, sweetie. You know they're putting on a show for you, for all the children, and we don't want to miss any of it, do we?"

"No." Karen pulled her head back out into the fresh air, but continued to search with her hands.

"I want her to have a completely happy visual and musical experience," Beth said to me, as if Karen had suddenly become deaf. "Quentin thinks that would be best. Kar?" Beth asked again, still gently, although on the edge of shrill. No matter how irritated or tense her daughter made her, she had to keep her cool. It could be a curse being friends with *the* outspoken expert on psychological blunders. A childless expert, at that.

Billy Obenhauser stood up and patted his stomach. C. K. also stood, but refrained from such actions. "We'd better be going," Billy said.

"*Kar,*" Beth said.

"They're my favorites, and I need them!" Karen's voice was muffled as she searched deep within.

"Maybe we could stop at a store and find new Markers," Quentin said, checking the time on her watch. She smiled expansively, but her radio voice was gone and soon she'd be audible only to dogs.

"Let me help." I tried to pull the bag toward me even though my niece was still lodged half in it. I estimated how many used tissues, receipts, and crumpled "to do" lists were about to be revealed, how much mortifying evidence of illegal snacks.

I reminded myself that Billy Obenhauser was interested in death, not in whether I was a purse-slob. My sister and mother would discuss, with superior regret, my messiness, but that would help pass their telephone time. "Karen, let go—let me—give me—"

"Aunt Mandy!" Karen pulled her arm, head and something else out of the feed bag. Her eyes were wide. "Where'd you get this?"

"This" was a gun. A revolver, or maybe a handgun. I don't know the difference, but it was definitely a thing designed to shoot and seriously injure living matter.

Beth screamed and rushed for her daughter, from whose hand it dangled.

Mackenzie looked at me, then at the gun. Billy Obenhauser took a deep breath and said, "Now, now, little girl. Karen, if you'll just—don't touch that trig—don't press down on—here, I'll . . ." And he removed it from her, holding it by the grip, not the way a TV detective would, but I didn't correct him. He held it until C. K. retrieved a plastic bag from the kitchen and Billy dropped it in.

During which time nobody else said a word, if you exclude Beth's gasps and screeches and Quentin's soothing noises.

"A gun," Mackenzie finally said. "Jesus! How come?"

"For protection, I'm sure," Beth said. "Living in this city." She shook her head and took Alexander from Sam, as if she could better shield him from the evils of the twentieth century than his father could.

"Perhaps it's another attempt to emulate, become the equal of you, Detective," Quentin murmured. "After all, you get to carry a gun." She also twinkled a conspiratorial smile, as if to say *she* wouldn't have any of those problems if she were with him.

"But I—" I tried saying.

Beth turned back to me. "You should have told me you had a gun in the house before I let Karen sleep here."

"I didn't. I don't. It isn't mine," I said emphatically. "I've never seen it before."

Billy Obenhauser made his fleshy features bland and unreadable as he looked at me. "A derringer," he said.

What did that mean to me? Cowboys used them, I thought. Or maybe it was gangsters in old movies. Or maybe a gangster had been named Derringer.

"The current thought is that a gun of this sort killed Jimmy Pat," Mackenzie said softly.

"How would you know?"

"One slug was still in him," Mackenzie said.

"What do you mean, a *slug*?" Beth asked. "That creepy snail-thing that—"

"A bullet," Mackenzie said. "One bullet exited, one didn't."

"Hey, hey!" Billy said. Obviously, we lay people weren't supposed to know anything, although I couldn't see what harm it did to know Jimmy Pat had been shot twice, and I was tired of being an outsider, first in South Philly, and now in my own home.

"We have to go," Beth said with an edge of hysteria. *"Now!"* She took Karen's hand.

"I don't have my Markers!" Karen shouted, breaking loose.

Billy stepped in front of her, pushed the pizza remains aside, and emptied my bag onto the kitchen table. The better to find other incriminating evidence of criminality or slovenliness. My date-book–life-record which theoretically holds everything important tumbled out along with a pile of detritus until the table looked like a landfill site. Amazing how many charge slips, junk mails, lipstick-stained tissues, ATM statements, and notched bus tickets a person could accumulate in a few days. Along with seven lipsticks, a bottle of nail polish, and—I counted them— thirteen ballpoint pens. Matchbooks from restaurants I wanted to remember. The paper bag with the rainbow-colored three-by-fives and pen I'd bought at Emily's. A ring of keys to the school, to here, to doors I could no longer remember. A paperback. Two of Karen's barrettes. A small can of hair spray and a folding hair-brush, a pressed powder compact. You'd think I would always be impeccably groomed, wouldn't you? Sixty-four cents in loose change. And oh, yes, five Magic Markers, which Karen immediately scooped up.

Beth put separate zippered bags inside her purse for makeup and car keys, and she probably filed receipts properly and promptly in something akin to an evidence bag. Nothing was loose or unmoored or without purpose about her, her home, or her pocketbook. Amazing that we share genetic stock.

"How . . . where do you think you got that?" Mackenzie asked. He didn't mean my ballpoint pen collection, either.

"The . . . gun?" It was hard saying it. It gleamed dully and re-pulsively in its plastic envelope. I shook my head. "Somebody else put it in there. I didn't."

"Who?" Billy asked. "When?"

"Today, I guess," I said slowly. "Or yesterday, at the parade. I don't know. I didn't know it was there."

My sister, her lawyer husband, and her two children stopped their rapid egress and stood like spectators at a primitive cere-mony. Quentin kept clearing her throat as a reminder of where they should be headed, but Beth seemed to have forgotten about her honored guest as well as about detraumatizing Karen at the fund-raiser.

"How could you not feel it?" My oftentimes beloved looked at me with less than full approval.

"For Pete's sake!" I censored what came naturally in deference to the young ears still in the room. "My bag isn't like one of your pants pockets. It's more like a suitcase. I wouldn't notice a boulder if it were dropped in there. First of all, I had a coat on, a muffler—there were layers of padding separating it from me. But even without that, usually I have a roll book in there, and at least one textbook, too. I don't always carry my briefcase, because everything fits in this. During vacation, it's been lighter than usual, and that . . ." I gestured toward the table and the plastic bag with its deadly contents. "I didn't feel it. Didn't register the difference."

"It's not heavy, anyway," Billy said. "Lady's weapon."

"Wait a minute—not this lady's, if that's what you're saying!"

"No, no," Mackenzie said. "An expression. It's small, see how short the barrel is? With a short range and not a lot of accuracy. Its advantage is that it can be concealed."

"Like in a woman's purse," Billy said with a sigh that was half snort. "Even a normal one. Normal purse, not normal woman, I mean." He not only looked at me with that impassive suspicion, but now he eyed Mackenzie with something less than full trust. Afraid Mackenzie was covering up for his murderous lover. After all, I'd known the prime suspect and was, in fact, his declared alibi, and now that I apparently was holding and hiding the murder weapon, my denials of ever having seen Vincent smelled suspicious. As in . . . accomplice.

Mackenzie felt it, too, looking at his co-worker, his friend, with a visible flash of alarm, followed by comprehension, and then, resentment. Except I wasn't sure which of us it was he resented.

Who had dumped a gun on me, when, and why? I could think of too many opportunities when I'd shed my heavy outerwear, along with my bag. I'd done so in Vincent's overheated house, at the beauty salon, at the Grassi house, and even at the card shop. It wasn't my fault—the damned places were steaming.

As for the freezing-cold parade—when could anyone have disposed of a gun into my pocketbook? In the Porta-Potty line? While I watched the parade? On my way home with Karen? But again and again and again—why? Why me?

"This is very interesting," Quentin said, looking directly at me. "Have you had episodes like this before? Times when you couldn't remember how you came to have something, or where you were?"

I stared at her.

"Not to alarm you, but this happens with multiples, you know," she said softly.

"Oh, for—"

"Multiplication?" Mackenzie said. "What does math have to—"

I shook my head. "Multiple personalities. Dr. Reed thinks I . . . never mind."

Beth inhaled sharply and spoke. "Oh, look at the time. We're late. We really have to go now." Her voice had returned to normal. "Thanks for letting us barge in on you to see this terrific place." Obviously, we had just all enjoyed a charming social call. With a gun thrown in for spice.

"I didn't find my purple Marker," Karen wailed.

"Mandy, if you need me, give a call," Sam said. "I've written down my beeper number as well. We won't be at this event all that long, and we're nearby."

I couldn't figure out how or why I'd need somebody to work on tax law with me, and then I realized that he meant I might need, simply, a lawyer. Sam had not gotten stuck on the mystery of how a gun got into my handbag. In his unassuming but pragmatic way, he'd accepted that the gun was on my person, and acknowledged that I might be in trouble. An offer of help was a kind and practical gesture, but nonetheless, my spirits crashed all the way through the floor, through the several floors, to the gallery below us. Reality often has that effect on me.

"We *have* to leave." Beth was stuck on that concept.

"Right," Billy Obenhauser said. "All of us." He held the baggie in his right hand.

He didn't mean me, too, did he? I lifted my eyebrows and pointed at myself, and he nodded.

"But—I don't know anything."

He tightened his mouth and didn't move. The plastic-shrouded gun dangled from his fingers.

"Couldn't Mackenzie—couldn't you take my statement right here, now?"

He looked like a piece of postmodern sculpture. Not exactly a cop, but a damned fine replica of one.

"Usually," Mackenzie said, "you want people in a neutral location. And it wouldn't be good for me to be with you during."

"Why not?"

Now it was Mackenzie's turn to look at me as if I'd failed an I.Q. test. I remembered again. Billy O. was now suspicious of both of us. He wouldn't want my answers tainted by Mackenzie's presence, or cues, or whatever.

Damn.

Here it was, late on the last day of my winter break, now telescoped down from the endlessness of two weeks to a few hours. Soon, it would be back to Renata's whines and laments. Her classmates' idiosyncrasies and idiocies. My principal's insistence on making a small private school akin to the Pentagon for bureaucratic tangles. And endless papers to mark in a futile, doomed attempt to improve language skills.

I deserved these last few moments of solitude and peace.

But my sworn statement had suddenly become urgent. Just because the murder weapon had fallen out of my pocketbook. Some people really overreact.

On the other hand, I knew I was innocence itself. Getting this over with and getting back to the sanity of a schoolroom suddenly became highly desirable. I lifted the suspect purse and retrieved my coat, then I winked at Billy O., and opened the door.

On the elevator, Beth pursed her mouth, Billy eyed me suspiciously, Karen wailed about her missing Marker, and Quentin-the-shrink mused on how very *interesting* this all was. I could feel myself and my life being reshaped as one of the "true stories" she used to amuse listeners.

I pressed *Down*, the only way left to go.

Nine

SCHOOL is a habit that is easy to break. After two weeks away, the building looked and smelled like nothing I'd seen before.

Small comfort that the rest of the faculty wore what-am-I-doing-here expressions that let me know they also suffered reentry bends.

The only one who looked elated to be back was Vincent Devaney, as well he might. His presence meant the police were still waffling. Even Philly Prep was preferable to leg irons.

I wanted to compare notes on being questioned by Billy O. even though my experience had surely been gentler, since I wasn't suspected of doing the dastardly deed, only of being a hench-person. Even so, it had been unsettling. I had pointed out, in vain, how ridiculous their theory was. If I'd been consciously hiding the gun, I wouldn't have let Karen root through my bag.

Billy was unimpressed, reminding me that I hadn't let her do much rooting, that in fact, I'd tried to remove the bag from her.

Mackenzie wanted to believe in my innocence, but I could tell—and be vastly perturbed by—what a struggle it was. He'd have been easier about helping me deal with the consequences of covering up for a friend or trying to subvert justice than coping with what sounded like deceptive nonsense. To him, I was the child with frosting smeared around its mouth insisting I hadn't been anywhere near the cake.

I didn't blame him. It sounded too stupid for words to insist I had no idea how a murder weapon happened to be in my pocket-book right after I'd seen the prime suspect. If Mackenzie did something equally inexplicable and incriminating, I wouldn't believe his cockamamie story unless I'd had a lobotomy. Still, I didn't appreciate the wordless head shakes, the requests that I go over everything I'd done the last several days one more time, the question—again—of whether the only places I'd been when I left the parade were the Porta-Potty line and the pretzel vendor.

It got so that I doubted myself, wondered if I could have con-fused taking my niece to a chemical toilet with the furtive swap of a gun. Maybe I did have multiple personalities. The Three Faces of Amanda. One of which looked like a gun moll.

I wondered whether Vincent had had a similarly troubled night. Did Barbs look at him sideways, on the sly, wondering?

The expression he now aimed at me was anything but the one given to an accomplice. Or even someone you trusted enough to use as a fake alibi. Matter of fact, he looked unhappy to see me. I felt hurt until I realized I was a question mark, a potential prob-lem because I was the only person at school who knew he was a suspect in the dead Mummer case. "Trust me," I whispered as I passed him. I was about to go on, to tell him that I, too, was be-ing watched by the police, that we were in this together, but I was stopped by a shiver of apprehension.

I was in this, too, because of him, because of his lies. It was acutely possible that he had not only murdered someone with the gun that wound up in my pocketbook, but that he or his wife had planted the weapon on me while I was at their house.

The strangeness resumed as I entered the unfamiliar room designated as *mine*, and encountered alien creatures who behaved as if I had forced them to spend time with me.

There is no real new year in a schoolhouse, at least not in January. Our year begins in September and ends in June, and winter break is a parenthetical insert, not the end of anything. So on this bleak morn there was an overwhelming sense of unwilling ongoingness, of sameness and moreness. Of the coppery aftertaste of two weeks that had looked infinite in length and possibility in December, and now in January were known to have been brief as an eye blink and not even as much fun.

The visitors from a far planet continued to shuffle in, their eyes bleary, as if irritated by the vision of the dark months stretching ahead with nothing filling them but school. One could hardly count the February closures to commemorate Martin Luther King and long-dead presidents. Single-day breaks weren't oases worth anticipation.

All that, and report cards three weeks away.

For my senior classes, there was at least a sense of finality. The three weeks ahead held the last exams and papers that mattered, the last performance records tallied into the last grades college admission committees would see. After that, they put their brains on hold. They might not have learned a lot, but one thing they knew was that from this report card on, they could essentially go on life support.

That was the good news, except for Renata Field, who had dug herself a deeply final grade of F.

As for me, I had three weeks, fifteen days, in which to do any possible teaching or to feel even a modicum of authority with this group. Three weeks from now, their individual dies cast, unable to change the past—except in Renata's delusions—they'd throw caution, humility, attention, and civility to the wind.

What the hell, each little mind would say as it went on cruise control till June. What the hell!

"Miss Pepper." Renata turned the relatively soft syllables of my name into a whine, a cry of pain.

"We agreed to talk after school," I reminded her. "Not during." As much as it annoyed me, her barrage of calls had forced me to argue the issue with myself. In the greater scheme, did it matter if I cut a deal so that Renata got a grade she hadn't earned, in fact had not *tried* to earn?

Truth was, no reputable college was going to admit her, and odds were against her lasting in even the most mediocre citadel of learning. The girl refused to work, except at cheating, conniving, and whining. She didn't need others to punish her; she herself was her own worst punishment.

But in the still greater scheme, would it be worth rupturing personal ethics in order to get Renata, her family, and, ultimately, my principal off my case? I wished I could confer with Mackenzie, but I didn't think the time was right for us to discuss sliding scales of right and wrong.

Eventually, as the hour inched on, the walls resumed a normal shape and the aromatic medley of tennis shoes, sweaters, tomato soup, perspiration, and chalk dust became my life-breath again.

Renata alternately sulked and attempted to compensate for a wasted four months, waving her hand hysterically each time I asked a question, even when it was rhetorical. "I wonder if anyone, anywhere, has ever kept his entire list of resolutions," I murmured at one point. Up went Renata's hand to address my wondering. When there was an actual answer in the offing, she never knew it, but responded like somebody speaking in tongues. I stopped rising to the bait and ignored her hand-waving. She sank into head-clasping depression. When I asked for a three-paragraph composition on what resolution they thought they might keep and why, Renata was in too much despair to lift her pen.

At the end of class, I walked over to the window. The view I thought of as mine seemed altered. The street looked diminished—used and abandoned—by the snow of two days ago. Its asphalt was marked by shiny runoff rivulets and edged with slush the color of watery coffee.

The snow in the Square looked equally left over and second-hand, the shrubs and trees, desolate and chilly. Only one pathetic soul, insulated with newspapers and presumably without warmer options, occupied a bench. I turned back.

Sally Bianco, the other player in the purloined essay caper, hadn't left with her classmates. "I'm humiliated," she said as soon as I was facing her. "I want to start the year right. I want to say . . . I'm ashamed."

I shrugged. "We talked this through before break. People make mistakes. That's how we learn."

"I didn't need to learn that way. I knew right from wrong."

"Sally, it's over, no need to—"

"It's just that . . . I worked so hard. Before I came to this school, I was a goof-off, I know. But I changed. Now, I feel . . . tarnished. My hard work was for nothing and my good name is gone. I shamed my family."

Tarnished. Humiliated. Shamed. Undoubtedly echoes of parental ranting. Sally was, indeed, one of our success stories, a child who thrived in our smaller classes and bloomed with increased attention. Her parents, always overly concerned with her every move, were—or had been—enormously proud of her turnaround. And now, they were obviously overreacting to her temporary fall from grace. "Nobody knows, Sally, except the three of us. I've told you. We've even worked it out—everybody gets to drop their lowest grade. Remember?"

"She shamed me," Sally said.

"Make it a learning experience. Let it help you with difficult decisions in the future." What else could I say? I didn't, don't, like cheats. Unless you do it on an enormous scale and write a bestseller about it, it hurts everyone.

"I didn't know she'd do that, Miss Pepper. I thought she was going to read my essay just to get the idea."

"I know," I said gently. "You've already told—"

"She said she was confused."

I knew all this, but let her go on. She seemed to be releasing a head of steam that had been building all vacation long.

"She said she couldn't understand the book, that she had heard it was about getting married. She expected a romance, like the ones in the drugstore."

The class had been given a free choice from a selected reading list. Both girls had chosen *Pride and Prejudice* on which to base their take-home exams.

"She said if she could read what I'd written, she'd understand the book, then she'd write her own essay. I never, ever thought she'd copy me word for word. I was still wrong, because I knew in my heart she was lying, that she was supposed to use her own ideas, that she hadn't tried to read the book, but all the same, I didn't want to seem mean, and I didn't feel like I was cheating."

I was sure that was what had happened.

"And then, okay. So we were punished, and we deserved it, and maybe then we could get past it, but Renata called me ten times over break. We're not that kind of friends. Then, worse, her mother called my mother. I can't stand it! They want us to go to the principal, they want to . . . to get you . . ."

Fired. That's what she was trying not to say. Get me fired. And they could. My principal's backbone melts at low temperatures. The threat of tuition withdrawals, the potential for bad press would outweigh any concern about cheating, school standards, and meaningless final grades. The world did not have a shortage of English teachers, either.

Unemployment beckoned. However, on this particular winter's day, that didn't sound all that bad. Perhaps I'd think of it as early retirement. It wasn't as if I'd need money, since my future would be spent in an all-expense-paid prison block because a murder weapon had been in my bag, so it wasn't the worst thing. It wasn't like being homeless, wrapped in newspapers on a park bench.

"I hate her!" the normally docile Sally said. "Her cheating gives me a bad reputation, too! I could kill her!" Her smooth, small features contorted.

"I hope you won't add murder to your extracurricular activities. Admission committees don't give it a lot of points."

Sally's anger wasn't assuaged by my feeble attempt at humor. Then the fire in her eyes slowly dissipated, and her facial muscles relaxed. "I got angrier every time she called. My mother, she . . ." She shook her head. "I mean, what I did was cheating, but I meant it like help, like peer tutoring, not the way it happened."

Her mea culpas were becoming as tedious as Renata's mea-not-culpas.

My ninth graders, who always looked diminutive after the seniors and enormous by the end of the hour, reluctantly entered the room. "You don't want to be late for your next class," I reminded Sally.

"I wanted to warn you what's going on, that's all."

"That was kind of you," I said, but she'd already waved good-bye and was gone at a gallop.

Renata wouldn't have left. She'd have dug in harder, whined still more, then asked for a late note.

What was I going to do about her?

I wasn't supposed to think about that now. My emotions and energy were supposed to divide amoeba fashion every hour. Kiss the rest of the self good-bye and carry no baggage. This was a new class, a new set of worries. Three students were absent. I was told that one had the bad flu going around. I could see all the other students instantly decide to get it. One, visiting her father in Chicago, had missed her return plane, and "Badluck" Dooney Scott had burned his right arm testing the CAUTION: FLAMMABLE warning on a sample lacquer spray his mother had gotten in the mail. He was reputedly hospitalized.

I was sure all three were actually basking on various tropical beaches, and they'd return with doctors' excuses and great tans.

I pushed my mind into the chore of this hour, stuffing synonyms into the young psyches and brain cells in front of me, and directed it to forget about Renata Field. Also whether Vincent had shot and killed Jimmy Pat. Also the gun in my bag. Also the murder story Emily wanted to sell me . . .

Unfortunately, synonyms are words and words have meaning

and meaning occasionally leads to thought. For example, there's nothing quite as bracing as starting an already marred new year with a string of words like *shortcomings, imperfections, faults, weaknesses, deficiencies, blemishes.* Followed not far behind by *ambiguous, vague, obscure, indefinite, loose, uncertain, dubious, questionable.* I hadn't made up the lists as an exercise in self-flagellation. They were next in the book, but they seemed targeted and mean-spirited, and completely aware of my moral waffling in class and my suspect morality outside it.

None of my other classes were currently working on vocabulary development. I talked with budding minds about poetic meter, about loaded words and propaganda, and about Shirley Jackson's "The Lottery."

Nonetheless, for the rest of the day, synonyms snaked through my brain.

Misery, affliction, distress, sorrow, woe, despondency, grief.

Suspicion, disbelief, distrust, doubt, misgiving.

Honor, honesty, integrity, morality, scruples.

Dilemma, difficulty, predicament, quandary, impasse.

MACKENZIE wasn't home when I called, and when I phoned him at headquarters, he sounded distracted as if, I thought with my new paranoia, he were removing himself emotionally and physically from my deceitful ways so that his buddies could arrest me.

Yes, he said, he'd see me later, but he couldn't say when.

It was four o'clock. I felt as if my skin had turned gray and oily, as murky as my mind.

I'd stayed after class for my Renata session. In the end, I compromised. Made a truce, conceded, settled.

Caved in.

But only halfway—she'd demanded not only a passing, but a *good* grade.

She was not a person to whom you wanted to give a second chance. Nothing in her generated hope or trust. Still, I'd done it. I'd assigned her a ton of writing, variations of every theme her class had written, to be begun every day during lunch hour, at the back of my room, then completed that night at home.

117

"If they are all of passing quality," I told her, "and on time, you'll most likely pass."

"Most likely?" she whined.

"If you do the assignments, and do them well." I counted on her innate duplicity to get us through. Her parents, or a writing tutor, would complete the essays. Then I could pretend to believe Renata had done them, and she could pass and I could remain employed. A win-win situation.

Or maybe lose-lose, because I have seldom felt quite as disappointed in myself, and the year only a few days old, too.

So, given the depressing weather, a briefcase packed with papers to mark, the cold night already shadowing the pathetic leftovers of afternoon, and C. K.'s continued absence, I did the logical thing. I went to the movies. Happily, there is a multiplex within a few leaps and bounds of school. I didn't even need to relocate my car.

There's something satisfying about going to the movies in the daytime. It's immoral in an innocuous way, a good kind of sneaking out of real life. The Puritan portion of my DNA springs into action, sending reminders about how the busy little bee doth spend her shining hours and fires-of-hell warnings about succumbing to sloth. This adds spice to the popcorn.

The movie was somebody's unbearable attempt to be lighthearted. Nothing worked. The acting was wretched, the lines strained, the story illogical. And the popcorn was stale.

Audience reaction was mixed. A woman, one of the handful of spectators, really liked the script. I know this because she had a habit of guffawing, then repeating the line that tickled her, so that she could guffaw all over again. She did this loudly and often. However, a grizzled man a few rows behind me was unimpressed. He fell into a deep sleep, full of snores that set the seats humming.

The complete cinema experience. By the time the credits rolled, I felt a whole lot better.

I walked into an early-dark night whose damp and windy bite found every engineering failure in my coat. Up the arms, inside the collar, and so forth and so chilly. I made myself as compact as possible and hurried toward the corner. There is nothing like a deserted street on a January night in Philadelphia to make a person feel stranded on this planet.

"Miss Pepper. Please, one moment."

I didn't recognize him, but I didn't think I should be scared. He was polite, his voice low-pitched and confident, and apparently he knew me. Besides, he was elegant. In his early forties, I thought, with prematurely silver hair uncovered despite the freezing wind, and looking none the worse for it. His topcoat was visibly soft, cashmere, I suspected, and his hands, encased in buttery brown gloves, held a leather-bound book with gold-edged pages. Automatically, I looked for the title, as if that were the key to something.

"*The Prince,*" he said. "Machiavelli."

A literate man, interested in the classics. Nothing to be afraid of.

"He's good to re-read every few years."

But Machiavelli. The admirer of Cesare Borgia. Wasn't he the ends-justify-the-means fellow?

Whether or not he knew me, I didn't know him. I was now chilled in an entirely new way that had nothing to do with the temperature. I put my arm out, warding the man off.

He laughed, either because my hand would have been of little use or because there was nothing to ward off. He didn't reach out or physically detain me. But there was a potential in his posture and that brief laugh that paralyzed my mind.

I was afraid to run, afraid he'd catch me, hurt me in some terrible way. If I made it to the corner and turned toward the school, the Square, the back alley parking lot, I'd be in even more deserted territory and in more danger.

I looked around, amazed at how empty the area was. No wonder the I-went-to-Philly-but-it-was-closed jokes. I thought those days had passed—but where was everybody? The five or six other cinema patrons had either relocated to another of the auditoriums or exited in the opposite direction.

"Who are you?" I asked, while I looked as discreetly as I could for escapes—brightly lit storefronts or restaurants. I wanted to appear in control, but I could hear my giveaway breathlessness.

"We haven't met before," he said in a crisp, well-modulated voice.

The city felt locked up and callous. Good citizens had gone home after work, not to a multiplex. Their doors were barred and they were safe, and I was alone on the street with a stranger. "How did you know where I was?" I worked to keep the desperation out of my voice. "How do you know who I am?"

"I was with you in there. And surprised, frankly, that a woman with your literary and educational background would seek such trivia."

"You followed me? Followed me into the movie?"

"Well . . ." he said with a small, almost-charming bow, "indeed. I was not the one snoring, however, although I considered that an appropriate response."

"Why follow me at all?"

"It's too cold to wait out here."

"No, I meant . . ." I didn't bother to finish. He was the best-groomed crazy I'd ever met. The calmest, most gracious sociopath. "I want you to leave me alone. Go away *right now!*" That was supposed to work. I'd been taught it in a class. It might have been more effective if my voice hadn't shaken on the *right now* part so that it sounded like a plea, not a demand.

"Go away or you'll . . . ?" he asked serenely.

"I'll—" He wasn't going to bait me, make the rules. But he wasn't playing by the rules. He was supposed to have already run away. *"Get away!"* I moved back from the corner. I'd get around him and race to the theater. It had somebody in it, and a phone.

He moved with me, as if we were joined by guide-wires.

I remembered a personal safety tip my mother had clipped and mailed me. *"Help! Fire!"* I screamed.

People were supposed to respond, people who wouldn't blink if I'd merely shouted "Help, police." People were supposed to worry that they might be in danger, and therefore pay attention.

No people. Not a peep.

"Fire?" The man looked around at the bare pavement, the concrete and stone building near us. He seemed on the verge of laughing again. "Where?"

"In Florida," I muttered.

"I don't enjoy the cold," he said. "I get sinus headaches, so let's get to the point, which is the gun." His voice wasn't loud, but each syllable crackled when it hit the chilled air.

The *gun*? I was so shocked, I forgot about fear for a while. He wasn't going to hurt me—he wanted the gun. But nobody except the police, my sister and brother-in-law, Karen, and Dr. Reed On the Air knew about the gun.

If he knew Sam and Beth, wouldn't he have said so? If he knew about the gun because he was with the police, where'd he get his wardrobe? But of course, he wasn't a cop. He was the other side, whichever that was. Which meant—who had spied for him at the police station?

"You're surprised," he said, answering my unarticulated question. "Don't be. This was easy. Have they given it back yet?"

I shook my head. "It's not mine, even if they call it a ladies' gun."

He nodded and looked encouraging.

"But it's not this lady's," I snapped.

My purse would have held a bazooka if I'd wanted one, but anything I'd carry would be a *woman's* gun. There were no ladies anymore, except in the British court. And I wouldn't carry a gun.

"It's not a put-down," he said. "Those little things are also called gamblers' guns. They're favored by people who want to hide the fact they're armed."

"That gun is not mine, and that's the only point." We had finished our business. The night seemed to thicken around us and I again remembered to be afraid. "I won't be getting it back. It's evidence."

"Of what?"

I wasn't up for a philosophical discussion, or for him. "You know what I know. There's a gun, the police have it, it isn't mine. End of topic. Now if you'll excuse—"

"Could you describe it?"

I backed up a step, but he closed the gap immediately. "A gun!"

121

I said, my voice shaky again. "A trigger, a grip . . . of course I can't describe it. They all look alike." Was that gun-prejudice? Would the NRA file a suit? Was I going crazy?

"They can be personalized, given a different finish, a fancy grip, markings, inlays—"

"A *gun!*" I said. "That is all I noticed. The kind of gun that killed Jimmy Patricciano."

"It's never smart to leap to conclusions."

"I'll think about that. Honestly. Now, let me—"

This time he actually put a gloved hand on me, but gently, on my forearm. "Stick to teaching," he said softly.

I tried to yank my arm back. He increased the pressure of his grasp. I wanted to speak, to scream, to scare him off, but I felt paralyzed with a fear born of nothing visible, audible, nameable. More like a force field, the sense that his exquisite tailoring and barbering was a disguise pulled over something misshapen and deadly. And he had crossed a line. His hand was on me. He was staking a claim that wasn't his.

"You're a teacher, not an investigative reporter," he said with the calm assurance of a guidance counselor. "Stay in your area of expertise. It's healthier. Let go of this Mummer story. Nobody needs publicity, more attention right now. You'll only fan fires. People are concerned."

The infamous article. How had it happened that I could be in trouble with Mackenzie about a gun I hadn't put in my bag, and in trouble with this elegant thug about an article I hadn't written?

I found my voice again. "There. Is. No—" I said each word separately, clearly, as if that were the key to getting the world's hearing cleared up. "Article. I. Have. Not . . ."

But what was I about to promise, to give away? I'd write it. If I felt like it. I was mightily tired of backing down, first with Renata, now with Mr. Cashmere. "I'm not writing about this murder, and that's enough about this—let me go and—"

"Murders, don't you mean? Plural. Those Mummers. Patricciano and Serfi." And he let go of my arm.

I shook my head. Connecting the two events was a TV news gimmick, nothing more.

"A man like Serfi, he doesn't voluntarily leave town before the parade. What do you think?" the silver-haired man murmured. "Is Serfi an ingredient in King's Sausage, the way people say?"

"I don't say. I never knew him, don't know a thing about him, and none of this has anything to do with me, or with that—my—article."

"And that's how it should remain. Stay in your own backyard, so to speak. But if they give the gun back to you, call me. I want to see it, that's all. Look at it. I won't keep it."

"Why?"

"It's a matter of honor, and I would make it worth your while." He handed me a card on heavy ivory stock with ARTHUR in raised gold script against an embossed gold crown. Below was a telephone number, also embossed and gilded. No last name, no company, no occupation, no address. I had the sense I was supposed to know who he was without being told, but I didn't, and I wasn't going to admit it. "I'll know if they give it back," he said, "so you might as well benefit. A look, that's all I ask."

And with a courtly nod, his hair catching moonglow that was evident nowhere else, he walked off.

I didn't stop shaking until, swamped with a primitive sense of relief, I reached home. I took a deep breath, rode up the elevator and let myself relax, inch by inch.

To my surprise, Mackenzie was there, eating Chinese food out of containers, surrounded by the day's mail which he mostly tossed into a nearby wastebasket. He looked near exhaustion, and none too happy.

I was learning that timing was as important in the everydays of a relationship as it was on the dance floor, and I decided that it might be best to let him get his day out of his system before introducing my encounter with Arthur.

"For you, Man," he said, sounding too tired even for my full nickname. He pushed forward a plain white box, the sort you can buy flattened out at Christmas time. This was the small *objet d'art* size, sealed with clear tape and tied with curly gold ribbon.

I smiled for the first time in hours. Mackenzie had anticipated what a bad back-to-school day it was going to be and had gotten me a no-occasion gift. A sorry-I-was-so-suspicious-last-night kind of gift. What a guy.

"It was outside the elevator when I came home. Messenger must have delivered it."

End of elation. Now I was afraid to touch it, so instead, I ripped open the envelope that had AMANDA PEPPER printed on it, and read its contents out loud. "It says 'When you wake up and smell the coffee, this might be appropriate. But please be aware that it, like many other things, is perishable.' I don't like the sound of it," I said. "And there's no signature."

Mackenzie leaned over. I turned the card toward him while I sniffed the box and shook it, then passed it to him for further inspection.

"You can leave it and I'll take it in later," he said, "but it doesn't have any earmarks of a letter bomb or anything dangerous."

So I untied the ribbon, tossed it to Macavity, and the box flaps opened.

I gasped.

Sealed inside clear wrap on a bed of green tissue lay a single bloated, mottled cylinder, looking like a short salami.

"Sausage," Mackenzie said. He looked at it more closely. "Blood sausage, of all things."

The Doomsday clock sat, showing me, graphically, that with every breath, I had less and less time left.

Ten

W E stared at the sausage.

"Odd thing to send," Mackenzie said. "Think maybe it's a late Christmas gift? Somebody signed you up with those food guys—Tom and Jerry? Dave and Harvey? Whoever's sausage-of-the-month club?"

I closed my eyes. He was trying to be sweet, to jolly me out of a severe case of the willies, but I felt patronized.

"You must be hungry," he said, "and I've eaten everything I bought."

"I had popcorn." The sight of the fat sausage took whatever

residual appetite I had away. Amazing what the overtones of a single cylinder of processed meat could do.

"How about I scramble you some eggs and brown this up with it?" he asked.

"What *is* blood sausage, anyway? Why is it called that?"

"Because it has a lot of blood in it." He retrieved a dog-eared sheaf of recipes his mother had given him when he went off to college. "Of course, we called it *boudin noir*. Other people call it black pudding. Ancient dish, served to Odysseus, according to Homer. Aside from onions, salt, pepper, and spices, it's a mix of pig's blood, lard, pork fat, whipping cream, and eggs."

"I'll pass. It's probably poisoned."

"It doesn't need anything but its own ingredients—it kills with cholesterol."

"Blood sausage," I said. "Don't those words have an all-too-familiar ring?"

"Coincidence."

"I think not. And that note—I'm supposed to wake up and smell the sausage which is, like many things, perishable?"

"You're paranoid. Those are expressions, and a reminder to refrigerate it. You have no earthly connection with the disappeared Serfi. Or did you meet him, too, when you were doing your . . . research?"

His tiny but deliberate pause galled me. I could almost hear him reluctantly snipping out the words *so-called*. So-called research. Just because I was still formulating ideas and really didn't have time to write.

"I'm not sure it matters what I actually know or knew or connected with or not," I said. "If people believe I know something, that's enough." Time to tell him about my encounter with Arthur. "I saw *Featherbreath* after school, and when I—"

"Was it as bad as its reviews?"

"Worse."

"Why waste your money?"

The fact that it had been a worthy investment, cheaper than mood elevators or psychiatric care, and that I'd appreciated the film's dreadfulness to the hilt involved lengthy discussion. Besides, I worried about Mackenzie at times like this when he lost hold of what was relevant and what was not. Mired in trivia as he tended to be, I didn't know how he ever tracked down a killer. He certainly didn't have a bloodhound style, nose to the ground, single-mindedly following a scent. "Later," I said. "The thing is, when I came out of the movie this man—"

"What man?"

"No, wait." I put my hands up in a referee's time sign. "This is when you *listen*, Cisco. Later on, I listen and you talk. Got that?"

"*Cisco!*" he shouted. "Cisco! I never thought—arrgh!" And he flopped off his chair, onto the floor, one hand clutching his throat, the other covering his eyes as he rolled hither and yon, continuing his *arrghs*. Precisely as I'd always envisioned Rumpelstiltskin when his name was guessed.

I'd actually gotten it. I leaped up. "*Cisco? Cisco K. Mackenzie!* I got it, I got it! I can't believe that after all this time, all those guesses, I actually—this is incredible! I hardly—"

He stood up and brushed himself off. "Apologies, Miz Pepper, but tha's not it at all, not even close. But after all this time, an' all those clever guesses, I thought you deserved the thrill of accomplishment, of triumph. Even if short-lived."

I took a deep breath, then I shrugged. He'd listened, which was all I'd really asked of him.

We both sat back down. "Anyway," I said, "this man I'd never seen before stopped me. He knew my name."

Mackenzie looked wary, ready to spring, ready to react, but he kept his silence.

"Turned out his name's Arthur. That's all I know." I fished in my purse, then in my pockets until I found the engraved card, and I passed it over to C.-not-for-Cisco. "He was carrying a leather-bound copy of Machiavelli's *The Prince*, and he warned me not to be an investigative reporter, and let me know he'd been in the movie."

Mackenzie frowned. "He's an actor?"

"In the movie house. With me. The whole thing gave me the creeps." I wasn't being clear, wasn't able to communicate the negative force field around Arthur, the fear I'd felt—even if it did not seem justified.

"Which aspect gave you the creeps?" Mackenzie asked. "His moviegoing, his taste in reading, or this pompous business card?"

"He'd followed me."

"When you say he stopped you, what precisely did he do?"

"Came up beside me, said my name, talked to me."

"Talked. In a normal voice?"

"Okay, right, yes—but that's not the—"

"Did he touch you?"

I shook my head. "Not then. Later, he touched my forearm."

"Touched or grabbed or held?"

"Touched, but I felt as if—"

"Did he threaten you?"

"We were alone. Nobody else around."

"Yes, but did he threaten you? Do anything intimidating?"

"He laughed at me, kind of." I was not going to admit I'd screamed "Fire!" in the middle of the street. Mackenzie continued to wait. "He said investigative reporting wasn't a *healthy* occupation."

"Luckily it isn't yours."

"The article, C. K. That's what he meant."

"The one you haven't written?"

I hated this. It wasn't as if he wouldn't care and didn't care, it was that I wasn't giving him any reason to care. "I was upset!" I said.

"Obviously. How can I help you? I'm not clear on this."

There was one part he'd be clear on. "He knew about the gun."

And indeed, Mackenzie sat up straighter. "*The* gun? The derringer in your bag?"

I could hear the lyrics of the new hit tune: "The derringer in Mandy's bag was a heavy, heavy load, oh, oh . . ."

"Is that what you mean?"

I nodded.

"Damn," he said. "That's weird. How'd he find out? Unless . . ."

"He wanted me to let him know if you returned it to me. He wanted to look at it, and he offered to pay."

"Thought it wasn't yours in the first place," Mackenzie said. "You acted like the sight of it gave you hives. Why would we give it back to you unless we were sadists?"

"You know what I mean."

He scratched his head, stood up, and stretched, a sight I usually enjoy watching, but the man's logic was getting on my nerves and the taller and longer and leaner he made himself look, the more of him there was to annoy me.

"Unless what?" I asked.

"Unless what what?"

"You wondered how Arthur found out about the gun and me, unless. You stopped there."

"Oh, right. Unless that's what—somebody mentioned that Dr. Reed On the Air's first 'true story' last night was about a high school teacher who taught in a privileged private school, insulated from the real world, but who identified closely with the armed, more violent segment of society—that's me—and got involved writing about a 'colorful subculture of the city' through a colleague, and through that activity, with a murder of her own. That's how she put it—seems I've got my murders and you've got yours. And this teacher-writer—Gladys, she called you—was named as an accomplice—"

"I never was!"

"That's what On the Air said—and a gun had been found on her person, but she still said she knew nothing, yah-ta-ta. Suggested all kinds of mental deviations, like multiple personalities, dissociation, pathological identification with bigger, braver folk— that's me again, I take it. Anybody interested, given enough brains to recognize which colorful subculture has recently had a murder, that person asks a few questions in that colorful subculture about who was writing something, that'd be it. The guy who mentioned it to me had figured it out. On the Air seemed to feel that your 'intimate relationship with a law-enforcer' and 'intimate knowledge of the seamier side of urban life' had so frightened you that you no longer were in touch with your own actions."

"I'm crazy? Is that what she said?"

"She said you found a gun in your purse that was most likely involved in a murder. Bet that's how Arthur tracked you."

He came around to my side of the table and massaged my neck. It felt too good and too necessary for me to cry halt even though

I could feel myself being not only literally but figuratively manipulated. He wasn't taking my encounter seriously enough, wasn't even taking Arthur's tracking of me via the radio-shrink as potentially frightening. If I hadn't been so upset by him, I might have even sunk into the pleasant twilighty grogginess his hands encouraged.

"Let me ask you," he said as he carefully kneaded. The muscles of my neck and upper back had been replaced by high tension wires at some point today. "Say you weren't such a city girl. How did this encounter differ from somebody passing the time of day with you?"

"He—I—there are rules about how people approach—the man knew I'd be frightened. He meant me to be. He'd been in the movie with me! He told me to stick to teaching!"

I could hear Mackenzie's deliberately slowed-down breaths. "I know teachin's hard and all, but I guess sticking with it is scarier than I am capable of understandin'."

"Never mind. You know he was creepy, and so do I. And that it had to do with this. These—because he referred to murders. Plural. Mummers. Plural. So Ted Serfi is somehow involved. He mentioned blood sausage."

"How?"

It was much easier to remember the fear, the uncertainty, the effect of the words than the precise order of what he'd said. I tried to reconstruct the moment. "He asked if I thought Ted Serfi had been turned into blood sausage the way people said." I did a double take. "You don't think that thing on the table could be—"

"I think Serfi's at the bottom of a river with weights on his feet. He ran with a fast crowd. Probably didn't run fast enough."

Still and all, I didn't want to look in the direction of the white box.

"I know it frightened you." Mackenzie's voice floated down to me serenely as his hands kneaded my knotted muscles. "Don't mean to dismiss that. But there's pretty much nothing I can do about it. I could call him and say, 'Hey, Artie, stay away from my girl.' "

I revved up for more precise objections, but he talked right over my hostile pfuts.

"I could challenge him to a duel, but that seems archaic. I could check him out, which I fully intend to do, an' whatever I find, I will heartily use against him for scarin' you. I will scare him back, I promise. But meantime, doesn't sound like a single thing he did's illegal, an' I'm sure he knew that. Creepy, impolite, not usin' city etiquette. But the rules say he has to break the law before I bother him."

"I wish I knew what's going on."

"He wants to *see* the gun, that's all? Didn't want to buy it or take it?"

"He said he'd pay to see it."

"He might well be involved in Jimmy Pat's murder, and he hid his weapon and can't figure how it turned up in your bag, and he has to see it to verify it."

"Unless he has to see it to verify it belongs to somebody else. He asked me what it looked like, as if he'd recognize some marking or whatever the police couldn't."

"I'd say let's set up such a viewing, except what you and he don't know," Mackenzie said, "is that the gun in your bag wasn't the murder weapon after all. It did not kill Jimmy Pat. Ballistics tests show completely different markings."

I swiveled around to see his face, check whether he was joking. He certainly didn't look it.

I stood up. The massage had been heavenly, and my neck and back did feel looser, but now I needed to move, to pace, to hope my brain kicked into gear. Luckily, the loft was a great pacing arena, with lots of sights around the course. I did the kitchen area, the living-room sofa area, the table area, the office—in each case, a piece of furniture or two equaled a room's worth of definition—the bedroom divider, the sound system, the TV, the bookshelves, which I suppose I should have called the library.

No metaphorical light bulbs blazed above my head. I tried saying it out loud. "Somebody planted a gun that isn't the murder weapon on me. Do I have that right? What sense does that make?"

"Frankly, I was hopin' you could tell me," he said with a sigh. "Of course, that was before this Arthur business. Now it is painfully obvious that you haven't got any more of a clue as to how that gun got in there than I do."

"You thought I did? You thought I lied to you?"

"Could we defer that fight?" he asked gently. "We're gettin' off track. Not lying. I thought you might have forgotten something, semi-consciously ignored somethin' injurious to a friend, say." He shrugged, giving up on that idea, deflecting the squabble I was itching to have.

"This Arthur's card," Mackenzie said. "Doesn't inspire faith, does it, with no last name, no business, no title, no location. That crown. Like *The Prince*, you think? Hard to believe he's for real."

"He looked like money. Cashmere and good teeth. The whole package."

"Probably has different cards—maybe different phones—for different needs." He pocketed the card. "Ted Serfi was said to be connected, you know. This Arthur might be part of that."

"He didn't look the type."

"What look is that?" The cat had sidled up to the love of his autumnal years, and was rubbing against Mackenzie's slacks. I could hear the purr as I held the refrigerator open and stared at its pitiable contents.

"You were maybe expecting a Damon Runyon character? Somebody in a striped suit with wide shoulders and, of course, a fedora? A funny-talking guy with his moll dressed in tight satin and a little hat with a veil? Something subtle like that?"

There is not much that's sillier than a mushy Southerner imitating a New York accent. Except maybe a Yankee woman who believes you can recognize the mob by their outfits. I hid my embarrassment by looking at the very back of the refrigerator shelves, not that there were any good surprises in the small containers there.

By the time I turned around, the two Macs, as I now thought of them, were on the leather sofa. Mackenzie was fiddling with the TV remote, and Macavity, who was obviously secure in his neuterhood, was obstructing his love's vision by lying vertically on the man's shirt, stretched up toward his face, which he assiduously licked. My roomie had become my cat's kitten. I didn't want to think about it.

"Truce?" Mackenzie asked.

"Sure." Dinner was going to be eggs by default, even though they reminded me of the sausage. What was I going to do about that, about anything?

"Then I'll entertain you. Ready for the stupid call of the day?"

I nodded and cracked eggs. There was nothing in the pantry worth putting into an omelette. Who was running this place? As egalitarian as Mackenzie was, he didn't qualify as a wife, and that's what we both needed.

"Woman calls nine-one-one, barely coherent. Turns out a man phoned and told her to cut up all the shoes in her closet as an act of faith because he was the owner of a new shoe store and as a special promotion, she'd been picked to get fifty free pairs of shoes." He paused in his narration. "What does any woman need with fifty pairs of shoes?"

"Shoes are a psychological issue unto themselves. Too much to deal with now," I said. "Go on." Not that I had fifty pairs—but it wasn't the worst idea I'd ever heard.

"The guy says he's coming over in ten minutes to check whether she'd had enough faith and if she had, she gets this certificate for the fifty pairs of shoes."

I carried my plate to the table. "Tell me she didn't."

"I cannot tell a lie. She did."

The cat decided that both he and the man were now clean enough and was snuggling into sleep at his side.

"It must be hard to slice shoes."

"Tough as shoe leather, I'll bet," he said. "Took sweat and effort, but she had the muscles and the faith. Yet amazingly enough, the so-called shoe-store owner never showed up."

The range of human behavior was stupefying. Not only was this woman a complete idiot, but one had to wonder about the caller, who obviously took perverse pleasure from the thought of sliced shoes.

Maybe his pleasure was based on power and nothing more.

With willing a woman to julienne her footwear. Like scaring a woman with an innocuous, if homely, sausage.

"When the nine-one-one call was answered, she was barefoot. She'd been afraid that if she left her last pair of shoes, the sneakers on her feet, intact, she'd show too little faith. One of those women with a perfectly organized house, nothing out of place. She had the shredded shoes in a trash bag so they wouldn't make a mess."

I finished my eggs and toast, rinsed my dish, and leaving the rest of the clearing up till later, I joined the Macs on the sofa. And I waited.

Mackenzie seemed blissfully contented with our silence, interrupted only by the buzz saw of the cat's purr.

"You know," I finally said, "that lady cut up her own shoes and called nine-one-one. I was accosted—politely, civilly, within the law, I realize. But all the same, it scared me and I'm not a ninny. I wouldn't have qualified for stupid call of the day even if I had called the police. Somebody put a gun in my pocketbook. Somebody followed me. I am not comfortable with this.

"Supposing I don't get killed and I remain a pre-homicide case. I know that's not your area of expertise, and I know you're going to check this Arthur out, but do you have advice as to what I should do meantime?"

"Let me think on that." He put his arm around me and the three of us snuggled and purred, until he said, "Okay. I think you should grade those papers you brought home so you'd have time to start writin' your article."

I sat bolt upright with enough force to make Macavity decide to leave the couch. He understood that there was going to be a homicide after all. I had been worried that I was being set up for the role of victim, but—surprise, surprise—I was going to be the perp.

Before I could strangle him, Mackenzie added a few thoughts. "Want to know what *not* to do? Anythin' that could get you hurt. Which is to say, don't go to lousy movies all by your lonesome, be aware of your surroundin's, and come home."

"That's . . . rather a primitive plan," I said. His protectiveness struck me as equal parts of loving concern, arrogance, and a desire to keep his life simple. "Sometimes your people skills make it obvious that you're used to dealing with dead folk."

"We don't know who or what Arthur is yet. Finding out is not your field of work. The thing is, my C doesn't stand for Carson, either."

"Huh? Like Kit Carson? Or, in your case, Carson Kit?"

"Wrong. Like Carson Drew, Nancy's father."

"I've never confused you with my father," I snapped.

"But maybe you've confused yourself with Mr. Drew's spunky daughter. Don't. Nancy Drew is fictional. That's why she always winds up okay. I'll find out about Arthur, but it's my strong suspicion I'm not going to find a whole lot because I suspect that he, too, is a fiction."

"You're doubting me again? I saw—"

"You saw somebody who said that was his name. Somebody who has a phone number which, when answered, will undoubtedly reinforce that impression. None of that necessarily makes it so."

"Why not?"

"Gut feelin'. Plus the lack of any information on the card. Plus his shabby way of approachin' you, which suggests a man steppin' out of the shadows, carefully stayin' within the law and yet deliberately managing to intimidate you. Plus his wanting to see the gun." He looked at me, his eyes as blue and deep as a loch in the land of his forefathers.

"I think," I began, "I think what he wants is . . ." I could barely bring myself to say it to this man, but there did seem to be a theme that repeated itself, lightly, inconsequentially, but regularly. ". . . that article," I finally said.

"What article?" he asked and to my horror, I realized that he was honestly baffled.

"The one I'm . . . not writing," I whispered. "But they think I am." It was painful to say that, since I also thought I was writing it. I was simply . . . blocked. I was so glad that articulate writers had made up a technical term for not doing their work.

"Like that joke about the charms used to keep elephants out of

135

Philly, and when the response is that I've never seen an elephant here, the answer is, 'See? They work.' "

"I've heard that joke."

"But you're seriously saying that man will go to great lengths to get hold of an article that doesn't exist? What could worry somebody about that? What do they think you know?"

I couldn't guess. I had notes about the history of the parade and its significance as an organizing principle for a sort of village within the city. I had notes on whatever Vincent and his friends had been willing to share, plus descriptions of places they'd shown me, and facts taken from a book about the Mummers, *O, Dem Golden Slippers*, by Dr. Charles Welch.

No dark secrets, not an incriminating or intimidating word.

"Of course," Mackenzie said, "doesn't matter if you really have somethin' worth their concern. Only matters if they think you do."

"Yes," I said, with an anticipatory sigh. "They seem to think the article is going to show their flaws in a hard light, to fan some unknown fire."

I took his hand and we sat in silence across from our unfanned but crackling fire.

"So you'll leave it to me," Mackenzie said.

I debated whether that was a question, decided it was not, and therefore let it go unanswered. He could think what he needed to, and I could do what I needed to. This way, everybody was contented. Even the feline.

Particularly the feline. I became aware of an extremely loud purr from the floor in front of my feet.

We both looked down as Macavity looked up, his paw in mid-face wash, his eyes dreamy with satiation.

The humans processed the clues at the same time, stood up in unison, turned, and looked at the white box on the table.

Empty, except for grease spots.

Macavity's purr registered a nine on the Richter scale.

Eleven

"I DON'T think I ever actually introduced myself." I extended my hand to Emily Semow. I had already removed my gloves and unbuttoned my coat. The place was still a blast furnace, smelling of heating ducts, dust, and cardboard.

I had called ahead, so I had to assume she expected me. Nonetheless, she raised her eyebrows when I spoke, and looked around me through the plate-glass windows, as if to check whether I had an accomplice lurking outside.

"My name's Amanda Pepper."

"Knew it," she said. "Unless you're called Associated Press.

You wrote it enough on the pen-testing pads. So, um . . . you're back again, aren't you?"

"Emily?" The querulous voice I remembered from my last visit came out of the back room. "Time for my pills."

"Busy!" she shouted. "A customer. They're next to you." There was no further response.

She was dressed in black again, this time suede boots up to her thighs, black tights, and a black silk tunic. "In mourning, I guess," I said, gesturing toward her ensemble.

She looked down to refresh her memory, grimaced, and then shrugged. Her face was nothing if not expressive. "No. Well, yes. Even if nobody believes we were getting married. Somebody even told me I should see a shrink to get a handle on reality. But of course, the somebody who said that was a Grassi. Won't leave me alone."

"I want to talk about something else," I said.

"I know. The story."

"Let me be absolutely honest. I'm a school teacher. I have no money."

"You came here to tell me that? Thanks a lot and join the crowd. You think we make money in this place? Some people, they act like I'm an heiress, I'll inherit my family business." She laughed harshly. "My father, he's not well. We pay the doctor's bills, and then there's enough for maybe a pair of stockings. I have to keep the store open whenever I can to catch an extra nickle or dime." She sighed, then looked beyond me, outside again. "Listen," she said, "did you pass anybody when you came in? Anybody, like, hanging nearby?"

I shook my head.

"I'm being watched," she said. "Since Jimmy Pat, maybe even before he died. It's weird, the person who . . . ah, maybe the Grassis are right and I'm crazy." Once again, I heard the mirthless sound that passed for her laughter.

"Now?" I looked outside. Nothing except a short woman pulling a shopping cart and a taller and younger woman pushing a carriage. Maybe Emily had delusions of persecution.

"People these days, they go to the discounters," she said. "Everything's falling apart for the little guy like me, and even

though I have ideas for how to make this place better, if he'd—"
she moved her head in the direction of the dark back room "—let
me, with wholesalers gobbling everything up, I don't see how . . ."

To my relief, she paused to glance out the window again, and
while so doing, and, like me, finding nobody watching her back, she
seemed to recognize that she had gotten herself off track. "My big
mouth," she said. "Like you care about the stationery business."

"It's interesting," I politely insisted. Fact was, I wanted to get
information and head home before dark, there to transfer whatever I learned to Mackenzie who would have, by then, found out
who Arthur was. I wanted to extract myself from all of it. So
Emily was right. My prime concern wasn't the woes of the small
retailer.

Unless, of course, the human side of it might make a good
article, now that I thought about it.

"My story," she prompted. "That's what you're here about."

"The bottom line is, I can't offer any money."

She tilted her head and raised her eyebrows and without utter-
ing a single word, lifted, lowered, squinted, shrugged, heaved, and
twisted her various parts so that she managed to silently chew me
out for wasting her time. I was awestruck by how varied, subtle,
and rich her body language was. If retailing dribbled into noth-
ingness, she could become a mime.

"I have another idea," I said. "A different approach to suggest."

She folded her hands across her chest, jutted out one hip, and
waited. A body shout of "Oh, yeah? Double-dare you to come up
with anything besides money that's worth my time."

"What if we did it on spec?" That sounded wondrously
professional.

"What the hell's a *spec* to do it on?"

"Short for speculation. Conjecture. Supposition."

"What the hell is all of that?"

"We do it without a contract, in the hopes of selling it."

Her arms dropped and she walked to the front door. I was
afraid she was going to open it and usher me out, but instead she
stood there, again examining the street scene. She leaned forward,
muttering to herself. "He's there. I feel it."

"Who?" I said. "Do you know him? Does he bother you?"

"Nah."

I didn't know which question she was answering, but before I could find out, she returned to the point of my visit. "You're saying I should give you my story. Free. Give it away."

"Not really, because once it sold, we'd split everything we get for it. Fifty-fifty, down the middle."

"What's that come to?"

"Varies."

"People sell stories to the supermarket papers for like a hundred thousand dollars."

I could kiss her information good-bye. I'd seen three cents a word mentioned in a writer's magazine. My mental math wasn't of the highest order, but I estimated that in order to make enough to pay Emily her hundred thousand, I'd have to write twenty-five thousand pages, and there's not a big market for articles that are longer than entire encyclopedias.

I had been lolling against the counter that held the cash register, but now I stood up straight. "Good luck with the story, then," I said. "I'd also like that kind of money, but I don't think it's going to happen."

"You're leaving? Like that?"

I translated that as meaning we had bargaining room.

"Emily?" the old man called out. "I'm thirsty."

"I'm working!" she shouted. Then she turned to me, waiting.

"Those big numbers, they're stories that get national press."

Emily shrugged. "My story's pretty big. Maybe."

With the "maybe," our positions, which had seemed wildly and unfairly weighted, shifted into potential harmony. But at that precise moment, the door, which neither of us had been watching, opened with the loud clang of the bell, and Dolores Grassi and I, mouths agape, stared at each other.

"*You!*" she shouted, as if I were the Black Plague. "*Again!*"

"Yo!" Emily said. "Do you mind? You buying something? Otherwise—"

Dolores swiveled toward her. "I'm here because you're such a bitch you didn't listen when my brothers told you to cut it out!

Who are you, you crazy old maid, to go around bad-mouthing me and my Jimmy Pat, saying he wasn't in love with me? Wasn't going to marry me? Was going to marry *you*? You're so desperate you have to *shame* me and my family—and a dead man—to get attention?"

"He wasn't going to marry you, and you know it."

"Liar!" Dolores looked at me. "Can you believe this? A girl's two weeks from her wedding, and this . . . this nobody talks trash about her." She pointed at Emily. "You can't stand it, you never could stand that he chose me, but that's how it was."

"He was marrying me," Emily said in a flat and final voice.

"What's the point of all these lies except to ruin everything—*everything*—for me and my entire family? I won't have a wedding, you go around insulting us, saying horrible things about the man I loved, who's *dead* already, and now you're ruining his funeral. Give it up. He can't marry anybody now, are you satisfied?"

"You saying I killed him? You out of your mind?"

"Everybody knows you wouldn't kill anything in pants if you thought it'd get you out of here. Not that I blame you for wanting something better." She sniffed, as if the air in the store were odiferous. "You're your father's slave, and you don't have a profession of your own, and—"

"Emily!" the voice in back called out on cue, as if anybody needed further explanation of what needed escaping. He had remarkably good lungs for an invalid.

"In a minute. More customers!" Emily shouted. Then, in a lower but no less harsh voice, she spoke to Dolores. "I'm not anybody's slave," she said. "And I'm not a baby the way you are. Baby tyrant. Your brothers are your slaves—like you're five years old or something, guardin' you. Act like a grown-up for once, why don't you? I know he told you."

"Never!"

"He told me he told you."

"Then he lied to you!"

"Never!"

I looked out the window above the faded and dusty school supply display, across the street, to a bus stop in front of a house with a cemented-over front lawn, a khaki-painted facade, and an aluminum awning over the front door. As I watched, a bus slowed and opened its doors. A silver-haired man in leather jacket and jeans shook his head and waved it on. He was staying.

Arthur was Emily's stalker?

Arthur wasn't going anywhere. Not that he was inert, but at best, he was semi-ert, positioned so that he could see everything that happened on the street, but it was not lounging weather. Everyone else out there hurried for shelter.

"Think you're so high and mighty you can flounce in here and boss me around, but you're wrong!" Emily raged on behind me. "This is private property, and I don't happen to think Grassis are above the law, right below God, the way you do."

"You've been jealous of me my whole life." Dolores sounded whiny now. "And I tried to be nice. When your mother died—"

"I didn't need your charity!"

"Yeah, right, like you didn't need my fiancé now, either!"

This was not age-appropriate behavior, as people of my ilk say. Without adult intervention, they could go on like this forever. I'd seen it on playgrounds. "Stop that right now!" my Miss Grundy voice snapped. "This is childish. You're saying things you'll regret and making yourselves feel worse, and—"

Dolores's hair was still a tall, dark confection, despite the wind she'd walked through. The dark tendrils weren't snakes, but the look she shot me would have done Medusa proud.

"She started it!" Emily screamed, maintaining the kindergarten level of dispute. "None of this is my fault! She came here!"

Dolores took a deep breath. "So now I'm leaving here," she told her erstwhile rival. "Believe me, this is the last place on earth I want to be. Gives me the creeps and always did. But I want you to know this." Her voice took on a nervous, knife-sharp edge. "Say any of this is true—*if*—then the shame is still on your head, because if Jimmy Pat wasn't going to marry me—"

"See? I *knew* he told you. I *knew* you knew!"

Dolores held her head up even higher. With the tower of hair, it was quite a sight. "*If* that was so," she said, "it wasn't because he loved you." She spat out the last three words and made a face, as

if they'd tasted poisonous. "It was because he was *afraid* of you."
She turned around and was out the door in a fraction of a second.
"He loved me!" she shouted as she left.

I expected shouts in response, curses, counter-charges, but instead, Emily, looking diminished and red-nosed, wiped a tear off
her cheek.

"What's the ruckus?" the voice shouted. "Call the police!"

"Excuse me," she said, going into the back room.

It seemed time for me to leave, too. I'd write a note, leave
Emily my number in case she ever wanted to talk. I rummaged in
my purse, found one of my many index cards along with the pen
I'd bought on my last unsatisfactory visit.

The doorbell jangled again before I got my first word down,
but business hadn't improved. Dolores, her face frosted pink
from wind and fury, was back. "And *you*!" she said, pointing
with one hand while she held the door with the other. "You're
the one stirring up the mess. Look at you, already making notes
about my private life! Let sleeping dogs lie. You write about any
of this, you disgrace my family name, and you'll be more than
sorry. My brothers don't take it lightly when people try to drag
us down."

"Hey, Dolores," I said, "I'm not responsible for any of this,
and I'm not writing about you or—" In the middle of my sentence, she turned and went back outside. Rude! I followed her out
the door as I finished what I had to say. Not a single person
understood the difference between a phenomenon and a tabloid
story about somebody's personal life. Maybe it was a forest-for-
the-trees thing. They were so much a part of the world of the
Mummers that they could only see, or even imagine, details and
current gossip. The big picture was an unquestioned given.

I followed Dolores down the street, walking double-time,
shouting at her back. "Twenty thousand people paraded," I
shouted. "If I wanted to write about one of them, there are nine-
teen thousand nine hundred and ninety-nine others beside Jimmy
Pat!"

She turned and pointed again. Nobody must have told her it
was rude. "Don't be a smart-ass," she said. "The others aren't as

143

interesting to somebody like you because they didn't get themselves killed."

"If you would listen—I'm writing about the tradition."

She shook her head. "Everybody knows about that. What's to write?"

I gave up that tack. "I wouldn't take advantage of a sad event like a man's murder."

She looked at me dolefully, then surprised me. "I wish *I* were dead," she said. "It could have all been so nice." And she turned and walked away.

I couldn't make sense of any of it, except for the implication that I should go home and forget about it. Which is what I prepared to do, as soon as I reclaimed my coat.

"So it didn't kill Jimmy Pat, after all."

I jumped, even though I recognized the voice and I had seen him earlier.

His hair still looked as if head-gremlins styled and smoothed it at all times, even during gusts of wind, when mine swirled and tangled and his jostled, then resettled perfectly. Maybe if I used the hair spray I always carried and forgot. Maybe I should ask him his brand.

"I wish you wouldn't keep scaring me this way," I said. He was once again carrying a copy of *The Prince*. He must be committing Machiavelli to memory.

"Sorry. I saw you barrel out of the store and I was afraid you might get on a bus." He waved at a departing vehicle, then did a double take, staring after it.

"Not likely, until I'm wearing a coat," I muttered.

"You see that?" he said. "You see what was on that bus? The poster on the side for King's Sausage? Some creep wrote on it."

Why act shocked? He'd mentioned the rumors the last time he'd accosted me.

The black and white ads showing sizzling sausages had been attractively understated advertising, with lots of white space and only HAPPY HOLIDAYS and KING'S SAUSAGE. But in the last week or so, I'd seen at least a half dozen of them, all altered the same way. A *whose blood* had been added along with *is in* and a question mark, so that the ads now read WHOSE BLOOD IS IN KING'S SAUSAGE? Now and then, a driblet of red paint had been added for further effect.

"Kids," I said.

"Not kids." The words were a growl. He shook his handsome head as if to rid it of the ads. "Enemies. People who think . . . You were going to contact me," he said, returning to his smoother voice.

I shook my head. "*You* suggested that. Told me to. You didn't ask me if I would. Besides, they aren't returning the gun to me. It wasn't mine in the first place. And—and I'm tired of being frightened this way."

"Didn't mean to scare you. I was in the neighborhood."

"Why?"

"Personal business. So I saw you, and I was about to come into the store when I saw Dolores Grassi."

"And?"

He shrugged. "Lot of issues those women have to work out on their own. The timing was inappropriate, although believe me, I'd have rather been inside, given my problem with sinus headaches."

"I'm having a problem with hypothermia, myself."

He wasn't interested in anything but his own woes. He pressed three black-gloved fingers against the center of his forehead, indicating how he was suffering for his sensitivity. "Whose gun is it, then?"

I sighed. "You seem to know everything else, including my address—"

"Me?"

"And ingenious ways of intimidating me, although why, I don't know."

"What are you talking about?"

"My cat ate it. And my cat threw it up later on. So much for the world's most stupid terrorist tactic." I thought that would upset him, at least insult him, but he only looked amused.

We had reached the front of the store. "Good-bye, Arthur," I said. "I can't see that we have any reason to meet again. And by the way, I don't appreciate being given a phony business card with no last name."

He raised his eyebrows. "It's a rebus."

"Spare me." I slammed the door behind me.

He stood outside, hands in his jacket pockets.

Emily was back in the store, sitting behind the cash register, holding a pink and silver paperback with a drawing of a long-haired, naked-to-the-waist man on its cover. "Skipped out on me to spend time with Cam, didn't you?"

"Who?"

"Him. Cam, short for Camelot. That's what he's called, didn't you know? Doesn't he seem from never-never land?"

That was Peter Pan's hometown, not Arthur's, but I didn't correct her.

"He has money and looks even if he's a little old, and he knows it. Always did."

"Who is he? What's his real name?"

"Arthur."

I was oddly relieved.

"Arthur King."

The rebus. He hadn't been kidding. The crown equaled king, and everybody who received the card was supposed to know that.

"They called him King Arthur, then Camelot, get it?"

"Part of the sausage people?"

She nodded. "Like I said, rich and handsome and smart, too."

No wonder he was apoplectic about the defaced ads, the gossip campaign.

King's Sausage. The alleged abductor-killer of Ted Serfi, heir apparent of the rival meat-clan.

But if Arthur had something to do with Serfi's disappearance, why was he playing tag with me and worrying over the gun that had been put in my bag? Unless it was his gun, unless it had been used to kill somebody else.

If it hadn't killed Jimmy Pat, had it—had he—killed Ted Serfi?

And how did that fit with his watching Emily? Why was he out there, given his whines about sinus headaches? I watched him light a cigarette despite the wind and several decades of government warnings. "You and he," I said, "you know each other?"

"Not nearly well enough," she murmured. "But ... don't laugh. I think he wants to know me better. He's been hanging around, watching me. Think he could be shy? Camelot?"

"Why else would he hang around?"

She gave me a cryptic sidelong glance. "There could be other reasons," she said, her attention back on the man outside, watching him almost hungrily. It was not the expression I'd expect of a woman in mourning for her one true love. Then she pulled her gaze back at me. "You ever been trapped?"

"By him?" I gestured to the outside.

She shook her head. "Trapped. For real. I mean, when it isn't something you could fix. Did you ever *know* you were trapped? Permanently? When I was a junior in high school, my parents, their car was hit by a truck. My mother was killed, my father was left ... like that." She gestured toward the back room, as if I could see the man. "I had to quit school and take care of him and the store, and here we are, six years later, in the trap."

My teacher-self kicked in. Suggestions flowed, as if she'd tapped a reservoir. As if she'd requested them. "You could get your equivalency degree," I began. "You're smart. Then, you—"

"Don't. It's not like I'm an idiot and never thought of it. But what then? A job that pays enough for me to pay somebody to take care of him, too? Doing what? A person who'd be willing to take care of him and his temper, anyway?"

"What if you sold the store and got cash that way?"

"Sell it to what fool? It's not worth anything, except it keeps us off the street because we live upstairs. Well, I do. My father, he lives back there." She looked at me and her eyes welled up. "Jimmy Pat was my chance out."

I wondered how far out. Gambling was sure to wipe out whatever profits Jimmy earned driving a produce truck. He'd have become just another trap. I felt that in my bones, but kept it to myself. Too late for it to matter.

"Now he's dead and I have some happy ending, right? A regular fairy tale."

Need I say this seemed an ill-advised time to jog her memory about the story she wanted to sell? Her only chance of a semi-happy ending, her one and only asset was whatever she thought she knew. And much as I'd like to believe we all make our own destinies and all that fascinating and uplifting philosophy, far as I could see—the girl was trapped. The only alternate destiny she could forge would be to put her father in institutional care and light out for the hills. It sounded both desirable and unkind.

She sat glumly, her glance moving from me, through the window to Arthur King, who kicked idly at a hummock of slush.

He still clutched his book. Maybe he was planning to hold onto *The Prince* until Machiavelli wrote a sequel, *The King*. For him personally. With a golden crown on the cover.

Then he looked up and over and I was willing to swear he exchanged a glance—the merest suggestion of a glance—with Emily, but it was a familiar, collegial, conspiratorial glance. A checking-on-how-things-were-going glance.

My sympathy for her psychic afflictions dried up.

The two of them were in collusion. Arthur's being nearby wasn't coincidental. I had called, announced my arrival, and she . . .

I looked back at gorgeous Emily. There was no mystery about a man following such a woman around. The glance was probably just that—a contact, finally, after he'd checked the waters. She had, of course, been seeing somebody else. She was supposedly in mourning. He had to play his cards carefully.

"I should go." Let them speak directly one to the other.

"Aren't you—aren't we going to talk about that article?" she asked. "About my story?"

"I didn't think you were emotionally up to it." I flicked another glance Arthur's way. With a last deep drag, he dropped his cigarette, shoved both his gloved hands into his jacket pockets, and walked off. I had stayed too long. Emily's eyes, tension-ringed and speculative at the same time, followed the man for as long as they could. Was it love, lust, or something else altogether?

"I'm in a hurry," I said. The light level outside was lower, my anxiety higher. "Another time, maybe. We got sidetracked."

"That bitch," she said. "Coming here and lying to my face."

"Let's not start, all right? Meantime, what I was thinking was that if you know who killed Jimmy Pat, tell the police. Then, after the trial, you could still sell your story—for big bucks, probably—to those newspapers you mentioned. If you can't write, it'd be an as-told-to. You wouldn't have to share any of the money, either."

"Stop already," she said. "I don't know who killed Jimmy."

"You're peddling a theory?"

"I never said I was talking about his shooting."

"Then what . . . why tell me?"

"You're the only writer I know. I thought you knew stuff."

"About Mummers. Maybe."

She lowered her lids and let her exasperation show. And be heard. "You're obtuse, you know? Not exactly a walking ad for higher education, if you catch my drift." She waved me away. "I have to think, okay?" She stood up, slammed down her book, grabbed a lipstick from behind the counter and applied it, and marched to the rear. Not a word of explanation.

"Fine, then." I wrote my number on a three-by-five. "Call if you resolve this. Or I'll call you if I get a definite offer from a magazine." Not that I had hopes of selling an article about a subject unknown to the author. "Dear Editor, I have this idea except I don't know what it is, but I want a lot of money for it . . ."

Emily returned, wearing a long black coat and a white angora hat that accentuated her pale eyes and made her look angelic.

Appearances aside, she grabbed the card with my number on it and ripped it up. "I won't be using it," she said, as the pieces fluttered to the floor. "Not worth it for the no-money you're talking." Her eyes were glittery, almost feverish-looking. "Besides, you gave me a better idea. Much. So thanks."

She flipped a square white sign from OPEN to CLOSED, and we made our exit.

And as she walked away from me, I could have sworn I heard Emily, the woman in black, she whose last chance at happiness and love had recently been murdered, chuckle to herself.

Twelve

THE next day, nature's mood had improved a lot more than mine. The sky had blown itself out of grayness into clear blue and the wind was taking a rest. The day had an edge of definition, a sense of itself I sorely lacked.

So far as I could tell, I had spent all this short new year rushing hither and yon to screw things up. Twice, Emily had offered me something important and I had not only failed to get hold of it, but I'd inspired her to give her secret to the attractive goon and possible murderer who'd intimidated me.

My friend Vincent was lying about me, trying to use me for disturbing reasons of his own.

The whole world, except Mackenzie, believed I was deeply into inflammatory journalism that endangered them. And I was still precisely nowhere.

I struggled to reach out to my classes from deep within the void where I was stuck, and succeeded only in establishing that I was not only a lousy sleuth, but a lousy teacher as well. "Take, for example, stupidity," I told my first-period class. "A stupid person or act could also be referred to, with slightly different shades of meaning, as dense, moronic, obtuse, slow, witless, imprudent, irresponsible—" the words piled into my skull with no effort, each one pointing a little finger at me "—reckless, asinine, pointless, senseless, and each synonym gives you a—"

A generalized murmur of interest rose from the seats. A girl giggled. A boy made the circling-finger-to-head sign indicating lunacy.

"*Synonyms*, remember?" And then I remembered. This class hadn't been studying them. "Just ... seeing if you remember what you learned awhile ago, given that a wide vocabulary strengthens your writing." I took their compositions out of my briefcase. I had graded them the night before while Mackenzie put on a stack of CDs and buried himself in an arch Thirties locked-room mystery, complete with diagrams, floor plans, and people who lived off inherited wealth.

These essays had filled my entire evening. There'd been no time left over to begin my article.

When class was done, Renata walked directly in front of my desk, head held high as she intrusively ignored me and flounced out of the room. I'd thought we'd reached a truce and I couldn't comprehend her haughty body language, but I knew she hadn't been sending warm and cheerful greetings my way.

Sally Bianco lingered behind. "Miss Pepper," she said softly, "I heard what you're doing for Renata."

"Doing? Me?"

"About making up the work. About writing during school, that business. So she can pass."

"And?"

"I'd feel better if there was something I could do, too. To make it up, what I've done."

"Sally!" There is nothing more annoying than a good person insisting she's a sinner. "For Pete's sake!"

"My mother says you'll never trust me again. Every time I think about it, I get so angry. My reputation—"

"Sally, I—"

"If only I had a chance to *atone*, to—"

I gave up. "Okay, I'd like a two-thousand-word composition from you on ethics. What moral ideas should guide our choices?"

"Two thousand?"

I nodded.

"By when?"

"Tomorrow."

"Tomorrow?"

"Absolutely. Not a moment later."

She exhaled. "*Thanks*, Miss Pepper," she said, and she made a brisk, almost exuberant exit.

The girl who'd missed the plane from Chicago was back—with a great tan. I'd been right about only one of the tardy trio. The flu case had no tan at all—just a ghastly gray hue and a lingering cough. And Badluck Dooney Scott was still out—"really burned," a friend of his said. "His whole arm. Spray bottle thing went up like a flamethrower, and when he stopped pushing on it . . . sucked it back on him. Really bad." I allowed myself a moment of repentance for having so cynically disbelieved. We'd do a class card, messages of good will, visits, although the boy needed a keeper most of all.

Today the class was discussing Steinbeck's *The Red Pony*, always a favorite. It's an unsettling, unsentimental work about coming of age. But let's face it: literary merit has nothing to do with its student appeal. For them, its prime and perhaps sole value is that at seventy pages, total, it is the shortest novel on any reading list in the known universe. To less than avid readers, it's the promised land of assigned novels, the chocolate fudge sundae on the scholastic menu.

Problem is, the kids are so dazzled by its brevity they can

think of nothing else. That's what they want to talk about—but not to me. They feel they are secretly pulling one over, but if they admitted it ("I loved this book because it was so short"), I might notice its abbreviated length. Their mamas must have taught them that if you can't say something nice—like "it's so short!"—say nothing at all. I grow fatigued trying to pull a discussion out of the book's wee body, but I keep it in the curriculum to avoid student insurrection.

"These stories," I said, "are about Jody's growing up, about what he learns during the process. Not all that he needs to learn is wonderful, or happy, either."

Duh, their collective eyes said, except for one girl who first tried out her thoughts in a whisper to her neighbor, who, in turn, nodded permission to go public with the idea. "It was harsh," she said.

Good. It was. Nature was. Life was. Sacrifice was. "Any harshness in particular you want to mention?" I asked. Would it be the unfairness of the pony's death after Jody had taken such loving care of him? The harshness of Jody's father's approach to life and child-rearing? Jody's loss of faith in adult omniscience?

The girl rolled her eyes. "Like when it *died*, the red pony. That was so sick with the cutting the lump and then, the buzzards eating its eye, oh, gross, yellow liquid and eye-eating! How could he write that? It was so harsh!"

Her female classmates nodded gravely. Her male classmates looked at her with contempt. *Girl*, their eyes said. They could take as much eye-eating as Steinbeck or I dished out.

Steinbeck pirouetted in his grave.

I pushed and prodded, and asked and answered questions until finally, the hour ended.

Teaching can be oh gross and so harsh.

And then it was back to poetic meter, a subject that is never wildly appreciated by people of the senior high persuasion. We slogged through iambic ta-*tums*, trochaic *tum*-tas, anapestic ta-ta-*tums*, and dactylic *tum*-ta-tas, eyes growing steadily glassier. With each new definition, I read a real-life, entertaining, illuminating poem they might like. My offerings were silently rejected. The class was much too worried about remembering arcane words to pay attention to silly things like poems.

"Dactylic," one grumbled. "Sounds prehistoric, like it belongs in a Spielberg movie."

They were building long-range anti-poetic missiles, and we hadn't yet approached an examination of the number of beats per line, something humans instinctively feel, along with the ta*dums*, until we make it part of the curriculum and slice the music into units from monometers to heptameters.

Sorry, I wanted to say, I'm not the one who decided to lessen your instinctive enjoyment by making you learn technical terms. Why can't that wait? Kids are born loving rhythm and verbal music. They bounce balls and skip rope and tease each other in homemade or learned rhyme. As they grow, they eat, sleep, and breathe music, the instrumentation of that rhythm they crave. So why do we squeeze it dry as soon as we can? Why not leave the technical business for after we have them hooked, when they ask how it works.

Maybe because if we didn't teach all those deadening terms and make it obscure and fearful, everybody would read and write poetry. There'd be a glut. Pretty scary.

We slogged on through the hour. Sometimes you aim merely for endurance, and don't dare think about inspiration.

I had packed lunch, trusting neither the cafeteria food nor the weather. But as my class stampeded out, I considered the landscape on the other side of the windows. The great outdoors looked as if it could finally support human life, and I hoped that fresh air might help, as I felt mentally mildewed.

Renata entered the room as I prepared to leave. I must have looked as surprised as I felt.

"You said I had to write during lunch period," she mumbled.

Had I thereby condemned myself to playing prison matron every noon? Until when? "I'll be back to check up on you."

"You aren't staying? You said . . ." She looked unduly horrified. Shouldn't she look happy?

"I'll provide the paper." I gave her the new year's accumulated flyers and notices. "Use the backs for your rough draft. I'll check at the end of the period." At least she'd have to copy over whatever it was she'd brought into the room.

"I didn't think I'd be alone," she whined.

"Easier to concentrate."

She slipped into her seat and put her head down on the desk.

"See you," I said. She looked up with the pathos of an unadopted puppy.

I managed to steel my heart and get out, only to hear a ruckus, a Code Blue something-bad-is-happening sound.

I slammed the door behind me, and trotted toward the noise. Caroline Finney, the gentle Latin teacher whose skin resembled tissue paper and whose thoughts should have been on retirement, not rumbles, also strode resolutely toward the room at the end of the empty hall. We carried scowls and disapproval as anti-riot gear.

We approached the open door from separate directions, hearing male voices ride over one another.

"I told you—think you could barge in here—Me! I'm not the one who—I didn't lie!—loyalty, all these years—pass it off on—the hell out of here!"

Caroline shook her head so vigorously her gray bangs jostled and rearranged themselves. "Boys, boys, *boys!*" she said before she'd even reached the room from which the sounds poured.

I was apprehensive, but not about the possibilities of real danger. This is a *good* school—our students fight the old-fashioned way, by hand. After they've spent their allowances on CDs, recreational substances, and sunglasses, they don't have cash left for heavy weaponry.

What worried me was a growing sense that the voices didn't belong to anyone Caroline could rationally address as *boys, boys, boys*. One was definitely familiar.

As we neared the open door, Caroline gave me a quasi-military curt nod. Ready—aim—fire. From within the room, the quarrel burst out in fragments. "—spying on—he knew—real friend wouldn't—money—"

Caroline continued the quaint teacherly remonstrations she'd learned in a different era. "Boys, boys," she crooned, "this is not—" She stopped herself for a moment of open-mouthed gaping at the sight of two definite non-boys. "Why, Mr. Devaney!" she said in a horrified whisper. "Mr. Devaney! I never imagined a teacher . . ."

Vincent looked at her, shamefaced as a kindergartner whose toilet training had failed. "Miss Finney," he said, "I, we—so sorry. Didn't realize we must have been so . . ."

"Caroline and I heard you," I began. I tried to sort it out, to sift retroactively through the barrage of words and get a handle on what was happening. Was Vincent under attack? Should I call the police? "Are you . . . is everything under control?"

"Fine," he said. "Thanks. Lot of noise, nothing. Little . . . disagreement. We'll be fine. Quiet and fine."

I looked away, troubled and embarrassed for his sake. In the far range of my peripheral vision, out of the classroom door, I saw Renata Field at the top of the stairs, gesticulating to someone below. She seemed to feel my eyes on her, because she turned around, glared at me, raised her chin, and moved back in the direction of my room.

I'd deal with her later, when I figured out how. Meantime, I studied the second man in Vincent's classroom. I had seen him before, and I hadn't liked him that time, either. I watched him pace around tables dotted with beakers and sinks and lined with high stools. Had I dated him? Worked with him? I came up blank, so I tried remembering from another angle. Vincent definitely knew him, perhaps too well. I must have met him through Vincent.

He clicked into place. At the club the evening I visited. Stitching large mother-of-pearl sequins onto miles of iridescent silky stuff, annoyed by my presence, although I was impressed at how steady his hand was—he threaded his needle with ease—despite having worked his way through a cooler holding a twelve-pack of beer. And then he'd been part of the group that went to the diner to help me with the phantom article, although I never knew why, since he continued to be uncooperative.

He'd been named for a South Philly singer. Not Mario Lanza. More rock 'n' roll. Bobby? Frankie? Chubby Checker? Fabian, that was it. Fabian Somebody worked with brick, and Vincent said he was a popular member of the club, but he was sullen around me.

I tried to remember what I'd heard between them, and the words *spying*, *lying*, *loyalty*, and *money* came back. An interesting and incendiary combination, but why here, why now?

This wasn't a student outbreak, but a disgraceful adult dispute. As long as these men weren't going to destroy each other or school property, we had no business here. "Excuse me," Caroline said. "I will no longer interfere with your . . . with you." She turned her back, ramrod straight, and marched away.

I waved adieu, lamely, and joined her. She shook her head, looked at me, and whispered. "A *teacher*. Imagine." As we walked toward the wide staircase, their voices rose again, as if our appearance had been nothing more to them than a long held breath.

Renata was at my classroom door, idling away her hour.

I glared in her direction. That should have been enough.

"Who can work with this noise?" she asked. "Is Mr. Devaney shouting?"

"Of course not," Caroline Finney snapped. "A teacher wouldn't carry on that way!" It was the only time I've ever heard her lie.

Renata disappeared into my room.

From down the hall came a furious shout. "Everybody knows!" I couldn't tell which man had said it, since anger distorted the voice.

Caroline shook her head wearily again, and we parted at the front door.

I crossed into the Square, passing a don't-drink-and-dress lesson: a man in a fur-trimmed satin Eagles jacket, a leather hat with earflaps, a tissue in one hand, a cigar in the other, and unbuckled high galoshes on his feet.

He was almost the only other person in the park, so I had my choice of benches. I sat unwrapping a leftover chicken leg from last night's take-out, replaying the angry snippets I'd just heard.

I tried to enjoy the bleak beauty of my surroundings, the colorless tree limbs that pushed against the hard bright sky with not so much as a leaf bud for ease, the dark, frozen earth below.

A gray squirrel was the only softness on the landscape. He hovered nearby, checking me out, and I felt guilty I wasn't eating anything he'd like. On the other hand, he wasn't sharing his cache of nuts with me, either.

Then Vincent Devaney, a muffler covering half his face, walked toward me. Alone. I wondered what had become of his sparring mate. I hoped nothing fatal.

He paused as he approached and cleared his throat. "Could I?" He gestured at the bench.

I nodded apprehensively. I didn't know this man nearly as well as I'd thought I had.

"I don't want you getting the wrong impression," he said. "I didn't want to involve anybody, trust me, but the police keep hassling me. I had to."

I was skeptical. He had involved me before anybody hassled him. Involving people came naturally to him. So did skirting the truth.

"It's illegal to withhold relevant information, isn't it?" he asked rhetorically. "Barbs said she was telling if I didn't, but then it wouldn't be as legitimate-sounding. I mean, I'm the one who knows him. I'm the one in the club with him."

"I'm lost, Vincent," I said softly.

"Fabian wanted to be Captain. He really wanted it. You know, wear the biggest cape, be up for a special award. So did Jimmy Pat."

"So did you, I understand."

I saw a brief flash of that ready anger in his eyes, then he lowered his lids, took a deep breath, and ignored what I'd said. "It means you're the best, not by City Hall judges, but by your friends, the other members. It means you wear the best suit and you develop your own style. The papers write about Captains."

"You're saying Fabian killed Jimmy to get that position?"

Vincent shook his head. "I'm saying that because of the competition being so out in the open, Jimmy Pat paid a whole lot of attention to Fabian, noticing what he probably wouldn't have noticed otherwise. And that's how come Jimmy found out about the missing money."

I offered Vincent the chicken leg, despite my having taken a bite out of it. He shook his head. I waited. After a silence, words poured out as if he'd turned a faucet. "It was gone, you see, and nobody knew why or how. All we knew was, we couldn't pay our bills. Somebody—Jimmy Pat was sure it was Fabian—was skimming from the till. You understand how horrible that was? You work all year to raise the money—everybody gives what they can. Nickels and dimes and raffles and door-to-door collections and bake sales and Atlantic City trips. *All year.* For one of our own—our treasurer, no less—to rob us! I mean the club, it's like family, where you belong. And suddenly, Fabian's saying we didn't raise enough, we couldn't pay for supplies—you know how much ostrich feathers cost? We were dead."

He grew contemplative. "I don't know," he said after a pause, "Jimmy thought it was a setup. That Fabian took the money so he could 'find' it and save the day and be a hero."

"And be voted Captain?"

He nodded. "Only before Fabian could pull it off, Jimmy Pat caught on that the money—lots of it—was missing, and he figured out who took it, and confronted Fabian. That's what I told the cops yesterday. That's why Fabian threw a fit today."

He stood up. "Any questions?" He sounded like a teacher again, winding up an important lecture.

"Anybody else know about Jimmy Pat's suspicions?"

Vincent shrugged. "It never got to the whole group, if that's what you mean. Jimmy was waiting until the new year."

"Did Fabian return the money?"

He shook his head. "Denied Jimmy's accusations, then, of course, he couldn't do anything, because it'd be an admission."

"Then how did the club get the money? You were in the parade, after all."

"Miller and Kovaks mortgaged their houses, that's how. Prize money would have helped pay them back, but hell, by the time we got to the judges' stand, everybody was so shaken up.... Most we could hope for was a pity vote, and they don't have that category yet."

"What would have happened afterward—if Jimmy had lived?"

"Who knows? It wasn't a closed chapter, is all I know. Still isn't, just all muddled up."

"Last question. Why didn't you tell the police right away?"

"They didn't ask. Besides, he's my friend, we grew up together. Like brothers, all of us are. You don't want to think wrong of your brothers. And in the end, there's no proof. A dead man's word, that's all. So I thought, let the police follow other leads, more logical leads, right?"

I didn't know the answer. I didn't particularly like this new Vincent.

Vincent put his muffler back up over the bottom half of his face. "Gotta go," he said, through the scarf.

"Wait—one more question."

He pushed the muffler down. "You said that was the last one."

"I lied, I guess. You told me you were looking for Dolores at the parade."

"I was."

"Then why'd you tell Dolores you were with me?"

He bit at his upper lip and looked distinctly uncomfortable.

"Why?" I asked again.

"She stood me up." His voice was constricted. "I didn't want her to think it mattered. That I even remembered about her. I mean, she didn't say she was sorry for not meeting me, so I played the same game. To save face."

Seemed to me there was entirely too much focus on face in this group. When they weren't hiding their faces behind masks, they were saving them. "Okay," I said. "That's it."

He pulled the muffler back up, covering his face although the day did not require extreme protection. "Gotta go to the library," he said, and he hurried on.

I sat worrying about Fabian and the missing money, and about Vincent and his lies. Fabian had a powerful motive, but I'd heard about it from Vincent, who'd wanted the same position, who had every reason to lie. I wondered how much the police knew. They were being very cautious about making a move. At the moment, there was a call out for home videos that might have captured the

Fancy Club and Jimmy Pat at various points on the route. The hope was to see something otherwise ignored, but so far, nothing had turned up except hours of jumpy and blurred amateur footage.

So Vincent could point the finger at another member of his club, suggesting that status and money had been the motives. Meantime, there didn't seem any way to prove or disprove the allegations—or even that there had been allegations.

Fabian could have committed the murder. Any of them could have strutted close enough to Jimmy Pat to shoot him low, hitting his stomach, before dancing away. Or, for all I know, have ducked into the frame suit for a call of nature, and heard nature call "murder."

That left the issue of the gun and its disposal, now that I knew it hadn't been the one in my purse. Of course, he—whichever he or she it was—could have left the parade later in order to chuck the murder weapon. I assumed the police had searched the multitude of trash baskets along the route.

Vincent, now at the far corner of the Square, looked innocuous and familiar, but I didn't trust him anymore. He wore a mask and disguise even when in street clothes.

A shadow fell on me, and the temperature dropped along with the light level. I looked up and saw the man from the corner, he of the satin jacket and leather earflaps, deliberately, resolutely approaching, one hand holding his cigar, the other half-extended in my direction.

I stood so abruptly, the remains of my chicken leg and my container of juice fell to the ground. I started to retrieve them, then decided that being a litterer beat being a corpse, and I stood up again and backed off.

"Wait!" he called out. "Hey! Don't be scared. You're Amanda Pepper, the teacher from across the street, right?"

"Why?" I eyed him from ten feet away. Unfortunately, from that position, I could also eye my pocketbook where I'd left it on the bench.

"I've been waiting to talk with you. I didn't want to intrude while you were teaching, or talking with that man."

"Are you a parent?"

He nodded.

"Whose?" I asked.

"Oh, you mean of somebody there?" He tilted his head toward the school. "No. Lookit—no need to be afraid of me. I'm with B.L.T. & G."

"Excuse me?"

"The law firm. Benthelwaite, LaVonne—"

"I'm sorry," I said. "It's just that . . ."

"I know." He looked sympathetic. "The world today, who can tell? I don't blame you a bit. My wife's the same way about strangers, and I say, good. Better safe than sorry."

"What is this about, then?" I moved closer to grab my bag. "What would a law firm want with me? I hope I've been named in somebody's will."

He cleared his throat. I dove, as unobtrusively as I could, for my possessions and in mid-swoop, he spoke.

"I thought you should see this," he said.

I turned toward him. He offered me a letter, and automatically, I took it.

"I thought you should see that," he said again, "so that you would be legally and properly informed that you are being sued by Phillipa and Thomas Field for excessive and unfair treatment of their daughter Renata, which has caused her and her parents grievous mental anguish and created insurmountable impediments to her future plans."

Sued? Me? Renata?

She'd been leaning over the railing at the stairs, signaling this man. Renata had let him know where I was.

That's why she'd been disappointed that I wouldn't be in my room during lunch. Not because of her desire for my company, but because she'd wanted to witness my being served the papers. I looked up now, and there she was, peering white-faced out of my classroom window.

No, surely there was another explanation. I'd lost my sense of humor. Nobody takes a teacher to court for a deservedly lousy grade.

"You're kidding, right? You aren't really a lawyer, are you?"

"Never said I was one. I'm *with* B.L.T. & G."

"You're an actor, am I right? One of those people you hire to pull funny stunts and practical jokes."

"No and no again," he said. The temperature dropped into a frozen, bleak hell. "Not an actor. Not a funny stunt. Real. A process server, you'd call me. Not a joke. You're in trouble, lady. Not a joke at all."

Thirteen

THE front door opened and a weary-looking C. K. entered.

"Sued!" I said by way of greeting. "I'm being sued over a grade! *Sued!*" As if repetition neutralized the word.

I sat facing the fire, finding no serenity in its flames.

"You're kidding, right?" He checked my expression, then shook his head, went to the kitchen, opened the refrigerator, and poured himself a glass of wine. "Want something?" he called out. "Who's suin'?"

"Renata's parents! And I've bent over backwards for her, given her a way to pass when she doesn't deserve even that!"

"Wine?" he asked.

I thought he was giving me permission to whine, for which I was grateful. I wanted to complain on an operatic scale, and endlessly. I explained the shameful ridiculousness of the situation in minute detail.

The legal papers said I had not sufficiently or adequately clarified my grading system, causing Renata to fail to meet arbitrary classroom standards. With no regard to her future, I had penalized her. It appeared she had been absent the first day of the semester and had apparently not heard my introductory speech on grading.

As if any school in the known universe considers cheating, plagiarizing, and goofing off acceptable.

Mackenzie patiently listened, and handed me a glass of wine.

"Sued! Me!" I waved the papers I'd been served. "It'll cost a fortune to defend myself, and I don't even know against what. Will the school back me? What do I do?"

"Talk to a lawyer," Mackenzie said. "Immediately. Do we know anybody who handles that kind of law?"

"Sleaze law?" His words translated into the dusty whoosh of money fluttering out of my hands. How many billable hours and minutes and seconds left on my Doomsday clock? "These things drag on for years." I'd read *Bleak House*, where the lawsuit dragged on until there was not a penny left in the till.

Nothing had changed since Dickens's time, except that I was starting out penniless and lawyers' fees were even higher.

"I had an interestin' day, too," Mackenzie said. "If you're done, that is."

Done? Not at all, and I resented any attempt to hurry the process. Besides, I felt incapable of responding to anybody else's news or problems until I was well and truly done. I was being *sued* for doing my job! "Don't you care?" I asked. It was not a question, but a charge.

He refuted it. "Of course." I was stressing him out, melting his speech, so that *I* became a soft vowel that dissolved into the words around it. "It's a frivolous suit," he went on, in a torrent of sinuous syllables, "brought by mean-spirited, ignorant people

165

who haven't a clue about the purpose of education, and it'll burn time, money, and emotions and wind up nowhere, and I'm sorry for the waste of your talents and energy this'll cost."

I must admit, I was impressed, weak with gratitude. I had a soul mate who took my woes to heart.

"But the thing is," he continued, "you asked what you should do and I said you needed legal advice, and soon. What else is left to say? The only law I'm conversant with has to do with dead bodies, rights to remain silent. Things like that. If you'd done away with Renata, I'd be of use. Otherwise . . ." He glanced at his watch.

Was he implying that having said everything about the topic, we could move on? What about carrying on? Actual, bona fide lamentations? I suddenly missed my little house shared with only the cat, who'd willingly endured—or ignored—as much obsessive self-pity as I provided. Time-sharing a life with a human had a real downside.

Even the feline soul mate was a turncoat. He half dozed, eyes open, near Mackenzie's favorite chair, looking bored with me, too.

Tough. I wasn't through. "Then there's her guilt-ridden accomplice, Sally," I said. Who needed to hear what had happened on *his* job, anyway, given that the answer would, always, be murder had happened. Again. "She's the complete opposite, demanding punishment, over-atoning . . ."

"Uh-huh," Mackenzie said. "You hungry?"

"Boneless chicken breasts on the counter."

He retrieved the plate. "What happened to them? Looks like roadkill."

"I tenderized them."

"Tough breasts? Isn't that an oxymoron?"

"Pounded breasts. Very California cuisine. After saying 'have a nice day' that's how they sublimate their pent-up aggression."

"It didn't do the trick for you, though," he said mildly. "Mind if I take over in here?"

I had enjoyed bludgeoning the meat, but I had no energy left, and was more than willing to pass the torch.

He busied himself in the kitchen, or in that section of the loft so designated since there really wasn't a room in which to go. We had a paucity of doors to slam, and not much place to hide. I missed my house again.

"Turn on the news, would you?" he called out.

"Why? You already know the big stories." He had a perverse need to listen to the media's distortions of the crimes he knew firsthand.

"You don't," he answered, "an' you might want to." I turned the TV on.

The screen filled with two perkies whose expressions suggested that they never once heard the headlines they read off the monitor. Just once, I'd like to see revulsion, horror, or miserable unhappiness mar their happy-news faces. Maybe if I told them about my lawsuit?

That wasn't a half-bad idea. It wouldn't touch their plastic hearts, but it could put the suit under the glare of scrutiny. If everybody knew what the Fields were doing, maybe they'd be too ashamed to do it. I had to find out how a non-celebrity, an ordinary teacher turned her woes into sound bites.

"Our lead story tonight answers, at least partially, a local mystery that has troubled the city through the holiday season." You could tell this was serious, not cute or human-interesty, because the male anchor had been assigned the telling of it. Sexist, but true. "For more than two weeks, a search has been on for Theodore Serfi—"

"They found him?"

"—who disappeared in late December after attending a meeting of his Mummers' club. There have been many theories and some allegations since then, but not until today has there been an answer."

"A real answer?" I asked. "Why didn't you tell me?"

"I tried." Mackenzie sounded weary. "But th' only news our wire service picked up was that you were bein' sued."

He was a tolerant man. I'd have to remember that.

The screen showed a large brick building, not unlike ours, but not like it, either. The on-screen place did not have near neighbors or trendy galleries at street level. It stood alone, in the

167

middle of a deserted parking lot. Windows were missing, and on its side, ERS was visible in outline, as if large metal letters had been ripped off the bricks. A reporter—female, this time—held a mike and tried not to shiver as she smiled at the camera. "We're here at the former home of Stanley Brothers."

Mackenzie hissed. A lot of the city responded that way to the name of the brothers whose candy plant—licorice was their specialty—had defined their neighborhood as its home for generations. Fathers, sons, and grandsons had filled spots on their production lines until the past March, when Stanley Brothers gave its one thousand two hundred employees seven days' notice. This plant, they said, had become "unnecessary." So had its workers. Licorice could be produced more cheaply elsewhere on the globe. And so died a lot of jobs and another chunk of city, and there weren't a whole lot of other licorice makers waiting to absorb the displaced.

Since March, the building had been attacked in lieu of its departed management. Those broken windows that had been boarded up had spiderwebs of graffiti on them. The bricks were spray painted as well, as was a pathetic FOR RENT sign that mentioned the square feet available. And all around the building, even as the camera panned, shards of glass and blooms of trash. It looked like what it was, the site of a catastrophe.

The reporter took it all in stride, stepping lightly through the ruins. That's how she kept from being as unemployed as the erstwhile candymakers. "Late last night, acting on an anonymous tip, police combed this empty factory, and in a storage room still filled with cellophane bags in which licorice was once packed, they found the frozen body of Theodore Serfi. Preliminary reports indicate the presence of multiple gunshot wounds, although police have not yet determined the time or precise cause of death."

The ghoulish camera switched to the grieving father, and an offscreen voice asked how he felt. What did they expect him to say? Why did they ask such things?

"I'm glad they finally found him. I knew he didn't run away or just leave before Christmas and the parade, the way people said.

My son wouldn't do that." He cleared his throat. "And now," he continued, "let him rest in peace. And I hope the police find whoever did this horrible thing." Then he waved them off.

The family, the reporter went on to say, has always denied any criminal connections and has no theory as to why this happened or who might have done it.

Speaking of which, the camera was now on none other than Arthur King, standing in front of his meat-packing house, as elegant a sausage maven as ever. "If you've driven around the city lately," the reporter said, "you may have seen somebody's idea of a joke, the defaced ads for King's Sausage and the inferences that they, or members of that family, had something to do with the disappearance of Teddy Serfi."

Arthur nodded. He wore a navy blue topcoat and a silvery white fringed scarf that looked color-coordinated with his hair. He wasn't carrying a book. Maybe he'd extracted everything he could from Machiavelli.

"You must be relieved by today's discovery," the reporter simpered.

How had they known to go to him? How had he known how to turn his private botherations into news? Would he tell me if I asked?

"We have mushrooms?" Mackenzie called over.

"Dried ones." Even without mushrooms, he'd created a mouth-watering ambience. Life was good as long as garlic perfumed the air.

"Everyone in any way connected with King's Sausage is relieved," Arthur said. "And exonerated. Maybe this will prevent others in the future from leaping to unsubstantiated conclusions and hurting innocent parties. Our long and honorable reputation has been grievously injured by the deliberate and organized slanderous campaign of people who may have been understandably upset, but who chose a bad way to express their worry and grief."

Enough already about the besmirched honor of sausage.

"For thirty years, we have stood for cleanliness and purity of product, and so it remains. All of us at King's Sausage hope this sordid affair and all the unjustified allegations are now a thing of the past, and that the long and honorable tradition of our company will be restored."

I'd known he was literate, but not what a smooth spokesperson he could be, gobbling up airwaves, giving his company enviable free advertising.

"Well, well," Mackenzie said. "Rumors that your competitor's bodily fluids are in your product must really hurt business."

Yes, but. Something about his performance bothered me, a something I knew—but couldn't reach, couldn't see clearly. It nagged like the early stages of a toothache, not altogether there, but uncomfortable and guaranteed to get worse.

"And now," the female anchor said, "turning to another neighborhood in shock after a bizarre explosion . . ."

How small a sound bite a murder generates these days—an ordinary, non-celebrity, gunshot murder. Standard-issue ghoulishness. Sorry, Serfi.

Might as well focus on my own life. Least I could do, given my man's good work, was set the table. I stood up and looked industrious, putting out cobalt placemats, blue and white napkins, and blue-rimmed white plates. They contrasted with the pale oak surface for a pretty, faux–French-country table.

I'd have remembered flowers, too, if it weren't for that damned lawsuit. Blue somethings, yellow and white daisies in a water jug. Blue candles. Our life as a pretty picture.

Choosing linens and pottery is kind of like grown-up finger-painting.

"Any interestin' mail or messages?" Mackenzie asked. He was like me in that—optimistic every new dawn about the day's postal and telephonic possibilities, disappointed every night with what actually arrived.

I liked that ridiculous hopefulness. I even thought we should get a fax and go on line with e-mail so as to double the possibilities of something interesting coming our way. And, I suppose, the disappointments.

"Only the message that I'm being sued," I said. "Have I mentioned that?" But this time I smiled at his groaned response, and then I realized I hadn't checked the machine. That damned lawsuit had blocked everything out of my mind. "At least I don't think so." I checked. Two messages.

"No," I said more positively when I heard the first voice. "Nothing important."

"You'll never believe this," my mother was saying. "Sid, you know? Dr. Landau's cat that was being taken care of by Violet who's nice, but flaky is the word. Did I tell you he got sick? Really sick. Of course, he's incredibly old . . ."

I tuned her out and wandered over to where Mackenzie was fluffing couscous and spooning onions and mushrooms over the chicken breasts. He'd even found still-living lettuce leaves and had made a salad with canned beets and a few orange slivers. "We should open a restaurant," I said. "Get away from teenagers and crime."

"We?" he asked mildly. "What part of the partnership appeals to you? Beating up chicken breasts?"

Actually, I saw myself picking pottery—maybe each table would have a different color scheme, different patterns. Then hostessing, smiling and leading people to tables. Interrupting their conversations to ask if everything was fine.

". . . *dead*," my mother's voice announced with great emphasis. "Too quickly for poor Allen Beth to see him at the end."

"Somebody died?" I asked.

"The cat," Mackenzie said calmly. "Aren't you paying attention? Old Sid. Ancient Sid. Remember earlier installments?"

"A guy's middle name is Beth?" I asked with some excitement. We actually were approaching equality, then.

"Well," my mother said, "here's the thing. First, I think it would be nice if you wrote a sympathy note. I talk about you so much it's almost like you knew each other, and I don't think people are kind enough about the loss of pets. That's Allen with a y—Allyn Beth Laundau, M.D., okay? Same address, apartment eight hundred six. She'd appreciate it. Me, too."

Allyn-with-a-y. She. Had her parents really, really, wanted a son, too? Now that I thought of it, was the late lamented cat a Sid, or perhaps a Cyd?

Was C. K., perhaps, a Cyd? Or something on that order? Was that his big secret? "Cyd," I whispered.

No response.

"Cynthia? Caroline? Charlotte?"

Nothing, except a puzzled look on Mackenzie and my mother's voice resolutely continuing with her saga.

"But," my mother went on, "the thing is, Violet won't give up his ashes. She says she was there for him in his last agony, and, well, she insists. Allyn Beth is heartbroken. She pleaded and pleaded, then she offered to split the ashes, divvy Sid up, half for her, half for Violet, but Violet said that was sacrilegious. Allyn Beth is so upset, she's flying back from her children's a week sooner than planned to fight for her rights. And you know what I say?"

I, for one, listened with interest for what truth she had extracted from all this.

"You have to be crazy to leave Florida in December."

Silence reigned in our speechless household until the next voice on the machine. At first, it was only vaguely familiar. "So look," it said. "Guess by now you know the news, being as it's on TV."

"Emily!" So she'd picked my phone number up off the store floor. It felt like a minor victory.

"So obviously," she continued, "there's no reason for you to keep after the story like you said you were going to because now there isn't any story left to sell, so if you meant like you said, that you were going to find out about an advance or a spec or whatever you called it, don't." She clicked off.

Mackenzie put a mound of couscous on a serving plate, plus the bedecked chicken breasts. His patience was commendable, except for the series of questioning looks he shot me.

I tried to piece it together, to answer his questions and mine in between delicious morsels and the compliments they generated. "You are a grand and instinctive cook," I said.

"Many thanks." And he waited.

"I was sure her story was about the parade, about Jimmy Pat," I said. "My mistake."

"She knew the whereabouts of Serfi's body," he said. "Odd."

And then I knew what had been nagging at me. I remembered her excitement as she shooed me out of the store yesterday. Her chuckle. The better idea I'd given her by talking about King Arthur, who wouldn't have had to search for an advance. Emily hadn't given him her story, she'd sold it to him because that's what he wanted all along—his sausage cleared of suspicion—and then he had notified the police. I explained it to Mackenzie.

"Guess that moves him far down on the list of suspects." I was disappointed.

"The gun, though. Why'd he want to see it?" Mackenzie shook his head. "You think she knew him personally?"

"Emily and the dead guy?" I shrugged. "Everybody knows everybody else in that neighborhood, and surely in the clubs. Everybody's connected to one another. And Emily's a Mummer groupie, living near Two Street the way she does. It's not only the extra parade they have there on New Year's, it's where most all their clubhouses are. She probably knows them all."

"That place they found him—that isn't close to Two Street. Doesn't seem she could accidentally stumble over him. Nobody did for more than two weeks, and it's not my idea of a love nest, surely not in December," Mackenzie said. "How'd she know?"

"Given her father, her home life, her standards of love nests might be . . ." But even I couldn't buy that rubble as her dream assignation spot. The woman read books with naked-chested pirates on the cover. That wouldn't fire the imagination for a bed of broken glass. So how had Emily known where Serfi's body lay?

"I think she saw it go down," Mackenzie said.

"Arthur didn't do it."

"Why not?"

"First of all—didn't you say it was a professional job? That he was Hoffa'd?"

"That was before they found him."

"But Arthur still doesn't make sense. He wanted to end the rumors, clear his company's name. He wanted to see the gun because if it were identifiable to him, if he could alert the cops to look elsewhere, it would be a way of clearing his name."

"Aren't you making a wide leap? How'd he know the gun had

anything to do with Serfi's death? How'd he even know Serfi was dead?"

I was stymied, then I remembered. "He assumed it. Always talked about two murders, two dead Mummers, because Ted Serfi wouldn't have disappeared before the parade, he said. He connected the deaths, thought the same person had done them. And he didn't do it—or why else would he call the police?"

"Which you don't actually know. Maybe Emily did."

"When'd you find out?"

"This morning. They got the call last night. Been working on it ever since." He poured the last of the wine. "But it isn't my case, and wasn't. He was a missing person until last night." He tapped his fingers. "I did find out today that Arthur with the crown was for real. But obviously, you found that out for yourself."

"Arthur King. Emily called him Cam, short for Camelot."

"And this Emily, she was eager to get to him last night?"

"Seemed that way."

"Any reason—anything she said—to make you think maybe she owned a gun?"

"Emily? We didn't talk about things like . . ." I put down my wine glass. "This isn't idle table-talk, is it? You're interrogating me. Why? You're making me feel like I'm on a witness stand, as if you suspect me of keeping something from you. Why?"

"I don't suspect you of a thing, except maybe knowing things that could be useful to keep other people from being suspicious about you. I'm trying to protect you."

"From what?" I couldn't believe this. Suspected? Of what on earth?

"Serfi was shot three times. Two of the bullets went through him, wherever it was he was killed. They're gone. No sign that it went down in that cellophane storage room. The third bullet lodged in his pelvic bone."

"Yes?" His way of savoring each step along the way of a story made me want to wave a baton, speed his tempo. I'd nod, faster and faster, hoping to subliminally hustle him to the point, but it never worked. "Sounds painful. Awful, but—?"

"That bullet looks like maybe it came from—"

I got it. "No. Too weird. It couldn't—"

"Probably could," he answered. "The derringer. A derringer."

The gun in my pocketbook. Again.

"Ballistics is testing it. The gun was still there, so they could move quickly. The gun that didn't kill Jimmy Pat very possibly killed Serfi. And that's why it couldn't have been a professional hit—not with that kind of gun."

Back to Square One. Or wherever we were when I was found to be packing a gun. One step forward and two steps back. Sherlock Holmes doing the Mummers' strut.

"They'll want a statement. Again. Tomorrow morning."

"I already—"

He nodded, looked terminally weary. "But not about Serfi."

Some days getting out of bed is the very worst idea you can have. I wondered why I had so many days like that lately.

Fourteen

I HAD to get somebody to cover my homeroom and first period class the next morning so that I could officially say I hadn't known this most recent victim, either. Hadn't known Ted Serfi, hadn't shot him, and didn't know enough about him to know why or how anybody else had, or why or how the presumed murder weapon wound up in my pocketbook.

"Duplicate my last statement," I suggested. "Change the names. The rest is the same."

That was not according to regulations.

"You say you have no idea." The sergeant sounded bored out

of his gourd. "No idea who might have put the weapon into your pocketbook."

"Just like I didn't have any idea about it last time." That wasn't a hundred percent true. I had an idea, but it didn't make sense, so I couldn't see the point of sharing it with this dolt. The night before, I had tried, unsuccessfully, with Mackenzie, who is anything but a dolt, and neither of us had been able to make it work.

My idea was that Emily was profoundly involved in this. She'd had the opportunity to plant the gun in my purse while I wandered through her overheated, underpopulated store. She'd wanted to sell me a story which I now knew was the whereabouts of the missing Mummer, and when I couldn't ante up real money, she sold it to a waiting bidder.

How would she know where Ted Serfi was if she hadn't been involved in putting him there?

But—a big, road-blocking but—if she had participated in the crime, why be so eager to publicize it? I couldn't figure out how she'd benefit by her own plan.

Finally, having wasted more of the taxpayers' money, the police were finished with me. I rushed out of the building, checking the time, and collided with a man in a brown overcoat and bright orange scarf. "Whoa," he said in a baritone. He gripped my shoulders with his gloved hands, keeping me from toppling onto him.

His eyes widened. He let go of me, loosened the orange scarf, and tilted his head. "I know who you are," he said. "Saw you here, when was it? After the parade, it was. About—yes! You're the one had the gun."

I shook my head. "It wasn't the gun," I mumbled. Not that time, at least.

"Right, right! The teacher, that's who you are. At the private school on the Square. I've got it in my notes."

Lucky me. Had he not come along, I'd have no idea who I was.

"I'm Henneman." His name and everything else he said turned into frozen puffs of smoke. "Henneman, crime reporter."

"Nice to meet you, but now, if you'll excuse me." I moved sideways so he no longer blocked me. "I'm running late."

He held his hands up, showing he meant no harm, and smiled with his mouth. His eyes remained squinted, suspicious. His face and posture cried out for one of those Forties hats with the white press card stuck in it. "Late, huh? Right. The thing is, why? Police headquarters during school hours, too, is my point. Why is that? What brings you back?"

"Asking questions about what's going on here is your job and all, so no offense, but this isn't my job, for which I'm late. Trust me, there's no story, and I have to go." This time, he did nothing to stall me. I made it around him and then I remembered how Arthur King had gone public with the blood sausage libels last night, and how well it had served him.

I walked back. "You want to know what's happening to me?" I asked. "I'll tell you, and I'll give you a newsworthy story. I'm being sued by a student's family because I'm giving her a C in English. A grade that is generous, if anything. What do you think of that?"

"I don't get it."

"Neither do I, but that's what we've come to. It's gotten so that people sue about anything. What's going to happen to our schools if teachers are afraid to give honest grades?" He listened intently. "Don't you want to take notes?" I asked. "And be sure and mention what'll happen to university admissions if they can't trust transcripts. Shouldn't people think about that? What about teaching kids to accept responsibility for their acts?"

He took a deep breath and puffed out a smoky cloudlet. "I meant . . . I don't get why you're here."

"Here?"

"Tough break, all that, but—shouldn't you go to a courthouse, or a lawyer's office? Why'd you come to the police station?"

"Never mind." So much for taking my story nationwide, letting the case shrivel in the glare of publicity.

"Gotta give you credit, though," he said. "That was clever, changing the subject that way. Also, I surmise, a little desperate. Too bad it didn't work. Civil suits aren't my thing, aren't sexy."

"I was being honest. That's the story; the one about being sued."

"Sure. And that explains why you seem to be in a lot of places with a homicide case. Homicide cases, that is."

"What do you mean?"

"I keep hearing your name. Like you work with the teacher who's maybe the key suspect, and you're his alibi, and you had the gun, and now here you are again. You're all over this. How come? You don't seem the type."

I didn't even ask what that meant. Mackenzie had told me about Henneman, a stringer for a news service, a semi-annoying but persistent scout for crime stories he could sell. I didn't like the idea of his noticing me. If this didn't turn out to be a big news day, I might find my name mentioned in filler stories all over the U.S.

"Coincidence," I said. "And . . ." Oh, why not? It was the only and easiest way I could think of to justify my inadvertent involvement and get me out from under his microscope. And it was more or less true. "See, I'm writing an article. Freelancing." His eyes squinched with worry: was I scooping Jimmy Olsen on his big-break story?

"Not about these crimes," I reassured him. "About the Mummers themselves. That teacher you mentioned works with me and is a Mummer in the same club as Jimmy Pat was. He—the teacher—helped me with my research. That's how I became involved with that particular club, and that's the only reason you may have seen my name. I'm interested in the Mummers as a cultural phenomenon."

"The parade?"

"Sure, but more than that, too. How their whole year is organized around getting ready, how they raise funds for the outfits and make them, at least the fancies. Or how the String Bands hire choreographers and designers and pay to have their suits made. And, you know, the history and . . ."

He had that glazed look I knew so well from Mackenzie, but damned if I wasn't going to make my point for once. "Do you realize we're barely into January and they're already revving up for next year's parade?"

"You know, that's interesting. That could be good."

"Thanks." I once again resolved to write the damned thing. It probably did have a market if it interested a man who wanted all his stories to be "sexy."

"I mean, you go snooping around so you can write something, you call it research, and it works: you unearth dangerous information, and suddenly, a guy's dead, two guys are dead, and you're smack in the middle of every—"

"Hey—that isn't what I said. That isn't what happened!"

"My editor would be interested in the article. Maybe it even has an important clue in it that you don't realize!" He loosened his muffler and let it hang. He was warming to the idea, literally, getting fired up over his stupid misinterpretation. "Could you get me a copy, fast?"

"I never said—"

"Under your byline, of course. I didn't mean to suggest—"

"All the same—"

"By, say, noon? I could get this in and—"

"I can't."

"You won't let me see it?"

How had I gotten into this mess? And how had I failed to produce an article?

"Then would you give me the gist of it? You know, local color, an anecdote? I'll credit you, of course."

"Sorry." I turned. I didn't have time to explain the many things I was sorry about.

"Is it because you're afraid?" he shouted. "You uncovered something that scares you? Is that why you're here again, now that they found Ted Serfi?"

I waved him off and kept moving.

"The paper would pay. I wouldn't steal your story!" I turned and saw him shake his head with disgust, then he wrapped his orange muffler up and around his head and over his chin for a cold-weather Arab effect.

Off my case. With any luck, he'd forget all about me.

I WASN'T able to forget him. The encounter bothered me all day. Having missed half the morning, I had less day in which to fester.

It was long enough for serious botheration. Finally, even this workday ended.

When, like a good teacher, I went to the office to drop off my plan book and retrieve late-breaking news flashes from my principal, I was surprised to find pink telephone message slips along with the customary memo-pap that grew like fungus in our mailboxes. I have no office or access to any secretary except Helga, who by no stretch of the imagination could be called *mine*, and use of the school phone is frowned upon. This little pile of pink slips felt almost as good as a full answering machine at home.

I saved the best for last and flipped through the memo-pap first. "Ms. Pepper, I have been notified of pending litigation being brought by the Field family concerning your proposed final grade for Renata. I would like you to schedule a meeting with me to discuss this tomorrow morning, (Friday,) so that we can fairly and objectively decide on a prudent course of action."

He spelled prudent e-x-p-e-d-i-e-n-t. Give the girl whatever she wanted, he'd say, although he'd pad that sentence in weasel words. I sighed and put the note in my briefcase.

I looked at my messages. If Helga were committed to clear speech and direct communication, she'd replace the *While You Were Out* with something closer to the truth like *While You Were Right Upstairs Whence I Could Have Summoned You Had I But Wanted To.*

Helga's meticulous script always looks written in a fit of controlled anger. *Please call Mr. Henneman at earliest convenience,* her raging handwriting said. Time, 12:17 P.M.

"Helga," I said. "When a caller says *earliest convenience,* do you think three hours should pass?"

"This was as early as it was convenient for me," she said. "I spent my lunch hour here, you know. Taking your messages."

A message from C. K. with no time on it said he wouldn't be back till late.

"Urgent, urgent," the third one said. "Emily wants to talk A.S.A.P. Closing store at five. Will be at Melrose Diner after. Can you meet her? Says you know who she is." Her number was in the proper space, as was the time of the call, 2:05 P.M. I was sourly amused that Helga chose to include the *urgent, urgent* part.

"As you surely recall," Helga said in her crisp, mean-spirited voice, "teachers are not encouraged to use this number for personal calls."

"So a good thing it is that none of my callers are teachers." I left, to call Emily from the hall pay phone, out of earshot of the Office Witch. Of course I'd meet her. Not only might I get information, but given that Mackenzie was out eradicating evil, I could also get a decent dinner that way.

EMILY SAT at the end half-table, drinking coffee and reading yet another novel with a bare-chested, long-haired hunk in ripped clothing on the cover. It was not the same title as the other day because this fellow had black—I should probably say raven—hair (probably tresses) and the other day's had honey blond.

When all this was cleared up, I'd give her a reading list. Particularly if she wanted to commingle with erudite Arthur King. Or maybe he'd provide it himself.

I slid onto the orange seat. "What's up? I thought you didn't want me to call anymore."

"I thought so, too." She put her book, open, face down on the gray Formica table. The pink cleavage of the heroine and the ravenlocks's tresses looked incongruous in this matter-of-fact wood and chrome diner. They had seemed more at home in the dusty store.

"But see," she said, "I made myself a new problem, and I wondered if maybe there's some way to help you take over the rest of the story."

The rest of the story. Emily doled out slices of crime as if it were a pie. This to Arthur King, this to you, and I must have said I only wanted a taste.

"Free," she said. "I'm not looking to sell the rest."

"You mean who did it? That's the only piece left."

"I need sweetener." She stood and went to the long back counter. Heads turned. She wore a black turtleneck that touched her chin and the base of her spiky hair and traveled down to her thighs, where it met patterned tights and laced-up boots. She could have modeled, if she could pull free of the store.

"Did Cam ask you out?" I said as she sat back down.

She shook her head, the spiky hair accenting the movement. "Not exactly. He was distracted, in a hurry. But he said he'd see me soon. Meantime, I'm tired of angry phone calls."

"From him?"

She shook her head and waited as two men who'd been sitting across from us in the other half of the booth put a tip on the table and left.

"They say 'let sleeping dogs lie,' things like that, leave messages, and they're angry about the cops knowing now."

"Who's angry? About the cops knowing what?" I'd missed a beat, maybe a whole line of melody.

"Knowing about Serfi. Where he is, what happened to him."

"But why would anybody be angry?"

"Maybe more scared than angry. Afraid I'll say who killed him."

"You know that? They know that?" I felt like a cold war spy. I had no idea about whom I was talking, who the 'they' were, but on we went.

"I think the callers are his friends," she said, "and I think they suspect. I tell them I don't know what they're talking about, like I don't know, either, but they don't believe me. The truth is, I'd like to see it cleared up and over. Cam King is one good catch and he'd like it cleared up and over, too, and then, who knows, maybe then the two of us . . . But I swore I wouldn't tell, and I'm not breaking an oath. So what do I do about that?"

"Let me get this straight. You know who killed Serfi but you promised his friends—"

"No, no. Jimmy Pat's friends."

I tried to make sense of that change, but couldn't, so I plugged on. "Okay, fine, you promised Jimmy Pat's friends you wouldn't tell even though you want it known. That's not a choice. If you know, tell the—"

She shook her head. "I don't think so, and it wasn't Jimmy Pat's friends I promised."

A waitress in a black uniform asked me what I wanted with

such warmth and enthusiasm, I was sure she could grant any wish. I was tempted to ask her to explain what Emily was talking about, but instead, I ordered a hamburger and coffee.

"Is this some kind of test?" I asked Emily when the waitress was gone. "If so, I give up, I lose. You leave a message that I shouldn't bother you any more. Then you call because you want to meet me here. Then—"

"Didn't want my father to hear. He'd never let go of it if he did."

"Okay, fine, but I've come for that talk, and what is it? That you know something you aren't going to tell. Give me a break!"

"The police. That's who I won't tell."

"Why wouldn't you, unless you're the killer?" Now there was an inspired remark. How was she supposed to respond? With a flood of tears and a confession? A maniacal attack on stupid me? Or a freeze-out? "And of course, you couldn't be," I quickly added, "or they—whoever they are—wouldn't be asking you not to tell."

"Like if I'd done it, I would really make sure the cops found the body," she said.

"I wasn't serious." Well, perhaps I was, a bit. I was sure money had been exchanged for the telling, so I wasn't positive as to purity of motives. "One more time. You didn't do it, but you know who did, but you aren't going to tell the police, but you want them to know. Do I have it now?"

She nodded rather sadly.

"May I ask why you won't tell them? The real reason?"

"Because . . . I have my pride."

That again. It was like a slippery possession easily misplaced. Pride was had, shame given, honor lost, face saved, reputation smeared, and always the wrong people concerned with it. Blood sausages and purloined compositions and broken engagements and now, Emily's pride, for reasons of her own, was endangered.

"Pride's a good thing," I said. "But I don't see why yours would be tainted by telling the police who committed a crime as long as you didn't."

She kept glancing at the empty other half of our table, as if, perhaps, invisible eavesdroppers lurked there, and when she spoke, it was in a whisper. "My engagement." I could barely hear her, but I could see that her eyes were suddenly too glittery, filling with tears she blinked back. "They'd know."

Who they? Know what?

"Jimmy Pat was my boyfriend first," Emily said. "After we broke up . . . let's be honest, after he dropped me . . . nothing, nobody . . . well, let's say I kept carrying the torch. I knew what I was doing, but like they say, all's fair in love and war, right?"

The waitress put my coffee and a thick platter in front of me. I busied myself with it, nodding now and then under the theory that if I let Emily talk, her loosely scattered thoughts would find each other like magnetic shavings and form a clearer picture.

"My life," she said. "My life is so . . ." She seemed to plummet into a private reverie. I thought of the dusty store, where the silence was more often broken by her father's commands than by customers. I wondered if that's what she was thinking about, too.

"I used to watch him at night," she said abruptly. "When the store was closed and my father was asleep."

"Watch your father?" What had that to do with anything?

"Sometimes I'd follow him, just be there, just see him. Sometimes him and the guys, sometimes him and Dolores."

"Jimmy Pat, is that who we're talking about?" I said it softly so as not to break her concentration.

Her cheeks were flushed, although I couldn't have said for sure which emotion produced the color. "I can't explain why I did it, what I wanted, except it was something to do."

I waited, studying the mural on the far wall. It depicted a pretty Philadelphia with scenes of the Delaware and a bridge—the Walt Whitman or the Ben Franklin, I couldn't tell—of the Schuylkill's Boathouse Row, and none of murdered Mummers. The clock in the middle of the mural moved forward a notch.

"I knew his routine," Emily said. "He came here around this time Thursdays, so I did, too. He wasn't hard to find, except when he went to the shore. The casinos. Then, I couldn't follow. But when he stayed in town, he played cards, took her out, had a few with the boys or went to the club Tuesday nights. The truth is, he didn't spend much time with Dolores. They were like old marrieds, if you get my meaning. Kind of dull."

185

It's always ironic to hear marriage maligned by those desperately trying to become part of the institution. Everybody wants the happily-ever-after bit but nobody wants to be an old married. Me, too, even though I haven't figured out how that could work.

"Dull doesn't matter, though, if you're a Grassi," Emily said. "She doesn't have to be interesting."

I still had no idea why the Grassis were spoken of with reverence. I wondered if anybody out of the neighborhood was even aware of the family, but here their status was real, a given in the equations of life.

"When he dumped Dolores and went with me, people said it was a shotgun wedding." Her smile was authentically amused this time. "That was funnier than they knew. It was, but not because I was pregnant, which is what they meant."

She was still whispering, barely audible, talking to herself as much as to me.

"They'll see I'm not pregnant, right? Which is why I don't want them to know the truth. I like being one up on Dolores Grassi for once. I'm not going to let her say he was afraid of me again. Her brothers—they act like they're the only ones with pride. They came to me twice now, saying I shamed them and their sister. Well, how about me?"

How about her, indeed. Her pathos was touching, but I held back. Emily said a lot, and I still wasn't sure if all of it was true, or if any of it was the whole truth. It was possible she had tried to sell the Grassis her story, in fact blackmail them, in exchange for keeping their family honor spotless.

"That night," she said, "I had no idea. It was cold and there were flurries. Nobody was on the street. I saw Ted Serfi was with him and I thought maybe they were going to have dinner, but then, it was so fast, I didn't think anything. Like that, they're shouting about money. That was no surprise. There was nothing much else to get mad at Jimmy about, but a person could get plenty mad about the money he owed. Probably to Teddy because he had cash and he was a good kind of guy. We were up near Broad and Washington. I hid, because I was scared. Jimmy's a good-time guy, a laugher. This angry Jimmy, he gave me the creeps. So I only heard the pop, a bad noise, and I thought 'no, please no' because it seemed impossible. And then another pop, and shouting and grunts and when I looked out, Teddy's in the street, not moving, and snow's falling for real, and Jimmy looks like he's dead, too, only standing, staring at the factory. Then he drags and half carries Teddy across all the junk and through a broken window, and in he goes."

Did this make sense, that Jimmy Pat killed Ted Serfi? I tried to think of reasons Emily would have to fabricate a story, but gave up, and she continued with her tale.

"I saw the gun, where he'd dropped it. It was already sprinkled with snow. Whatever blood there'd been was, too. Just the littlest pink marks there. I think maybe Teddy's coat and scarf and all, I think they were soaking up all the blood at first and whatever came out, it dissolved in the new snow, you know? So, anyway, I took the gun."

Two girls of around fourteen slid into the other side of our table. The convention seemed to be to pretend we were separated, not to acknowledge our table-sharers, but it was impossible not to be aware of them.

I put my hand to my mouth and whispered. "You kept the gun?"
Emily nodded.

The girls exploded in laughter. "He ran away soooo fast!" one said, and the other put her head down on the table and pounded with her fist.

"Hid it in the safe in back of the store," Emily said low and quickly, under the cover of the girls' hysteria. "I didn't think the police would find any trail or tracks with the snow. Ted Serfi could have just left town. I called Jimmy that night. Now do you understand? What would people say if they knew what was really meant by a shotgun wedding?"

"So then—so *then*," the girl across from us said, "I ran after him!" They shrieked and doubled over once again.

"You blackmailed him?" I whispered.

Her eyes grew wide. "That's for money. I made a trade. I give silence, he gets me out of that store, gives me a life. All it costs him is inconvenience, telling Dolores."

"You'd marry him even though you knew he murdered his friend?"

"That wasn't the real him." She shook her head, to reinforce her words. "That wasn't Jimmy Pat. That was just a man pushed too far, a man in a bad jam."

"And you'd marry him even though he was in love with somebody else?"

Her eyes sparked with anger. Murder was a mistake, but what I'd suggested was an outrage. "He was engaged to Dolores, but he didn't love her, he loved me. It was just that stupid breakup of ours, saving face. And I wasn't as much of a bargain. Look at her family and look at mine, and that's the truth. She could bail him out of his debts. Probably did. Certainly would. But as luck had it, I was given something to equal things out, because even Grassis can't get you out of a murder rap."

I thought I had it so far. But . . . "Why did you put it in my pocketbook?"

"My reputation," she said. "I have to hold my head up in the neighborhood. I don't care they find out who killed Teddy. I only care they don't find out I witnessed it, what that meant. When Jimmy Pat died, what did I need with it? I wanted it out."

"Thanks a whole lot."

"I swore to Jimmy that I wouldn't tell about it while there was breath in my body. That was our deal. But if *you* wanted to suggest that somebody should ask Mrs. Patricciano if there was a gun like that one around her house after the uncle died, I think the police could tie this all up."

Her features hardened. "So this is how it winds up," she said. "I don't have the gun or the man or the life or the future, so I'm sure as hell not going to lose my last bit of respect, too. It's up to you. You've got the answers. All of them."

It wasn't until we'd paid our bill and gone our separate ways that I realized she'd been wrong. I didn't have all the answers by a long shot, because if Jimmy Pat killed Ted Serfi, but nobody knew that until last night, then the original question remained.

Who killed Jimmy Pat? And why?

Fifteen

"**G**o through that one more time," Mackenzie said, his fork poised over a steaming plate of *fettucine tutto mare*. "And a little more detail this time."

He had to say it loudly, because the restaurant was participating in the great psycho-physics experiment of trying to ascertain how many sound waves can bounce off hard surfaces before diners go crazy. The noise level gave the place atmosphere—the atmosphere of downtown Rome at rush hour.

We were there because it was nearby and reputed to have excellent pasta. Also because Mackenzie turned out to be home and hungry after all. The phone message in my mailbox today had been called in last year, before winter break. Helga was setting new lows for when it was convenient for her to pass on a message.

I had ordered a "garden fresh salad." As opposed, I have to assume, to a salad made of rotting compost. Whence came the mushroom garnish, I was not sure. They chose not to put that on the menu. I twirled a garden-fresh green and speared a basement-grown fungus and spoke again. "I repeat: Ask the Patriccianos about the gun. The word is, it belonged to an uncle. Isn't that enough?"

He speared a shrimp, but gesticulated with the fork instead of putting it in his mouth. "*Whose* word?"

"Pointing seafood at your date is a sign of bad breeding, and I already said I wasn't telling. What does it matter, anyway?"

His eyes rolled ceilingward, seeking divine assistance, but the Lord was dining where it was soundproofed and She could hear Herself think. "You know for a fact, and I should take it on faith, that Jimmy Pat killed Serfi?" he finally asked.

"Not for a fact. But I know he had a major gambling habit, is said to have run up debts he couldn't repay to his friends, of which Ted Serfi was one, and that might be a family gun. Put it together and it spells . . ."

"But you won't say how you know this or why you're sayin' that, am I right?"

"Reliable sources. Can't betray my journalistic confidences." The way I figured, if the police traced the gun to Jimmy Pat's house, they'd glom onto the obvious, and Emily could keep whatever dignity her community would allow. That seemed worth a serious attempt to keep my mouth shut.

Mackenzie leaned across the table. I caught a whiff of his after-shave and I wished we were having a different sort of conversation. I became almost nostalgic for the days when he was injured and disabled. "Do you also know who killed Jimmy Pat, then?" he asked. "An' why?"

"If I did, I'd tell you."

"The way you just told me that? Can you at least say whether the second murder was revenge for his killin' Serfi? An' who did it?"

190

"I don't know. But since nobody even knew Ted Serfi was dead until last night, I don't see how it can be revenge. If somebody had known, wouldn't they have said so, called the cops or the papers long ago?"

"Maybe not until they got theirs on Patricciano," he said.

I thought about slick Arthur King and considered his maneuvers in this new, Machiavellian way. Were they to distort, hide, turn attention away?

"Maybe I'm lucky you don' know more." Mackenzie put down his fork, sighed, and drank wine. "Because when you do know somethin', so does the whole world. What a day."

"Do you assume you are making sense?"

"Of course. You, on the other hand, are not the easiest human being on earth to comprehend."

The chemistry of attraction has a precarious balance of elements. I wondered which aspect of Mackenzie would dissipate first—the captivating part or the insufferable part? How soon might I look across a table and find no trace of sexy, cute, lovable, or smart and instead simply see a professional bully and interrogator?

"Do you believe people who love one another have to trust one another?" he asked.

"Of course. Why?"

"Because you're acting like Mata Hari."

"Gertrude Zelle."

"Who?"

"Her real name. Takes the mystique away, don't you think? Anyway, there's no correlation. Gertrude took secrets. I'm offering you non-secrets."

"Offerin' 'em with one hand held behind your back. Not trustin' me enough to be open with it. All of it."

"I can't explain. It's nothing criminal and nothing about you. Or us. It's . . . a girl thing." I surprised myself with the sisterhood-is-all loyalty I felt for Emily, but there it was, and I wasn't going to tell her secret unless I had no other option. She had so little else going for her, it seemed the least I could do.

"Is everything all right with madame's meal?" the unctuous

waiter asked. His name, he had told us earlier, was Angelo. We had not told him our names. I squelched a keen urge to inform him that everything except the general noise level to which his interruption added was quite fine.

Of course, that wouldn't be true. Things were not fine and not according to Hoyle. Mackenzie and I were sparring, and Angelo had a right to be concerned.

"Fine, fine. Her food's delicious," Mackenzie said, as if he could know that. As if we had once discussed the food. As if I were mute, or non-English speaking. "Hold on there," I protested, but he interrupted me, thereby compounding his intrusions on my autonomy and rights.

"—and to further complicate everything," he said, "I cannot understand why you—"

"And your meal, sir? Is everything all right with it?" No wonder Angelo still hovered nervously. Mackenzie no longer even bothered to lift his fork. At least I was prodding my greens. "If there's any problem whatsoever, the chef and I will be delighted to—"

Once again, Mackenzie exhaled excessively. "It's fine, okay? Absolutely. You did your job excellently!" he said loudly enough to be heard over the din of the room. But he did lift a few strands of fettucine. The waiter beamed at both of us and backed off, all but touching his forelock during his retreat.

I was in no rush to know the end of a sentence that began with "And to further complicate everything, I cannot understand why you . . ." making me sound like a chronic delinquent or mental case. What had happened between us in my absence?

"—would expose yourself that way," Mackenzie said.

Images of flashing some innocent passerby flickered experimentally behind my eyes. Could I have done that and forgotten? Was he telling me I had the beginning of dementia? Or was On the Air right and I had multiple personalities? "When? Where? To whom? What are you talking about?"

"Bad enough to have a shrink make you a radio case study but this . . ." He shook his head in hopeless grief.

I had no appetite now, couldn't bear to see the ruffly, jolly

garden-fresh lettuce leaves, the cellar-fresh mushroom bits lounging on them. I pushed my plate away. The indignation diet. Anticipatory indigestion. This did not bode well for anything except
my waistline.

"You didn't see it?"

"What?"

"Didn't read it?"

"You're making me so—"

"Nobody mentioned it?"

I stood up, fully intending to leave. "I can't stand teasing. Isn't
it obvious I have no idea what you're talking about?"

He pulled a newspaper out of a soft leather pouch that he had
taken to carrying. I didn't like the idea that he had exhibits backing up whatever was making him so angry.

I sat down again and pulled a minuscule piece off the crusty
bread to keep busy. But my mouth was too dry to chew, my
throat unable to swallow. I switched to wine, instead.

"Couldn't help but have my eye caught by a feature article,
signed by one Marv Henneman. The headline reads SCHOOL-
MARM SLEUTH MONITORS MURDERS. Marv has a fondness for
alliteration."

I hoped I was having a bad dream, but Mackenzie read on and I
had a deep suspicion this was for real.

> Imagine, if you will, a situation that sounds like the "high
> concept" idea for a film, or at least for a knockoff of a TV
> drama about a writer who becomes an unlikely and acciden-
> tal sleuth.

"Dear God." A crusty crumb stuck in my throat. I coughed.
Angelo rushed to my side, arms outstretched, ready to perform
CPR, the Heimlich maneuver, or if all that failed, suicide. I shook
my head and downed still more wine while Mackenzie looked at
me thoughtfully.

"He's twisting everything around," I said when I could speak.
"Made it, made me, sound frivolous, phony. A laughingstock."

Mackenzie sorrowfully shook his head and continued:

Amanda Pepper, a thirtyish English teacher at Philly Prep, claims she only wanted to experiment with a second career, that of journalist. For her first topic, she chose the city's venerable Mummers, an eccentric group with a long and interesting history.

She threw herself into her research, interviewing people, visiting clubs as they prepared, gathering personal and group histories. But instead of finding herself in print, Ms. Pepper found herself in hot water. In fact, involved in a murder—or maybe two—and several go-rounds with and questionings by the police.

And what of the story her journalistic sleuthing turned up? What does it say? What does she know? That remains to be seen. At this time, it is still not sold and its contents are known only to its author.

"Talk about purple prose, hack writing! Making things up!"

"Worry less about style and more about content," Mackenzie said.

"Puffery and lies. Anybody can see that! I didn't say I'd uncovered secrets. I said I didn't want to give him the article, and look what he made of that."

"The article," Mackenzie muttered, followed by another of his overly expressive sighs. "Ah, yes. Well, he didn't print our address, guess that's somethin' to be grateful for." Mackenzie's pronunciation was disintegrating again. I seemed to have that effect on him often.

Having said and read his piece, he finally noticed his dinner and with great deliberation, ate the shrimp on his fork. Once it was chewed, he spoke again. "The omission, however, is probably 'cause he didn't know it. How'd it slip by when you told him everythin' else in your life?"

That emerged as *Thomshin whirrs prahly causee dinknowt. Howdislipbah* . . . And so forth. I spoke fluent Mackenziese. If the South ever gets a seat at the U.N., forget journalism. I'll have an exciting career as a simultaneous translator of the crisp-syllable-challenged.

I pleaded my case. "I barely said a word. He bumped into me when I was leaving the police station—which your stupid regulations made me go to again today. He recognized me, realized who I was, knew—unlike the police, obviously—that I should have been teaching at that hour, and made the connection. And then he started in. He made up the girl-sleuth business. All I said was—"

"—that you were writing an article, but why'd you keep sayin' that, given that no matter how you're urged, you never do it?"

He was undergoing a chemical change, his cuteness factor ebbing, obnoxiousness on the rise. This was how endings began.

"The misunderstanding is partly my fault," I admitted.

Instead of wondering what I meant, he nodded instant and hearty agreement, which made me want to throw my mushrooms at him, but it's a pity to waste portobellos. "I thought I could use him to publicize the lawsuit, make the Fields so ashamed of themselves they'd go away. So much for my ability to manipulate the media."

I needed to talk about the suit, about Havermeyer's probable response, about the possible loss of my job, about what I should do. "Why don't we forget about that hack's fantasy? I'm concerned about tomorrow. Havermeyer wants to see me, and I'm afraid—"

Maybe it was the acoustics, but apparently, Mackenzie didn't hear. "I'm afraid for you," he said. "Real worried. The hack made you sound like you know too much. Once and for all, tell me true—do you know who killed Jimmy Pat?"

I shook my head. "No idea. Honestly. Cross my heart and hope to die."

"Not a good expression, given the situation."

"No idea. Honestly."

"Not even a theory? An overheard whispered rumor?"

"Not even that."

He leaned back. "I wish this article made it clear that you don't know squat. It's obvious Henneman wasn't crazy about you. What'd you do to annoy him so much?"

"I didn't tell him why I was at the station. I didn't give him my, ah, article. Then he left a message at school, so there's probably something else I didn't do, but this time it was unintentional."

"What did he want?"

I shrugged. "For me to call him at my earliest convenience. Helga didn't give me the message till three hours later. He'd already have been past his deadline. Maybe if I'd returned his call he wouldn't have been so creative with the facts."

Mackenzie's turn to shrug with cynical disbelief. "If he was going to do a hatchet job, I wish he made you sound like an idiot instead of Amanda Pepper, Ace Detective. This way, whoever killed Jimmy Pat is likely to misconstrue. Believe this. You emerge soundin' like you hold the keys to this thing. I was convinced after I read it, which is why I was so annoyed with the games I thought you were playin'."

It was a relief to belatedly understand his early testiness.

"But I'm not anybody for you to worry about," he went on. "On the other hand, somebody out there does not want those keys he thinks you hold to unlock anythin'. I don' want you to have anything to do with that somebody. Understand why I'm worried?"

I understood. He was on my side. Sometimes I forget to trust that. Force of habit.

"Care about you, tha's all." It took even me awhile to decipher those words which slipped by in a single soft syllable. He cared. Really cared.

The charge in the air dissipated, the miracle of ancient chemistry cleared his features, and the attract-repel factors returned to their original tilt in his favor.

FRIDAY ARRIVED ahead of time. We'd stayed up late trying to pull apart the confusing web of facts and suspicions about the two murders. Pretty much the only result of the effort was excessive fatigue the next morning.

My classic Mustang was not, for all its charm, the most perfect vehicle for a frigid January morn, and my heater never felt that my commute time was worth the effort and energy to rev up and make a difference. With all the whistling air leaks, I might as well have driven the kind of mustang that had a mane and a whinny.

I pulled into my parking spot and sat for a moment, temporarily—I hoped—overwhelmed by the challenges of the day ahead. Looming above all was, of course, the lawsuit. I was about to walk a job-related tightrope, and I wished I had more confidence in my balance and ability to make it to the other side. I wished, in fact, that I knew which other side I wanted to be on.

And of course, there would be the Henneman article repercussions. Last night, there'd been a blather of reactions on the answering machine. My friend Sasha wanted to know why I hadn't asked her to take photographs so the article could be a joint venture. Emily left a cryptic, worried message—I recognized her voice, because she didn't leave her name as she questioned what precisely was in that article. Vincent Devaney left an inarticulate, half-completed message ending in "never mind." The only thing clear was his anxiety about the contents of the mythical article. Billy Obenhauser was much clearer, if not on what I might know, then definitely on my obligation not to withhold whatever it was unless, of course, it might incriminate me.

And that wasn't even the lot of them. Luckily, my mother's subscription copy of the paper hadn't reached her yet, so I was spared that call. But a concerned aunt filled in for her. Shrink Quentin offered reduced-fee post-trauma therapy—free if I'd go on-air with her and discuss it. One former colleague wanted to know if I was leaving teaching because of this new career and if so, was my position open, and an actor I'd dated in college wanted first dibs on the movie version of my story.

People say newspaper readership is down. I say nonsense.

The only heartening message was from my sister. After expressing obligatory horror, outrage, concern about my growing notoriety, and admonitions to leave the city immediately, abandoning my possessions if necessary, her voice softened. "By the way," she said. "I, ah . . . Dr. Reed, On the Air? Quentin? Well, she's no longer . . . well, we won't be seeing her anymore. I was angry about how she used you as a 'true story,' and I could see how she twisted things. And to be honest, Karen said she was annoying her. So, I, ah . . . told her. And when she put up this big fight, saying Karen was seriously damaged, I threatened to tell people she was really a foot doctor."

I laughed out loud hearing that. "Your sister's all right," Mackenzie said. "A little stiff, but all right in the clinch."

I could hear Beth take a deep breath before continuing. "She used me as her true story last night. Called me 'Louisa May'—you like that?—an abusive mother who wants to appear to help her child, but who really subverts . . . oh, you know." And then she giggled. "What a creep!"

And Bea's daughters would be friends still longer. And Karen would be safe from On the Air's meddling. All was semi-well.

Remembering that, I screwed up my courage and willed myself out of the car and into the school. Once upon a time, the only thing I faced, feared, and anticipated at the start of a teaching day was teaching itself, which seemed quite enough, thank you.

I opened the car door, then bent toward the passenger seat to retrieve my pocketbook from the floor where I leave it to make it harder on stoplight muggers. When I straightened up I yelped. The door was still open, but my exit was blocked and I faced a pair of slacks, a winter coat, a man inside them. He had his arms out, up on the convertible top, to block any possible egress.

"Hey!" I shouted. "What's this? Who're—" I was getting tired of the shouting business. Besides, it didn't seem to work.

I craned and looked up at his face. Mostly, I saw flaring nostrils and a chin that needed shaving. "Let me out right now!" I snapped in my most authoritarian voice.

It is an archetypal voice, generally reducing grown men to weepy memories of being tiny and helpless, of having Mommy give them over to a stern teacher replacement.

This time it had no effect. This guy had definitely gotten over the kindergarten blues. "Listen," he said, "whatever you found out—"

I didn't have to ask what he meant. "I didn't! That article—"

"You'll destroy me. What I did was wrong, but a mistake, I swear, a big one, and I'll make it good. You think you know things, you have your high and mighty code of behavior, but you don't, you don't know."

It seemed too late to ask who he was when we were already deep into heated disagreement. Besides, he was impossible to interrupt, although I tried so often that my *but—but*s sounded like an outboard motor.

"You—you live in this comfortable, steady world. A teacher kind of world, but other people—"

I slowly edged my feet more securely in the open door, estimating my skill and limberness, his position, and the odds of success. "Get away from me," I said. "You're making me late."

"You could ruin me, understand? You could destroy me, and for what? Vincent's so scared he got me into—"

Vincent. The connection. The schoolroom fight, the missing funds, the question of whether or not he'd taken them. I had only heard him shouting last time, hadn't recognized the speaking voice or the nostrils.

"Fabian." I tried the remembered name on for size.

"I told him it wasn't like it looked. I wouldn't kill—"

That's who it was and I didn't like him, never had. That first night, over coffee, all I had felt was anger coming off him, anger and dislike of me. "What do you want with me?" My feet were on the door opening. I could have used an old-fashioned running board, but I slowly edged my rear around until I was pretty much facing him.

"Don't act stupid! You know what I want—the article before anybody sees it, before you push me into doing something I don't want to do. I'm at the end of my—"

"No." I was fighting over an article that did not exist. Freedom of the hypothetical press. And the man frightened me. There was something steely and cold at his center. "Don't worry about it. There isn't any—"

"Hand it over or I'll—"

That was it, then. "Don't threaten me—now—last chance, get out of my way!" I looped my bag over my shoulder.

"I swear I'll—"

"*I said don't threaten me!*" I screamed it, I'd been trained to—

but you know, men have a lot of trouble around the issue of listening to women. Including him. So while he sputtered about what he might do to me, I gave up on verbal communication. Instead, I visualized myself as an Olympic gymnast, small, strong, and compact. I pulled my knees toward my chest, then as fast and hard as I could, I swung my feet up and out. Aimed for his manhood, as they say.

And thus did I render my first lesson of the day.

"Oof!" He doubled over. "Jeez, you—why'd you—didn't have to—what is *wrong* with you?" Then he merely groaned.

He was the one with time to contemplate answers. I was late for work and in enough trouble. As he staggered, doubled over, grunting and gasping, I jumped out of the car and ran toward the back door of the school.

"Fabian! Mandy! What the hell is going on? Did you just—I thought I saw you—"

I'd been so intent on going for the gold, doing my personal best, I hadn't even heard him pull up, but now, Vincent stood beside his still-running car in a position that suggested he'd leaped out of it. Its door hung open as he looked from one of us to the other. I don't know why he was astounded. Hadn't he been in a shouting match with the selfsame Fabian earlier this week?

"She—" Fabian shouted, or more accurately, gasped, pointing at me, still doubled over.

"What now?" Vincent asked me.

"Now? *Now?* As if I've—"

"The article, isn't it?" he said. Fabian grunted assent. "Listen, Mandy, stop thinking about yourself all the time. *Your* credits, *your* résumé, *your* income. If you drag our names through the dirt—"

I stared, trying to really see him. He was my professional colleague and, I'd thought, my friend. And I didn't know a thing about him, except that he had a mercurial temper, he'd lied to his wife, lied to the police, and in a definitely unfriendly act, used me as his alibi. This was not good stuff to know.

I didn't know if Vincent Devaney was a killer. I didn't know if Fabian was an embezzler and a threat and a killer. Looking at the two men this morning, I did, however, know that no matter what either or both of them had done, even to each other, they were on the same team and I was an interloper, an intrusive outsider. I don't think Vincent would have rescued me from Fabian if I'd needed him to. He hadn't made a move, just stood there and been testy with me.

I was a threat to both men, because I wasn't one of them, and because of an article that was actually a figment.

But a person who is perceived as a threat is in danger.

That, unfortunately, was no figment at all.

Sixteen

THE Office Witch didn't say "Gotcha!" but she might as well have. She didn't bother hiding her malevolent triumph, either. Caught me as I tried to walk past the office. "Dr. Havermeyer's waiting for you."

"Now?" I was disheveled and trembling from the encounter outside. I wanted to call Mackenzie, tell him about Fabian, get the man off the streets.

Helga nodded, folded her arms over her chest, and gloated. Being summoned to the principal's office had the same effect on me as it would have had twenty years ago. "I was supposed to make an appointment with him this morning for—"

"He's *waiting*. You were supposed to arrange this appointment *for* this morning, but you left in a big hurry, as I recall." She would have made a great prison matron.

I couldn't contemplate, let alone face, Maurice Havermeyer immediately after mad Fabian. Too much terror for one day's dawning. "My homeroom, I have to—"

"We've sent a monitor to take roll and maintain order." She glanced at her watch, making the gesture a condemnation even though I wasn't late and hadn't done anything wrong except misread a poorly worded memo.

I stood tall and refused to be intimidated, or at least to look intimidated. Fabian had rattled me, but after my kickboxing round with him, I was also as cocky as my shaking nervous system allowed. Don't mess with me.

Unless you're Maurice Havermeyer, He Who Authorizes the Paycheck. I took a deep breath, nodded, and went to meet my fate.

It wasn't only He Who I faced. Renata Field and her parents were also in attendance. That's why the meeting had to be now.

The day kept getting better and better. At this rate, I wondered if I'd survive it.

"Miss Pepper, good to see you!" He Who said, as if this were a surprise social gathering. "Have a seat. Of course, all of us here know Renata, but I also believe the rest of you have met Miss Pepper, Renata's English teacher, Mr. and Mrs. Field?"

I hadn't met her parents. They'd waited to make contact until now, when their daughter's negligence was out of control. Nonetheless, we nodded and sat back in our chairs, pretending to have a prior relationship. I, for one, didn't want to go through the motions of introductions, particularly as it might involve something as hypocritical as smiles and handshakes.

"Mizzzz Pepper." A sign of desperation when Havermeyer lengthens my name as a delaying tactic. This is a man who will do anything to say nothing, and when, as now, he's faced with a charged situation, his armory of hot air and euphemisms isn't enough. He needs to drag every syllable through mucky resistance. "As I have already told Mr. and Mrs. Field, and as Renata surely knows, Mizzzz Pepper is one of our most popular teachers. And, I might add, an outstandingly gifted one as well."

Litigation. The way to Havermeyer's heart. Or at least the appearance of a heart. I had suddenly become a Class-A teacher with Maurice as my cheerleading team. I'd have to remember that the next time I was up for a performance review.

"This is therefore quite unusual." He sat behind his enormous desk, leaning back so that his scholastic key—it looked like Phi Beta Kappa, but was not—glinted in the cold, early sunlight. "Unique," he went on, "I might say, in the truest sense of the word. Indeed, this entire, ah, proposed lawsuit, is the first such action against her. Or, I hasten to add, against any of our excellent staff. Gradewise, we have heretofore never been impugned, so you might call this an historic event." He chuckled.

Apparently, the stern-faced Fields did not find any of this amusing. For all I know, they were puzzling over the word *impugned*.

I allowed secondary muscles to relax. Bossman was championing me, defending our record, albeit in typically garbled style.

"You can imagine my consternation and amazement when I first was made aware of your distress," he said, swiveling toward the Fields. They were an unhandsome couple, but compensating for nature's minginess with everything money could buy. He was fit and elegantly coiffed and tailored, and his nails looked as if they'd been buffed. She was all gritted-teeth effort. Hair in a hard, geometric cut, plain features burnished with a practiced hand, workout-enhanced body in a precision-engineered suit. Not to mess with.

And rich.

But I had justice and perhaps Maurice Havermeyer on my side.

"Now, as you have every right to assume, there is a definite set of standards against which our students are measured, and such standards are necessary in order to preserve the integrity of the very idea of education as well as our own school's accreditation," Havermeyer said. "I'm sure that's why you chose this school for your daughter. And within that structure, Miz Pepper's academic standards, I have been assured and have personally observed, are equitable and reasonable."

Renata pouched her lips and emitted an explosion of sneering air. A raspberry, as if we were in a ballpark.

Everyone overlooked, ignored her rudeness. I figured her whole life had been handled that way.

"That is one great part of the reasons," Havermeyer said, "that and her excellent teaching, of course, that we have been so proud to have Miz Pepper as an integral, important part of our staff for these several years."

I felt less comfortable. We'd slithered into the murky realm of the too-effusive. I heard the first hiss in Eden. A "however," large, fat, and lethal, lurked behind his flowery words. The muscles I'd relaxed returned to near-spasm.

"Let's get to the point, Doctor," Mr. Field said with such familiarity and self-assurance that even my earlobes clenched.

"Of course, of course."

"My child's entire future is at stake."

His child sniffed victory and smirked at me.

"I am, of course, aware of your concerns, and, of course, aware of the significance of a student's grade point average."

"Particularly a senior's." Mrs. Field's voice had a razor-edge.

Havermeyer nodded.

I knew I was dead meat.

He cleared his throat, still nodding, then spoke. "All of what I said was by way of making clear that this is why, as soon as this was brought to my attention, I realized there must be some grave perceptual or conceptual error on one or the other of the parties' parts, or perhaps, on both of them. I am, however, more than positive that this is an issue we can resolve here and now, and amicably. After all, the teachers, students, and parents of Philly Prep are a team, all of us working together for the greater good, isn't that so?"

The Fields, my purported teammates, stared blankly. They really didn't get it. Renata wrinkled her brow, giving the impression of one puzzling through what he'd said, and even I nodded once before I stopped myself. The action felt too much like lowering my head to the guillotine blade.

"Excuse me," I said, "but Renata and I have already worked this out. There's no need to involve the legal process. I don't understand why any of this is necessary."

Mrs. Field tilted her head as if I were a ridiculous but interesting specimen. "This is necessary because a C is not a satisfactory working-out," she said, her words slicing through the office. "A C"—she outlined the letter in the air, for fear, I assume, that I had not yet learned the alphabet—"is a mediocre mark, an ordinary, middle-of-the-road mark. My daughter is neither mediocre nor average. A C is not a first-rate, college-level entrance grade, and it will seriously impede and perhaps change the entire course of our child's future."

I waited for Havermeyer to interrupt or redirect her.

"A C is not the sort of grade Fields get," Mr. Field said.

Fields? We were talking about one girl named Renata. Was her poor work now pulling down her entire family name? I imagined the conversations between the Fields and Sally Bianco's mother. Doom, doom, family name ruined, like a bad opera.

Havermeyer did nothing except nod encouragingly to both of Renata's parents.

"We cannot allow one teacher's blind spot, rigidity, and stubbornness to destroy our daughter's future or ours," Mrs. Field said. "We have plans for Renata, dreams that are now seriously threatened." She shook her head. "I will not allow that to happen."

Having delivered her prepared speech, she tapped a long fingernail against the arm of her chair and watched me, a vulture waiting for me to die.

Havermeyer harrumphed. Once, I'd thought that was a sound only comic-book characters made, but the choking, coughing, throat-clearing exhalation that bought time and meant nothing was his favorite word.

I waited for him to say something more about grades, about fairness, standards, about anything, but instead, he looked at me. "Mizzzz Pepper?" he asked.

I had no idea what response he had anticipated, so I murmured a noncommittal "Yes?"

"Do you think there might be some way for us to take another look at Renata's record and recalculate the grade for the semester so as to . . ." Even he couldn't think of a graceful, dignified exit from that sentence. So as to placate her parents? So as to once and for all sell out, lose your last vestige of teacherly pride? So as to keep your job? All of the above?

"She . . . she didn't do her work, not at all."

"You lost it," her mother snapped.

"No, I—"

"My daughter says you lost it! I trust my daughter."

More fool, you, if that's the truth. But I moved on. "The one assignment she did hand in was copied. Plagiarized. Both girls therefore shared the grade, which would have been excellent, had only one of them written it, but was a failing grade of 50 when divided in two. They both knew the policy. So the C—that's not even guaranteed yet. First, Renata has to make up a whole lot of work, and—"

"From what I read in yesterday's paper, you're not exactly committed to the classroom," Mrs. Field said. "It's a career in journalism you're after, isn't it?"

Havermeyer looked in need of major analgesics.

"No," I said, "that was a—I—what that man wrote has nothing to do with my classroom practices. Or the truth."

Mr. Field spoke directly to Dr. Havermeyer. "If what I'm hearing from you and your staff is a *no*, then consider our daughter withdrawn from this school, and speak to our lawyers from this point on." He stood up as he spoke.

"Please. Have a seat. This can be worked through." Havermeyer's voice and entire history made it clear that we weren't going to work this through via the Fields. *I* was going to work this through, i.e. give Renata whatever she, her parents, and my headmaster wanted. Do whatever it took to keep the tuition coming in and prevent a lawsuit.

The air in the room and even the supply stored in my lungs

had been siphoned out. How was I going to live without a job? How was I going to live *with* a job as a performing pet willing to do any trick that pleased the people with the money?

And the world wasn't exactly begging for impractical, dreamy-eyed former lit majors. I'd wind up with the displaced licorice factory workers.

"Miz Pepper?" Havermeyer let the real question hang unsaid.

"I—I—" I couldn't frame a sentence, couldn't agree with this bargain with the devil and couldn't afford to refuse it. I was working hard to avoid crying with anger and frustration. Mrs. Field tapped the wooden arm of her chair. Mr. Field smoothed the crease in his slacks. Renata considered the wall, studied it.

Havermeyer, however, looked concerned. It is possible that he noticed that I was on the verge of either hysteria or catatonia. "Perhaps you'd like time, Miz Pepper, to work out the way we can best handle this?"

I nodded.

"Then this will, ah, be handled?" Mr. Field asked.

"Of course, of course. Didn't I say so all along?"

"She's my child, after all," Mrs. Field said. "We only want the best for her. A parent's duty, after all. An A would certainly help on her application form."

I had heartburn without having eaten anything. "My class," I said. "Have to get to . . . first period's about to . . ."

Havermeyer nodded. "Of course. Far be it from me to hinder a dedicated teacher from fulfilling her obligations."

"Thank you for seeing to this," Mr. Field said to Havermeyer. "We appreciate your taking the time."

"It's my pleasure and obligation," my leader said.

I nodded by way of farewell and bolted out of there. Helga barked my name. "Messages. You have more. You're supposed to pick them up first thing each morning, as you should remember."

My mail box was, indeed, loaded. Mackenzie had been sarcastically impressed that the article spared mention of my address, but of course, it said where I taught, so the end result was the same. Anybody could find me.

This time I heard from Andrée Jansheski, the hairdresser, who hoped she hadn't said anything out of line, and reminded me that her salon was not a place of gossip, and what was it that I was planning to put in my article, anyway, and if I still wanted a haircut, it'd be on the house.

And from a girl I went to junior high with who thought I would have been married and have changed my name by now, or was I staying with the maiden name for feminist reasons, but anyway, she was collecting for a violent-crime victim's charity and thought I might want to donate memorabilia.

"I really *wish*," Helga began.

I nodded. "I'll just bet you do." I walked out of the office, still flipping through pink slips. The one that caught my attention said only, "Grassi wants to talk."

I called Dolores at lunchtime. "Yeah?" she asked. "What?"

"I don't know. You called me."

"Me? Oh, that. I was blue, so Stephen called for me. I nearly forgot."

That family was an odd organism, treating Dolores like an eggshell-thin piece of porcelain when she seemed anything but. When last seen, she hadn't seemed too debilitated to lift a phone. In fact, she'd been swaggering and royally pissed with me and Emily Semow both. And the time before that, she'd seemed pretty much perked up by the idea that Vincent Devaney still carried a torch for her.

I envisioned that torch as real, not metaphorical, and pictured Vincent as an Olympic runner with the flaming object in his hand, racing for Dolores, trying to pass the torch on New Year's Day. I had to think more about that.

"About the message," I prompted. "You wanted to say . . . ?" I waited. Nothing. "Do you want to come here, to the school, and talk to me?"

"Your school?" I heard a shudder. "I really don't feel up to travel."

As if I were phoning from Kuala Lumpur, instead of two handfuls of city streets away. She was playing Baby Grassi. "Well, then?" I asked. "You want to talk now?"

"I, ah . . ." I thought I heard her say "that teacher" to someone, but her hand was over the mouthpiece of the phone and her words were muffled. "Okay," she said when she returned. "I wanted to tell you that I hope you're not saying anything in your article that would be . . . embarrassing. No, *wrong*. My family has suffered enough with the talk going around."

"That is certainly not my intent," I said.

"Then, you aren't going to say anything about my engagement?"

"Why would I? I've said it a hundred—I'm not writing about you or any specific Mummers."

The awful thing is, the more I had to protest this very point, the more interesting Jimmy Pat's life and death became. He'd lived and died a Mummer. Born into the tradition, a neighborhood boy, gambled with and borrowed from other Mummers. Fought with Fabian over Mummer embezzlement. His friendship with Vincent was twined around the Mummers, and Vincent's alibi was locked into parade behavior. He'd make a great symbol to hang the article on. I felt excited about the possibilities of the article for the very first time, and I could see a shape to it.

"Because it isn't true," Dolores said. I had trouble remembering to what she referred. "You've been with Emily so much maybe you think . . . but it just plain isn't true. Jimmy Pat and me, we'd have been married next week."

I could still hear male rumbling in the background. "Jimmy Pat never would've shamed me and my family that way. To call off a wedding after everybody's invited, everything is done? Because there's suddenly somebody else? That's impossible. Worse even than leaving a girl at the altar. He wouldn't do it." Her voice lowered. "He wouldn't *dare* to do it."

My mind spun with the possibilities of a feature about him, but that didn't mean I'd have to touch on Dolores's tender pride. Maybe.

"Because if you printed anything like that, it would be . . ." I could almost feel her hand cover the mouthpiece for a moment. Then she returned, ". . . slander. Libel. One of those. I would sue."

Goodie. I could have dueling lawsuits and wind up not only unemployed in my real profession, but also in one that was completely imaginary.

"Don't drag my name in the dirt," Dolores said. "I know journalists get weird about sources and things like that. I watch TV, I know about the ethics thing. Just don't. It wouldn't be good for me. Or for you."

"What do you mean?" I said softly.

"What does it sound like I mean?" And she hung up.

Had I just been threatened, or had she simply meant it would defame her supposed honor and do me no good to be sued for libel?

I mused over this, one eye on the frosty door pane, deciding whether to brave the outside for quality sustenance or to simply rehydrate one of the instant-soup tubs stashed in my desk drawer. And while I peered outside and pondered, Vincent Devaney came down the stairs.

For obvious reasons, our relationship had grown strained, and we both sighed at the same moment. And then there was nothing to do but attempt a smile. Assuming his innocence, and I so wanted to, time would cure the impasse if we kept our balance during it.

"Sorry about that business with Fabian this morning," he said. "He's a little on the edge." He nodded in the direction of the lunchroom.

Fabian wasn't on the edge. He was in free fall without a net. Vincent was much too forgiving of his clubmate's behavior, and that made me still more leery of my co-worker. I also hadn't retrieved the soup, but I walked with him because I wanted to talk about this morning. About lots of things, in fact.

"He's crazy," I said. "And dangerous. He admits taking money, and he's terrified somebody's going to tell the cops, and Jimmy Pat knew about it."

"You think Fabian?" Vincent said.

I didn't commit, but I tilted my head a bit so as to suggest that I surely wasn't ruling that out.

"You're not going to do something dumb now, are you?" Vincent asked.

I shook my head. "I don't want anything to do with a murderer, if that's what you mean."

"Ah, he wouldn't . . . Fabian's loud, but . . ."

"You guys really stick together, don't you? Everybody's angry with one another—but protecting one another, too."

"Like family, I guess," he said. "You fight, you make up, you say things, but in the end, you're one thing, and you stick together. Take care of each other."

"Well, somebody took care of Jimmy Pat, all right."

We walked in silence. "I'm going to the club tonight," he said. "There's stuff to take apart, store, you know. Fabian'll be there, most likely. Maybe he'll say something, I'll know more."

"And then what'll you do?"

Again he said nothing. Didn't matter. I knew the answer. You didn't turn on family. Unless, of course, it was your neck or theirs.

"Any, ah, news?" Vincent finally asked.

I shook my head. "And that business in the paper about my article? It's rank nonsense. I haven't started writing yet."

Vincent looked overly grateful.

"And if—when—I do, I won't put anything in about you, what you told me. The Dolores stuff. You know that, don't you?"

"I think that, but you never know what's going to turn up in the press."

I thought of what the reporter yesterday had written and nodded. "But there is something I'd love to know," I said. "For my own curiosity, not the article."

"So this'd be off the record?"

"Sure." Where was that record? When had I become Brenda Starr, and what did this say about how we judge people? Was it that easy to create a persona? I say I'm something and *voilà*! I am? "Off the record," I said in a saucy journalistic tone. "Look—no tape recorder, no notebook." No reporter, if he had any common sense left.

His turn to nod, giving me permission to ask away.

"How did you find out that Dolores wanted to see you the day of the parade?"

First he looked surprised, then he frowned in concentration, shaking his head. "I don't remember."

"Did she phone?"

He frowned some more. "No," he finally said with an air of discovery. "She wrote."

"To your house?"

"To the club, around a week before the parade."

"A letter with a stamp?"

"Why? What kind of question is that? I don't . . . yeah. Sure. It must have. It was a Christmas card, actually, a Season's Greetings."

"You said she wrote."

He nodded. "On the card, not separate."

"You remember what it said?"

We were near the lunchroom, but we paused at its door for more privacy. " 'Two o'clock, January first, my corner.' That's what it said."

"My corner?"

"Hers. I knew what she meant. And then it said, 'Please. Important.' And then, *D*, with a heart around it." He sighed. "I knew she was going through something bad. This was after I saw her crying that day, you know? I mean . . . I was her . . . old friend." He apparently no longer saw himself as her Romeo, and it seemed to diminish him. The possibilities in his life had narrowed since last we'd talked about Dolores and her summons.

"I assume this message was in her handwriting." We went into the faculty lunchroom and spoke in low tones as I turned the heat on under the kettle.

He shrugged. "Sure. Been awhile since I'd seen it. A little more grown-up now, I thought. Besides, you could tell she was upset. It was a little wiggly, like she was nervous, know what I mean? Green ink."

"But her writing, correct?"

"What are you getting at? I think so. But it's not like we used to write letters. In high school, if she sent me a card, it always had a heart around a *D*. So that was her signature, sure." He retrieved a paper bag from the refrigerator and unwrapped a sandwich. "Why?"

"Just wondering." The kettle shrieked, and I had to run upstairs for the soup-stuff.

I found the cardboard containers and chose corn chowder, closed the drawer on the remaining tub, and once again left the room. Not a memorable lunch, but it would get me through the day.

My path was blocked by Sally Bianco. "Did you read it yet?" she asked. "My essay?"

I hadn't. "I, ah, skimmed it. I'm looking forward to a closer read tonight."

"I'm so nervous you won't like it. My mother, she said my ideas about honor, like you asked for, were tarnished."

Her mother sounded like the Fifth Horseman of the Apocalypse. "Oh, please. You have honor aplenty. You've atoned enough, been punished sufficiently for your sins. Let go of it. I have." This was a blatant lie. I was being sued, pressured, possibly endangered by the aftereffects of her fall from grace.

"My mother says if you lose your honor, you lose—"

"I'm sure she means well, and she's raising an honorable daughter, but you both have to lighten up a little. Honor is . . . honor is, well . . ." Honor was getting tedious, to tell the truth. Honor was everywhere, pulled on as everybody's favorite cloak, excuse, disguise. I'd heard too much about it.

"Honor is who you *are*," Sally said. "My moth—well, that's what I think, too. Honor is what you can't give up without losing a part of yourself. That's why I wrote that in the essay."

Her words bounced off the nearby marble steps, the high ceilings, the long corridor, and boomeranged into my center, where they echoed for quite a while.

I looked at the girl. She was smug, she was brainwashed, she was anachronistic, she was going to grow up to be the hope of the planet or somebody's insufferable next-door neighbor. Maybe both.

But she was right.

"Where's Renata?" I asked.

"She said she'd taken care of it. I thought it was all settled."

"It isn't smart to trust her opinions. And too bad, then," I said. "A C is better than an F. And by the way, I like your definition of honor. Tell your mother." I marched down the stairs, bearing my corn chowder tub like a beacon as I pushed open the door to the office.

Helga looked startled.

No wonder. I was smiling. I was elated. I was *right*.

Thanks to the barely sufferable Sally and her intolerably rigid mother, I had my honor back. "Helga? Please get a message through to Mr. and Mrs. Field and Renata. And a copy to Dr. Havermeyer, too."

She pursed her lips and took out a pad.

"It's simple," I said. "Short. Three words. And they are: 'So sue me.' "

And with that, I swiveled around, propelled by the forces of might and right, and I made my exit.

I would miss this place. But it wasn't a vital organ being amputated. It was something I could survive losing. Unlike my honor.

Ask Sally Bianco.

Seventeen

"$$S$$ INCE when do we celebrate impending unemployment?" I nonetheless clicked my champagne glass against his.

"That isn't it at all."

Mackenzie and I were burning up whatever resources we had left in an old-fashioned, unchic restaurant near South Street. Its food was solid and without theme, its room starkly decorated, but soundproofed. Plus, a jazz combo played standards in the background as we toasted each other. "This is Sid's memorial service," he said.

"Who?"

"Your mother's neighbor's cat."

"Ah, yes. Allyn Beth Landau, M.D. I owe her a sympathy card."

"Your mother called."

"About the card?"

He shook his head.

"But there weren't any messages. I checked."

"We spoke in real time, on the phone, and she updated me on the saga."

"Okay, when last I tuned in, the poor cat was cremated, his ashes coveted by the cat-sitter, and his brokenhearted owner flying home to recover them. Did she succeed?"

Mackenzie shook his head and chewed on a salad green. "It appears that Violet, still afraid she'd be forced to divvy his ashes, took them and flew the coop. When Dr. Allyn got home, Violet and Sid's remains were at large, address unknown."

"Sad."

"It grows sadder still. Allyn Beth opened the paper the next day and saw a news story. Seems young Violet got off a train in North Carolina carrying her precious box of Sid, and she was robbed. Her suitcase, her pocketbook, and worst of all, the poor cat's remains. She begged the thieves to leave that, but they thought Sid was cocaine." He lifted his champagne glass. "Sid is truly free at last. May he rest in peace, wherever that is."

I hoped he wasn't up a robber's nasal passages. Then Mackenzie raised his glass again. "And to Amanda, as well, because she's intact and we know where she is and we're celebrating her return from limbo."

I'd drink to that, for sure. "I survived Renata-fever. That waffling and uncertainty was like losing a chunk of myself, the way Sally said."

"Out of the mouths of babes."

"How do you know she's a babe?"

He ignored that. "Now if I could get closure, too, we'd go for vintage champagne."

The gun Emily put into my pocketbook had, indeed, turned out to have once been Uncle Lou Patricciano's, passed on to his favorite nephew. Circumstantial, but Jimmy Patricciano was assumed to have killed Ted Serfi, and that case was considered closed.

That didn't answer the looming question of who had then killed Jimmy Pat, and it annoyed the hell out of Mackenzie, who was positive the murders were related, and therefore both should be tidily cleared up by now.

I didn't see the connection. Jimmy Pat was involved in both, true, as was wrongly placed money. But given that Jimmy was the killer on one, the corpse on the other, that the money was owed on the one hand and stolen on the other, the linkage dribbled down to nothing. Apples and oranges.

It also annoyed Mackenzie that his pet suspects had fallen by the wayside, one by one. He constantly double-checked his A-list's eligibility. It was becoming a litany. "Arthur King," he said now.

"Wanted to clear his name," I finished for him. "His sausages' name."

"Emily—"

"Had every reason to keep Jimmy alive."

"Dolores—"

"Little Dolores, the darling of the Grassis?" I was pleased that her poor-me appearance hadn't bamboozled him.

"She'd been dumped, shamed, duped, disgraced."

"So you think she knew."

"Full well."

"That was probably what Vincent saw—he claimed she was crying, a few days or a week before the parade, that her brother said she was going through a bad time."

"Therefore, why not do the cad in? She'd have more status in the community as his grieving fiancée than as his stranded-at-the-altar, egg-in-her-face dumpee. Only one flaw—how could she do it, get into the middle of the parade? Jimmy was in that massive suit—he never left the route the way Devaney did. Besides, she was blocks away at City Hall, on the bleachers at the judges' stand, waiting to see her brothers and Jimmy Pat. Her mother was beside her, neighbors behind her."

"You still think it was Vincent, don't you?" I said softly.

He shrugged. "There's the Dolores connection. The lifelong competition."

"Fabian," I said. "Fabian, Fabian." And I returned to this morning's scare. "He's a hotheaded crook. He had opportunity and motive, and he's got the ugly personality to do it. Why keep looking for a Ted Serfi connection? Out of real fear of exposure and disgrace, loss of everything he holds dear, including his place in his club, if not prison, Fabian did Jimmy in. Don't you see?"

I could discuss Fabian logically, but inside, my autonomic nervous system ranted. I could pump myself up and think of the encounter as my kung fu debut, but my intestines and heart knew that my escape was based more on Fabian's early-morning stupidity than on my cleverness or agility. If he'd been quicker or had more smarts and less smugness, he could have done whatever he wanted to and with me.

I poked at my Caesar salad, trying to think of ways in which I could better protect myself in the future. Mackenzie worried out loud about how safe my school's parking area was.

"Doesn't matter," I said. "I'll be booted out of there soon enough." I wondered whether I should bother marking the tenth graders' compositions. Trying to improve student writing often equated trying to tune up their thinking, a task that Sisyphus would have quit. What a waste of effort to go at it again if I were about to be kicked out.

"He hasn't put back the money, am I right?"

"Who?" My mind was still on the tenth graders who were the cognitive equivalent of illiterate. They could write, but not make sense. Given that handicap, they had few career options and were probably doomed to become lawyers.

"Fabian. What else were we talking about?"

Wasn't worth describing my mental meanderings. "He said he was going to pay it back, not that he had."

"Did he say how? Didn't you tell me two guys took out mortgages to pay for the costumes?"

"Suits. Don't call them costumes."

"Doesn't he owe them?"

"Indirectly. They don't know where the money went. Not yet.

If they can get additional funds together, they're going to hire an accountant to do an audit. But Vincent said—"

"You know what I hope he said? That he did it and that the case is now closed. It would make it so tidy."

"Too bad." The waiter silently put down my grilled salmon and Mackenzie's pork chops. He didn't tell us his name, he didn't hover, and I thought I might adopt him. "What Vincent said was that they're taking apart their suits tonight. See, the Fancies are allowed to reuse them, or parts of them. String Bands have to be all new from the undergarments out . . ."

My beleaguered buddy had long since O.D.'d on Mummer lore. His eyes were glazed, his attention elsewhere. If I didn't stop, he'd remind me of my phantom article, the reason I had for collecting that data.

For the rest of the meal, I was mum about Mummers and death. Amazing, but when you gave it a real try, there were one or two other topics available.

THE WEATHER had lightened up. It was still cold, but dry and windless, and the sky was filled with stars. We walked around the corner to South Street and ordered frozen yogurt for dessert, then negated whatever healthy points we gained through that by topping it with fudge. "Hot fudge—food for a cold winter's night," Mackenzie explained.

We sat in the shop, its windows steamy and comforting, and I was almost able to believe that the entire evening was going to be like this, lazy, fluid, and open-ended with Mackenzie truly off duty and all mine.

Until he said, "Here's the thing."

When spoken by that man, *the thing* seldom signals lazy times or laissez-faire. I spooned up the last of my hot fudge sauce and waited.

"I'd like to visit, given that he'll be there."

He. There. Visit. Fill in the blanks.

"I don't like anybody roughing you up, and I want to know more about the money connection."

Fabian.

"Do you realize he's the only one with the temperament, the opportunity, and a solid motive?"

Could it be I realized that because I'd expressed it an hour ago? Maybe we'd been together too long if we no longer could differentiate between who thought or said what. On the other hand, maybe it wasn't supposed to matter under whose name each idea was registered.

"If you're finished with your yogurt, I'll drop you off," Mackenzie said.

Now there was an idea I hadn't originated. It was an idea that stunk. "Why?" I asked. "Are you expecting mayhem?"

"Doubt it."

"Then let me come along."

He shook his head. "That's unprofessional, hokey, like I'm bringing proof of what I'm saying. I'll drop you off at home."

"Home is the wrong direction."

He shrugged.

"We're in the neighborhood already."

Another so-what shrug.

"You think you'll be long?"

"Don't intend to be. Doin' it now because it seems less intrusive than going to his job or home. After all, one of their own was killed. It's not odd that I'd want to look around again, ask more questions about how they run the place, things like that. See where it takes me."

"Then how about if I keep you company? I won't get in your way." I hated the idea of being counted out, dumped off for another solo evening by the hearth.

"You're not going to have an attack of heroics?"

"Puh-lease! Don't act as if I have a compulsion to play cops and robbers. Maybe I'm about to be fired, but meantime, I'm a teacher. I don't ever want to see Fabian again, let alone have anything to do with him. It's the end of a hard week and I want to be with you, that's all. I *am* with you and my number-one wish would be that you would put off detecting for another day. But if not, then if you take me along, you might be more apt to wind it up quickly and get back to me."

"How can I resist? Flattery will get you everywhere, even South Philly."

THE CLUB was housed on Two Street, behind and above a vacant former dress shop. Basically, the quarters were one large all-purpose room with storage in back, a bar along one side, and a dazzling photographic display of what was worn in parades past on the walls. Once Vincent had recovered from his surprise at seeing Mackenzie and me, and once he had realized that despite a penchant for privacy, a club with a murdered member would be wise to let in a homicide detective, he'd explained that the room was used for dances and other fund-raisers and when not in such use, for sewing and planning and general hanging out. They stored their larger creations in rented garages nearby and, as long as the dress shop was vacant, downstairs as well.

Unlike the String Bands, whose uniforms were most often sewn and designed by professionals, these men—with help from wives—stitched their suits and built their frames and headpieces. Tonight was a careful first salvaging of this year's garb. A suit could have a hundred and fifty pattern pieces, Vincent explained. Feathers were expensive, as were the fabrics. You saved and recycled what you could.

Only a small portion of the members, about twelve men, sat at tables, carefully ripping stitches from strips that shimmered, glittered, and gleamed while they joked and idly talked. Tuesday night was their regular meeting. This was optional, Vincent said.

Among the dozen, I recognized Fabian, who glared at me, and Stephen Grassi, who always looked like the tragedy mask of drama, along with a freckled redhead to whom I'd once been introduced but whose name I couldn't remember. He remembered me, however. "Look who's here," he said. "The writer-lady. The one's gonna make our club famous."

I was too tired of repeating my protests, too tired to correct anyone on that same point.

I could almost hear the click of eyeballs as the men glanced from me to Mackenzie and back as he made conversation. I decided I should become less conspicuous and go where testosterone was not at flood level. I murmured that I'd wait in the car. Mackenzie seemed relieved.

I went downstairs, but momentarily detoured into the erstwhile dress shop, now eerie with robes and gigantic headpieces of parades past hanging from hooks on the wall. Some looked cannibalized, half-gone, or conspicuously lacking trim, but what was left glowed.

Outside, the street was almost monochromatic, subtle shades of brick and flickering TV lights through windows providing the palette. But inside, even in the dim light reflected from the street, the finery twinkled and gleamed emerald and amethyst, silver and coral. In one corner sat a black and silver helmet surrounded by spikes of feather-backed sequins. Next to it, a yellow-gold and mirrored-petal daisy that must have been six feet high. I tried to lift it, to try it on, but it was too heavy and I was afraid of hurting it, or myself.

But in touching it, I again sensed the wonder of becoming something splendid, eye- and mind-boggling one day a year. One day, won by fifty-two weeks of labor. It seemed like the short-lived and finite reward given in a fairy tale. One day to become your own fantasy, grotesque beauty, anything. One day to provoke open-mouthed admiration, be a hero, the symbol of pride.

And then, back to the pumpkin coach. To workingman's uniforms and time clocks, blue collars, dark wools, and work boots. But that one day of golden slippers was so resplendent, it was well worth it.

Which made Fabian's embezzlement, which put everyone in jeopardy, even worse.

I left the storage room and made my exit to the street, my hand searching for car keys. Pocketbook Braille is a female secondary sex trait, but tonight, I was unable to read the bag's contents. Twice I pulled out mouth spray in lieu of keys, once a string of paperclips.

I gave up and looked the amateur's way, with my eyes. Still no keys. I opened the bag all the way and tried excavation instead, clearing the rubble by putting items on the car's hood. I moved quickly and kept my wallet inside the bag, even though this was not a dangerous street and no one was around.

I removed flotsam. My emergency stuck-in-a-line book of short stories; a folding hairbrush; a plastic container of mints; the small can of hair spray I lugged all over and had used only to immobilize a yellowjacket trying to carpool with me; five lipsticks; countless pens; two matchbooks. I hadn't smoked in well over a year, but matchbooks were how I remembered good restaurants. At home, I tossed them into a large bowl. Rooting through it was like having a dining-out Rolodex.

I removed the ubiquitous packet of fraying three-by-fives, neatly wrapped in a rubber band. A rupturing audiocassette. A container of floss and a still-wrapped toothbrush from my last visit to the dentist. My roll book.

No keys. Even with the bag half-empty, I could neither see, nor hear, nor touch their comforting metal. Mackenzie must have used mine and automatically put them in his pocket when we parked.

Keyless, generic urban discomfort took over. I felt exposed, a city turtle soft and vulnerable without a shell of dwelling or car to protect me from the night.

Be brave, I counseled myself. I had already faced down the Fields and The System, and Mackenzie was taking care of Fabian.

That should have made me calmer than it did. There was something wrong there, something incomplete I wished I could identify.

It was stupid to stay out here. I'd have to go back in and be the intrusion I had promised not to be. I put the paperback and my roll book back in the bag—it didn't make sense to call it a pocketbook, since the only pocket it would fit was a marsupial's. Whatever its label, it now seemed a catalogue of the pieces of my life. I wasn't yet a bag lady, but I definitely was the lady of the bag. The reader, the teacher, the female vain enough to tote five lipsticks. And the three-by-fives. What part of me were they? The eternal wanna-be? The goof-off? She who teaches because she can't do? What would I tell my journalism class?

What was it that so nagged at me? It almost had to do with

Sally Bianco and her code of honor, almost had to do with Fabian, with something wrong.

And then the thought was displaced as the cards and the bag were ripped away from me, nearly dislocating my arm.

Mugged!

Scream!

But all sound was stuck somewhere below my neck. Nothing but windy silence came out. And terror. My attacker loomed over me, enormous, monstrously so—eight feet, nine feet tall—and huge-headed. I tried to back off—but the car was behind me, blocking me, and I pressed against it, one hand on the hood where the pitiable droppings of my life lay, the other on the door handle—the locked door handle.

He—it—had my purse, my wallet—what else?

I looked at it again—and this time, I placed the enormous head. The silver and black helmet, the spikes and the feathers. I'd just seen it inside on the floor.

I found my voice. It was hard to take a Mummer mugger, even one who'd taken my purse, altogether seriously. "Who are you?" I demanded.

Silence.

Fabian. Who else? Furious, as always. Recouping his losses. But I was better off, safer, if he didn't think I'd recognized him.

Except. I still couldn't finish the idea. "You have what you want, now get out of my way." Maybe I could bolt for the door and get it open and scream before he'd tackle me. If he listened to me and got out of my way.

I studied his running shoes, trying to remember if I'd seen them before. Of course I had, on ads, a million times. This was a ridiculous waste of time, and I knew it as I was doing it. I studied the bottom lip, the semi-visible chinline below the helmet. I tried and failed to remember what color eyes Fabian had, not that I could see through the mask's eye slits.

Except.

"Didn't want to have to do this." I didn't recognize anything about the voice except crazed anger. He moved closer. "You should have quit."

Except! Never in this lifetime would Mackenzie have let Fabian out of his sight!

My hand searched the hood of my car. Surely I had taken something out that could become a weapon. Why, this one time, didn't I have a file or scissors or a can opener—anything!—those keys would have been my weapon, a set of brass knuckles, a gouge. Instead, my fingers touched my hairbrush with its rounded plastic-tipped bristles and I nearly wept. I moved on to the hair spray. Great. His eyes were too protected for me to try to temporarily blind him with it.

He tossed my bag toward the building, reached behind him as if tucking in a shirttail, and brought back a gun. A bigger, nastier gun than the one that had been in my bag.

"Help!" I shouted. Somebody had to hear, didn't they?

"Shut up." He cocked the gun.

I could hear TVs through closed windows, and I knew those people could hear nothing else.

My searching fingers were on automatic, not giving up despite the futility of their hunt, despite my mind's running around and around on its own track—who was this? Because I knew, at some place in me, I knew, and I had for a while.

Except I couldn't remember.

I touched a loose lipstick, a few packets of artificial sweetener, then a matchbook. I squeezed it in farewell. I'd never eat there or anywhere again, and the waiters had been so quiet and polite!

My last act on earth was going to be crying.

But no. I was brave, I was woman. I had honor, thanks to Sally. And that was the part you couldn't lose. That was you.

"Did you sell it?" he demanded.

"It?"

"It's not sold?"

I shook my head.

He nodded, slowly, his enormous helmet bobbing up and down. I had pleased him.

"Where is it? In your bag?" He waved at the pavement behind him without turning his head. He gesticulated a lot, emphasizing his points, his bewildering questions with his hands, one of which, unfortunately, held a gun. I didn't know much about firearms, but he didn't seem in control of his. The gun could go off with any of his angry sentences. It could go off by mistake. Maybe he wanted to terrorize, not kill me. If so, he was succeeding. "Where is it?" he demanded again.

The article. He wanted to know if I'd sold it. The freckled one had said something upstairs and I'd let it ride. "Listen, there is no article, never will be." The sentence made me oddly sad, ridiculous given my current situation. "I have notes, that's all. Those, there on the pavement, see them?" They looked pitiable, multicolored cards in their rubber-band halter. That's all there was. Nothing.

"You're right—there isn't ever going to be an article, because you aren't going to be around to put us on display for laughs."

"I was never going to write about you!" The *writing*, that was it, the thing I knew I knew but couldn't remember. The writing! Oh, God, I knew who—"Don't be stupid," I said. "Don't make it worse. You can—"

"Shut up!"

My fingers gripped the matchbook.

And his fingers grabbed it from me. "Only that, only those cards, but it'll never be because I'll burn them!" He backed up a step, still aiming the gun at me, and flipped up the matchbook cover. "Burn every one of them!"

He bent down a match and lit it with a flick of his thumb, that one-handed macho act I never conquered, even when I smoked. He held the matchbook up like a torch, while he bent to lift the index cards.

The torch. I thought of Vincent and the torch he carried for Dolores. Her note. The writing. His mission during the parade. I thought of Vincent and school.

School, that place where I soon wouldn't have a job. Because of Renata. I thought of my soon-to-be-former students. Of Sally. Of Badluck Dooney Scott, the mad little scientist. By the time he recovered, I'd be gone. I hadn't realized how much that mattered.

Dooney, I thought. Dooney Scott. And a child shall lead you.

I had to pay attention, because one chance was all I was going to get.

"I'm not sorry," the masked man was saying, talking faster and faster. "He deserved it. No respect for—" The index cards were too bulky to ignite as quickly as he must have intended. "Damn!" he shouted as the match singed his finger. He blew on it and promptly lit another.

My chance. My one chance. I grabbed the hair spray and aimed it at the match's flame.

And it worked. Dooney's experiment worked. Those warnings on cans were true. They were indeed dangerous near flame. The entire arc of hair spray ignited, and I stood like a long-distance welder, my flamethrower burning all the way from me to him. Bless you, Dooney. I aimed for the headpiece.

The man in the mask screamed.

As well he might because he was on fire—the lowest feather of his headpiece catching a spark and flaring, lighting the cardboard inner support of the sequined masterpiece. A lethal halo formed around him.

He screamed again, louder, and dropped the gun, which went off with a shockingly loud sound. The noise made me scream, too, and when I turned, I saw the right front tire of my car exhale and deflate.

The kids had told me that Dooney's can exploded in his hand after he released pressure on the nozzle. The flame had been sucked back inside. Let that be a lesson. I couldn't let go of my nozzle.

Not let go and hold on, that was. "Sorry!" I screamed as I tossed the flaming canister in the direction of his feet.

It exploded with fiery noise and light.

The man screamed even more and while he was so occupied, I ran to the gun, stepped on it, then carefully bent to retrieve it, fighting my revulsion at touching such a thing.

My attacker danced, shrieked incoherently, and pulled at his headpiece, now a circle of flaming feathers. I knew he'd get it off—he'd gotten it on quickly enough, hadn't he? "If you'd calm down," I said. "Calm down!"

He didn't.

I pointed the gun at him, waiting.

And the door to the club opened and men poured out, all of them making *whazzis* noises, shouting at the sight of me with the gun, then even more at the sight of the man in the helmet. They seemed hordes, filling up the sidewalk, much more than the dozen who'd been up there. The eleven who would have been left.

And Mackenzie at the front of them, rushing to me. "You all right?" he shouted before he was even near me. "Heard a shot, an explosion—what the—"

"I got him," I said. "This is who killed Jimmy Pat."

"No," Mackenzie said. "It's—"

With a last yank, the man pulled free of his flaming helmet and dropped it to the pavement, gasped, and doubled over.

"He was trying to burn my note cards," I said. And inadvertently, was about to succeed, as what was left of the headpiece landed directly on them.

To my amazement, Mackenzie ran over and stomped the little pyre, then gingerly lifted it. The cards looked charred around the edges, but mostly intact.

Front doors opened up and down the street. People, women pulling on sweaters, came down their front steps.

"Ruined the headpiece," somebody murmured sadly.

"For the love of—" Mackenzie's mouth hung open. *"You?"*

Stephen Grassi, gasping and pale, stood upright with difficulty. His eyes seemed wild and inflamed, either from the smoke of his fuming headpiece, or from the sight of me.

I looked away. It felt an intrusion to look directly at him. At the far corner of the street, I saw a willowy woman in black, a fringed shawl pulled around her. I was sure it was Emily. There was a figure next to her, tall and silver-topped. So she had, at least for now, met her prince. Or, more accurately, king. Nice.

I looked from her to Stephen Grassi, and then back at Mackenzie. "You were right. They were connected."

"What?" Mackenzie asked. "Are you talking about the mob?"

"The murders. You were right. And wrong. And so was I."

We'd talk it through later. But I knew what I meant. The two murders were connected, but not in any way we'd thought of. Jimmy Pat killed Ted Serfi and because of that, because Emily was then able to blackmail him into breaking his engagement, Jimmy Pat was killed by a man convinced that the broken engagement shamed his sister and besmirched his family name. He'd said it often enough, to enough people. I, who'd been grappling with questions of respect and integrity and honor all along, who'd heard gentle Sally say she wanted to kill Renata for shaming her, should have realized those values, no matter how interpreted, were also other people's issues. All of us felt naked, exposed, and shamed when the mask we want the world to see is removed. The difference is, some of us handle it without bullets.

Vincent Devaney looked like a man under a spell. He moved toward Stephen Grassi. "You sent me the card, didn't you?"

I nodded. That's what I had realized earlier. The shaky almost-familiar writing on the Christmas card. The easily forged *D* in a heart. Stephen telling Vincent that Dolores was going through a bad time. Dolores's absolute ignorance of Vincent's whereabouts during the parade. Dolores had never contacted Vincent. It was Stephen, always Stephen, obsessed and driven.

"You wanted me to leave the parade," Vincent said, "so you could take my place." With each word he advanced a step, and all of us watched, as if equally bewitched. "So you could kill Jimmy and make it look like I did it."

"Stop!" I shouted. "Vincent!" Another disaster would happen if he reached the man who'd set him up.

His friends, fellow club members, shook themselves out of their trances and grabbed hold of him. His shoulders slumped and he looked near tears.

And at the far end of the block, Emily and the King of sausages faded back into the night, to live, I hoped, happily ever after.

I DIDN'T get fired. That would have been too assertive and definite an act for Havermeyer. And the Fields, double-dared, turned out to be cowardly playground bullies under their masks. It probably also mattered that their lawyer told them theirs was a frivolous case that would last, if the courts didn't throw it out altogether, until Renata was long past college age. They did, however, pull Renata out to seek greener, less demanding pastures. I can't imagine where.

Nonetheless, that's what I call a good way to begin a new year. And without her calls, and with my packet of broiled three-by-fives, I had the time to write my article. Its scope had expanded. I wanted to build it around Jimmy Pat's murder at the parade and end with its solution at his club.

"I think I'll start it off with the night my mother called," I told Mackenzie. "The night she said we'd catch our deaths."

It struck him as a good idea, too.

About the Author

GILLIAN ROBERTS is the *nom de mystère* of the mainstream novelist Judith Greber. Winner of the Anthony Award for Best First Mystery for *Caught Dead in Philadelphia,* she is also the author of *Philly Stakes, I'd Rather Be in Philadelphia, With Friends Like These . . . , How I Spent My Summer Vacation,* and *In the Dead of Summer.* Formerly an English teacher in Philadelphia, Gillian Roberts now lives in California.

X

DISCARDED